# THE NOVICE

## MARIBETH GARRETT

The Novice

© 2021 Maribeth Garrett

Print and eBook editions published by Admission Press



eBook ISBN 978-1-955836-00-5

paperback ISBN 978-1-955836-01-2

# PROLOGUE

*First, the foreplay.*

He placed the double-sided tape precisely along the edge of her eyelid with his gloved fingers. One by one, he positioned each eyelash to its best advantage. She must look as exquisite in death as she did in life. He so enjoyed this ritual.

He arranged each specific detail. Then he ripped off another adhesive strip to tape the left eyelid open and repeated the process on the other eye. The game would soon begin.

He brushed her red hair until no tangles remained. Each strand he combed into a perfect semicircle after her head rested on the small pillow beneath. He bent over and inhaled the white lilac scent near her throat. The smell enticed him. His penis stiffened, but he must not rush this production.

He took the table that leaned against the cement-block wall and unfolded the legs. He placed it beside the gurney and covered the top with a white linen tablecloth. From his pocket, he removed a gold, heart-shaped locket and laid it on the surface three inches from the left corner. With the chain, he formed a heart.

Next, he lifted the scalpel and smiled while he remembered the smooth feel the blade carved through his last creation. The instrument felt warm and comfortable in his grip. He placed it on the right side, where the overhead light reflected from it. The green-handled tree pruner he positioned across the bottom. Condoms centered on the table presented the final touch.

He set candles in strategic points around the basement. One by one, he lit them until the walls danced. The flickering light required music. He prepared the CD player, stripped off his clothes, and left them neatly folded in a pile near the stairs. Ready, at last, he wanted to begin.

He leaned over her unconscious nude body and nudged her softly in the ribs—no response. The next push, he nudged a little harder. Still no sign of—wait. He leaned closer, his ear near her lips. She moaned. Then silence again. He poked her much harder, and this time, a red mark formed on her ivory skin.

Her tongue licked her dry, lower lip and hunted for moisture. He stood at the foot of the gurney. Her first sight must include him. The scene always started with their amazement—a precious time but not his favorite.

The muscles in her eyes twitched. Her left hand tugged against the binding which held it fast. Dream-filled eyes became seeing. Recognition entered them before confusion chased the acknowledgment away. Both wrists pulled against the restraints. Her legs fought their war and lost.

He had victory. She recognized him. He smiled at his achievement.

He grasped the scalpel and put it between her breasts. She would see it there, and she would know. She couldn't help but know. The alarm came first, and panic always followed. Anticipation soared through him.

He caressed her foot. Lust infused him. He stroked higher up her leg. She remained alert and watchful, but stoic. The resentment and dread were absent along with fear and terror. She should plead with him. She should promise him, but she only studied him without response.

*No music.* She needed to hear the music. He returned her delicate ankle to the gurney and flipped the switch on the boom box. The driving beat flowed out into the night. The song, filled with dark, demonic guitar riffs, sunk lower with each strain. The melody sounded so strong and powerful. How could she not feel afraid?

Then he turned around, and her lips moved again. He couldn't hear the words for the sounds that surrounded him. He moved closer to her and made out, "Yea, though I walk through the valley of the shadow of death, I will fear no evil, for thou art with me." Then she turned her head away from him.

She ruined everything. He should kill her now and not complete the rest, but that would not feed the hunger which drove him. He craved the screams, the terror, the release he needed so desperately. Fury consumed him. He drew back his hand to slap her but stopped midway.

No. He would start this scene over. This performance would fulfill his fantasies. She would suffer for her insolence. His gratification would cause her maximum pain.

He turned the dial, adjusted the music, and listened intently. His body swayed with the macabre notes for several moments before he broke the spell. His finger hit the left arrow button, and a chilling silence filled the candle-lit room. Then he pushed play, and the garish sounds permeated the atmosphere again. After he stalked back toward her silent body, her lips barely moved. They beguiled him. He craved to know what they said and to bring her to his will.

As he neared, her words flowed like music to his ears. "Jesus loves me, this I know." He could make out most words. Her voice sounded pure and clear. She displayed no hint of fear and spoiled his fantasy.

He picked up the scalpel from between her breasts. The metal felt hot in his grip and burned him as he attempted to grasp it. He remembered the words. She sang a childhood song from his past. "Jesus Loves Me" taunted his ears and tormented his mind.

He threw the surgical instrument against the far wall and ran his fingers through his hair. He paced up and down beside the gurney while his loud music sounded a crescendo. He'd had enough. She would not win.

He grabbed the piece of metal from the floor, lifted both hands high above the table, and brought the blade smashing down.

**1**

---

Paige Stone pulled her Chevy Cavalier along the curb on Twenty-First Street. Three patrol cars sat on the street with flashing lights. An officer waved traffic around the illegally parked black-and-whites. At 2:37 in the morning, no one cared. Gawkers and bystanders weren't allowed at murder scenes, and these squad cars would leave before the morning's rush hour.

The deceased resembled a sacrifice placed in front of the *Appeal to the Great Spirit*. Since the mid-eighties, the Indian statue on the pony gazed skyward, arms outstretched, in Tulsa's Woodward Park. With the darkness, and the harsh lights shining on him, the warrior in full headdress couldn't bear to gaze at the display below. That's how the homicide detective's first case appeared from her car.

She crossed the distance between her and the obscenity. Up close, she noted the offering's eyes. The perpetrator taped both lids open, which made the prey appear startled. Someone had carved a heart shape from the right one, removing most of the iris. Fluid dripped from the cavity. A scalpel stood upright in the left eye. That caught her attention. The instrument seemed to contain its own light source from the reflected Klieg lights.

"Sick, depraved bastard," she mumbled and rolled her lips inward to apply pressure with her teeth—anything to keep them from trembling. She'd seen a hundred or more dead people from the files she studied with Hank since her childhood, but this time it felt different. Photographs didn't make her stomach heave the way this young, mutilated woman did. She forced her shoulders back, determined to get through this without throwing up or giving her fellow officers more to criticize behind her back.

A heart, about nine inches across, sliced deeply into the center of the female's chest. Her titian hair fanned out in a perfect half circle. The white body, appropriately positioned for a casket and burial, laid naked upon the dirt below the bronze sculpture. The feet bottoms were clean. The killer carried her to the site.

Red streaks marked what remained in the eyes. A dark, angry bruise surrounded her neck. Strangulation, most likely the cause of death, but Sam Cartwright, the medical examiner, would give the official cause of death later.

Sweat trickled down Paige's back. She stood and tucked her blonde hair behind her ear with her gloved fingers. She longed to close her eyes and shut the scene from her view, but the time for that had passed. Each detail she locked in her memory. Weakness wouldn't serve her purpose. She needed to show Hank and the captain she was ready for the gruesome details this job would encounter. The officers on the force couldn't wait for her to fail.

She shook her head and brought her mind back to current matters. Something nagged at her. The idea lingered out of her mind's reach. It would come to her later. Hank Gettering entered her peripheral vision.

"What does the evidence suggest to you?" He motioned toward the deceased.

"A psychopath at work. Strangulation, probably COD." She glanced up at him and knew her answer didn't contain the specific words he wanted to hear.

"Are you sure you're okay? This case is a bad one. The worst I've seen." Hank paused.

She recognized he gave her time to adjust.

"I've seen as bad in car wrecks before, but this is different." She couldn't help but compare it to the scene she'd witnessed six months ago. The one that brought Hank and her such loss.

"We'll run point on this. After we get back to the desk, let's check for any MO that appears similar. I don't see any hesitation marks. The carving shows confidence, and he took his time. Our guy has done this before. Others exist. We need to locate them. Keep your mouth shut. Everyone will expect you to screw up. With a case like this for your first one, you could learn several lessons most detectives never get a chance to during their lifetime." Hank reached down to rub his calf muscle.

She nodded in the stifling night air. No breeze, nothing to dissipate the stench death brought. Flies landed on the corpse. One crawled inside her nose.

"Check the surrounding area for every tiny object. Make sure forensics does an exceptional job. Nothing must go wrong." Hank walked the adjacent grounds and searched for any trace the perpetrator left behind.

"I'd like to get my hands on this guy for about ten minutes," she murmured, then she ran her teeth over her bottom lip and nibbled one corner. Her eyes scanned the terrain for any tracks or detail useful for the case while she picked her way around the section that surrounded the body.

"He's a traveler. This crime appears too sophisticated for his initial one, but we haven't seen any like it in our jurisdiction. If he's crossed state lines, our priority will change to nil. They may apprehend him anywhere. He could travel to LA, New York, or God knows where in between." Hank massaged his knee several times.

"It displays the signs for a serial killer, so I figured he has other prey," she said.

"Since more victims are probable, the FBI will more than likely get called in. After that, it will turn into a chaotic nightmare. We'll do the best we can. You know the procedure." He pulled off one glove and strode back toward his Crown Vic. "Make damn sure we follow it to the letter."

She turned to walk back over toward the ME. He hadn't left yet.

"Hank wants a thorough check this time." She took a step closer and examined the ligature marks on the deceased's wrists.

"I hope there's not another any time soon. Do you recognize her? I can't place her, but she seems familiar." Sam appeared unfazed during his work on the dead female. He'd worked as a medical examiner for many years.

She observed the woman's face for the first time. Before, she'd mainly studied the wounds and how the murderer positioned the corpse. Then she remembered what bothered her. "I think it's Heather Balentine. You know, the movie star from *Four Moons* and *The Honey Drop*. Why do you suppose she came to Tulsa? I didn't hear about her coming here."

"Couldn't be her. She can't move without being followed and photographed everywhere she goes. How could she visit here without the press in tow?" Sam lifted Heather's arm and slipped her hand into a sack. Then he tied it securely with a small rope to contain any DNA evidence inside.

"I don't know, but I should tell Hank. If he'd recognized her, he would have said something. Check absolutely everything. The whole world will watch this one." Uncertainty filled her mind during the trip across the grassy patch to the street where she left her vehicle. What did she get herself into? Publicity for this case would label Tulsa for years. Stars didn't come any bigger than Heather Balentine. She'd followed Heather's career from the beginning. She and Crissy got tickets to the opening night for the movie *Far from Alabama*. That film remained their favorite. She longed to call her best friend and tell her the news about Heather, but she couldn't.

Hank removed his old camera from the trunk right after she arrived slightly out of breath.

"You know who she is?" The strobe lights from two black-and-whites made Hank's face change colors as she spoke.

"Not a clue." He seemed unconcerned and more interested in the Canon adjustments.

"She resembles the film star, Heather Balentine. You know who I mean?" Though she struggled to, she couldn't keep the excitement from her voice.

"Who doesn't, but it's probably a look-alike. If she stayed anywhere in the vicinity, the press would show up in full measure." Hank continued to adjust his camera. "What would she do in Tulsa, anyway?"

"I asked myself the same question a few minutes ago."

"I'm ready. I know the crime techs will shoot photos, but I always like to take my own. Sometimes details will bother me that others don't notice. If I make mine, I can remember exactly why it caught my eye. It's helped me more than once to clear up what people remember and what happened. You may decide you like to do the same, or you may develop your own particular routine.

Each detective investigates in a specific way that works for him. Of course, the defense can use my pictures for evidence, too. Let's go check again since the shock value has worn off a little."

"Sure."

Hank moved back in the direction toward the victim. She attempted to keep her mind neutral while they walked in silence through the oppressive heat. The long night ahead loomed before her.

"We didn't find any identification for her. The perpetrator probably has it since we didn't discover her belongings around here, but I admit, she does resemble Ms. Balentine." Hank leaned over the corpse and snapped off two shots.

"I think it's her. If we locate her hotel room, we might discover the murder scene. You never know." Sweat dripped down her spine.

"When we leave here, we need to check the local hotels to learn where she stayed. I don't know for sure, but she probably didn't use her name. Figure a way to word it, so the press doesn't hear about it."

She nodded. "Gotcha."

"I'd start with the more expensive ones, but if she didn't want people to know she came here, she could have used a cheaper one." Hank snapped a picture of the female's wrists.

"I agree. Especially, since no one seems to know about Heather's presence."

"We'll give it twenty more minutes, then go back to the department to get the Incident Report started. Make sure you take good notes and sketch every detail correctly." Hank moved over to the statue and searched around and behind it, but he didn't bag any more evidence.

The IR gave details for what happened on the first day of the investigation. It's always the next page after the table of contents. She took her note pad from her pocket, jotted down the information she would need for the report, and started a rough drawing of the crime scene.

PAIGE APPROACHED Officer Danny Baker where he stood guard outside the taped perimeter. He stood over six foot. Bright red hair topped his slim frame. He appeared close to her age.

She offered her hand, though he gave her a disapproving expression. She ignored it and went on. "I'm Detective Stone. I need to ask you a few questions. I understand you discovered the victim early this morning. That correct?"

"Yes, ma'am." He nodded and held onto her hand longer than most people. Finally, she removed it from his grip. She figured many officers believed she received her promotion because Hank wouldn't partner with anyone else. His attitude confused her. Was he flirting with her or suckering her in for the kill shot?

"How did you discover her?" She retrieved her small notepad from her jacket pocket.

"I turned right off Twenty-First Street on to Peoria and moved south. My lights caught a flash of white by the statue." He motioned toward the deceased more than forty yards away. "I figured kids probably put something there as a prank, but I came back around and went to check it out. At that time, I found the woman."

"What time did you find her?"

"One fourteen this morning." Danny patted his pocket. "I checked my cell phone immediately before I called it in." He cocked his hip and bent his knee as if he posed for a calendar shot. She wondered who he thought he would impress out here in the dark.

She disregarded his cheesy stance and pressed on. "So when you called it in, what did you report?"

"I called dispatch to report a dead body, female, in Woodward Park. I believe I reported the DB on the corner of Peoria and Twenty-First near the warrior on the horse statue. Then the dispatcher said she'd get the next detectives right on it. She said to stay put and secure the place with tape, which I did."

She noted belligerence in Danny's words and expression.

"Did other black-and-whites arrive at this location?"

"Two more units arrived at one twenty-six. They helped me put up the crime scene tape."

"Did they go near her?" This issue was important. She needed to know what happened.

"They got within ten feet, but I told them to clear out. We needed to keep the area clean."

"And did they listen to you? Did they clear out?"

"Yes, they did."

She believed him. "Did you observe anyone else around the park? Did kids hang out nearby?" She paused for a moment. "I'm aware the gates close at eleven, but you know how teens do. Was there anyone suspicious?"

"No, ma'am. The darkness." He shrugged. "But I didn't see anyone else around."

"What about cars? Any vehicles leave the vicinity? Any person lurking around?"

"No. I didn't notice any, but the stiff startled me for a few seconds. I didn't expect one there." His combative tone dared her to press the subject any further.

"It's understandable, but if you do remember any little detail, it could be important. Did you spot objects close around her? A candy wrapper, a cigarette butt, or anything?"

"No, ma'am. Nothing. You got any more—questions?"

She could tell he wanted to say *stupid* questions but caught himself in time.

She nodded. The attitude rankled. It got more noticeable since the news broke she made detective. She took two steps away but turned back. "You need to follow protocol on this. File your report, but don't notify anyone else until my superiors tell me. We still need to contact the next of kin and give this a thorough review before we release a statement."

Danny nodded. "Sure. Anything for *the princess*."

She'd never wanted to punch anyone so much in her life, but she forced a smile to keep from belting him one. "I'm sure Hank will want to question you later. Thank you for the information." She went back toward the Klieg lights that lit up the park. She assumed everyone on the force felt the same way he did. No one else showed as much blatancy as Baker, at least, not to her face. She rubbed the back of her neck and wondered if Hank found any answers yet.

PAIGE FELT *the heat though snow fell steadily to the ground. Her feet waded through a good ten inches. But the smell terrified her. She must get to them. Arms grabbed at her and pulled her away, but she knew she must save them. They would die if she didn't. She smelled flesh burning. She fought the arms that held her captive, but the sound of music finally made her realize she fought blankets.*

She barely caught two hours rest when the clock radio woke her up. Still groggy with vivid dreams, she slapped at the alarm. It crashed to the floor and jarred her wide-awake.

"Shit, I think I broke it," she said then got up to inspect the damage. She placed the clock back on the nightstand and walked into the bathroom. In the shower, the hottest water possible beat down on her and washed the final cobwebs away.

The case got colder by the second. It wouldn't wait for sore muscles or the exhaustion that persisted. She loved her job, but it still sucked a little at times.

She stood and gazed into her bathroom mirror while her eyes searched for her father's familiar photo in dress uniform. The picture sat on a shelf on the opposite wall, positioned to reflect in the upper right corner. She'd started each day with the ritual for fourteen years. His face looked over her shoulder and always brought her comfort. It reminded her who she was. She speculated how different she might have turned out if he hadn't died. She smiled and left the bathroom, and his presence, behind.

As she walked into the station, Hank sat at the computer and used his two-index-finger approach to input information. She opened her desk drawer to place her bag inside then she saw the drawing. The work of Artie Jones shocked her. He remained the best artist on the force. They sometimes used him with witnesses to make a suspect's facial likeness.

She figured Harley Judd put him up to it. The picture showed her performing fellatio on the police chief with her hand grasping a detective shield. Harley considered himself the next detective to make it into the homicide squad. He might deserve it, too, but Hank refused to work with him. This antic typified him, and the main reason why. Harley had to get his way, or his peevish attitude showed itself. If slighted, he always let everyone know.

"Find anything similar yet?" She ignored the latest installment to protest her promotion and joined Hank.

"No. I just got here. I barely got the computer booted up. You look like shit this morning. You out late last night or something?" He gave a dry chuckle.

"You know exactly what occupied my time in the early hours this morning." She leaned on the desk and watched his hunt-and-peck typing.

"Yeah. Tough night for me, too. I carry more years than you. Why don't you type in this information? You're a lot faster on the keyboard than I am." He moved away from the computer and gave her access.

"I thought you'd never ask."

She traded him places and entered the data into the Violent Criminal Apprehension Program, better known as ViCAP. While she waited for the site to bring the results they needed, she lifted her Pepsi can and took a drink. "Do you know what time Sam plans to perform the autopsy?"

"You still drink little kid's pop?" Hank nodded at her beverage choice.

She grimaced, smiled, and held the can up for spite.

"In about an hour, I think. I'm not sure, but Sam planned to do it first when he got here this morning. It will depend on what time he gets in. He didn't get to bed any sooner than we did." Hank leaned down to rub his leg.

She hesitated and gave him a meaningful stare. They'd discussed this before. Hank refused to talk about it anymore. "Don't remind me. I'm still trying to tell my body it got plenty of sleep. Right now, it doesn't believe me."

"I know the feeling."

"So what do we start with today?" She finished her soda and dropped the empty container in the wastebasket. "I'd like to confirm the victim's identity."

"If it's Heather Balentine like we think, it shouldn't take too long, but we'll need to stay extremely careful with the media. Leaks can and will pop up. Don't open your mouth to anyone. Not even another cop. The media pays top dollar for anything on these high-profile cases. So don't talk to anyone. Run everything through the captain or me. The only two words I want to hear come out of your mouth until we complete the case are 'no comment.'" Hank stared her directly in the eyes. "I'm aware you know the standard protocol, but I'm serious on this. You don't understand the extremes the press goes to on something this big."

"I got it."

"The only good to come from this murder case is that you'll learn a lot from it. These multiple-victim cases show you who you can trust. People rarely turn out the way you think. It's one lesson I wish you didn't learn because it's hard to unlearn. After, you will have difficulty trusting anyone." Hank said.

The computer screen flashed, which signaled they found murders with corresponding MOs. After it stopped spewing out information, she hit print to get it into hard copy.

She handed the first printout over to Hank and waited for hers to finish. The third would go in the murder book. He started through his listing, marked with his pen, and made notes. She couldn't tell what he wrote, but she figured if she stayed patient, he would show her. She'd only been on the job with him since Monday, so he remained in teacher mode with her. Hank took her in after her father's death. Through childhood, she'd watched him when he brought work home, so she understood how he worked cases. This was the first time they had completed the whole process together.

After Hank quit writing, he turned his head and glanced up at her.

"Well?" she asked.

"Do your own. Let's see if ours match. I won't always spoon-feed you, you know." Hank paused. "I'm going to go drain a quart of the coffee I drank this morning. Work on it until I get back."

She lowered her head and started through the printed

pages. The program suggested various similar cases. Most didn't appear closely related but bore resemblances. Without the actual cause of death, the matches weren't a certainty. But COD was most likely strangulation. The marks around the neck appeared dark. The eyes displayed petechial hemorrhage.

She circled two that were obvious and put question marks by a couple of others. They weren't identical, but several details seemed like they fit. Often serials took time to develop their MO while still evolving.

When Hank came back, he carried another coffee cup. He stared over her shoulder for a minute. "Why did you decide on these two?" He pointed to the ones with question marks.

"They are reasonably close. Both women strangled and minor celebrities. The dates ran older on them," she said.

"Looks like you learned something from what I taught you. I think we're probably on the right track here. I'm glad you recognized the strangulation marks on the neck and the eyes. It will probably stay the COD, but we're never certain until the ME has ruled on it. You picked up on the same ones I picked. Paige has turned a page."

She beamed. Hank used the phrase often after she'd demonstrated improvement. Even though the saying sounded hokey, she loved to hear it.

"Let's see what Sam tells us. We need a COD and a confirmed identity."

Her smile lingered as she followed him from the room.

## 2

---

*Two weeks earlier*

Betty Greenway sat and looked down at her expenditures. The stack on her mahogany desk grew daily, the figures astronomical as she totaled them. She gazed back up at her computer screen. Not a single listing moved in over three months. She was depleting her reserve funds at an astounding rate. She couldn't continue like this. The three thousand dollars she had left wouldn't pay her bills for the next month.

She tapped her fingers on the desk twice then got up to tidy the room. When situations seemed their worst, she needed to work off her nervous energy. If she cleaned, her anxieties quieted. Besides, she loved to keep a spotless office and home. If her car didn't get washed and waxed at least once a week, she didn't feel right.

Her assistant, Stella, had left a magazine laying on her desk again. Betty grabbed the publication and returned it to its place on the coffee table. The *Good Housekeeping*, with Heather

Balentine on the cover, went after April and before June. She placed it straight in a row where it belonged.

She heard the Instant Message notification sound from her desk. She hurried to the computer screen and glanced to see who contacted her. She didn't want to chat about silly gossip and prayed it was a new customer.

*I'm interested in using your services for a unique project in the area. Can you help me?*

*Tweet Tweet*

She didn't know whether to take the message seriously. Would a child make a joke? What was the deal with the Tweet Tweet?

*More information, please. What special project?*

*Betty*

She waited for a reply.

*I need a place to stay for a month or two. I am an established actor. I want a break from everyone. A remote location away from other homes would work best, so I'm not recognized. Last time I finished filming, I couldn't get away to relax without the world on my trail. I want some privacy. Will you help me out?*

*Tweet Tweet*

As she searched her brain for possibilities, she typed an answer.

*What do you require for your stay? I assume you want to rent a house, but what specifics are necessary?*

*Betty*

Several minutes later, the IM sounded again.

*I need a basement with trees around the house. An attached garage works best. Privacy is the essential requirement. I don't want anyone to find out I'm there. Last time the press kept me cornered. They followed me everywhere. I need a break for a month or two. This desperate guy needs your help.*

*Tweet Tweet*

*I'm sure we can work something out. How can I contact you if I find what you need? In Tulsa proper or a neighboring area? What you described, I would likely find in a rural setting.*

*Betty*

They exchanged several more messages. He gave her the information to find what he wanted for his stay. She could barely contain her excitement after she signed off the last time. The answer to her dilemma came in an IM and a promise of twenty-five thousand dollars if she could keep her mouth shut.

She'd feared she would have to let Stella go. Her helper worked only part-time, but she needed her, and Stella wanted the work. The extra income would push the problem into the future for a while.

She hummed while she searched through her files for the perfect place. She smiled as she considered how quickly the market changed in the real estate business. When she got up to get a fresh cup of coffee, she remembered a place that might work.

~

*Three years earlier*

Tony Strete hated Grant Windsor and his grandiose visions for their picture. They'd wrapped the last scene. The film was in the can, thank God. Grant ruined a dozen of their scenes with his ridiculous ideas. He hoped those got edited out in the final cut.

"I think we made a great movie here, don't you?" Grant's words stopped him between steps, and he faltered.

"I certainly hope so." He swallowed the words he wanted to say. If he could only escape the blowhard, he'd be a happy man.

"I think the tension between you and Sarah presented well. Were you intimate during filming?"

He hated the leering expression on Grant's face. "You need to ask her."

"Oh, come on. It's obvious. Her eyes devoured you every time you turned away from her."

"Perhaps she just acted. That *is* what the scene called for."

"I suppose, but I'd put money on an affair between you, and it made the scenes more intense. Believe me. I'm for anything to improve our project. Tell me, does Sarah scream?"

He wanted to choke the giant hulk who stood before him, but he didn't want to contaminate himself with Grant's slimy brashness. "Again, ask her. I have people waiting. I need to go."

He hoped his career didn't suffer because of the director's inflated ego. For now, he only wanted a six-pack to wash the disgust away and company that didn't require sixteen retakes for something they'd gotten right the first time. He'd known men like Grant before. They liked to hear themselves talk.

As he walked farther from the lot, he saw Josh Stuart and Ben McCall meander toward Ben's trailer. They'd share a few beers before they left the set for the last time. He figured he would join them and stopped by his place to grab the Miller Lite from his small fridge.

When he opened the door to Ben's place, they both held up their beer bottles. "Thanks. I'm so glad you waited for me."

"No problem," they both said in unison.

"Glad to know you care. Hey, what's the plan since we've finished this fiasco?" He opened a beer from his six-pack and took a drink. Then he moved into the kitchen and placed the rest in the refrigerator.

"Wait. No. It's an *expensive* fiasco. An I-wish-I'd-never-signed-on fiasco," Ben said with his legs crossed at the ankle while his butt rested against the kitchen sink.

"God, me too. The screenplay read great until Grant, the hack, got hold of it." Josh sat on the small green sofa.

"I've got to agree. It's probably the worst film I've worked on. How the hell did we get hooked up with this one?" Tony deliberated for a few seconds. "For me, the ten million and not carrying the single lead. Plus, I wanted to work with you both again." He took his seat in the recliner, which Ben usually guarded for himself, then ignored Ben's dirty look.

"So you guys never answered my question. What plans do you two have since we finished?" He downed the rest of his brew.

"I start *Walking on Eggs* in two weeks. I'll likely hang at my house in Malibu. We should get together and burn three large steaks on the grill." Ben walked over and sat on the couch with Josh on the opposite end.

"I could handle a huge one straight from the grill. Sometime next week would work for me." Josh got up and put his empty in the trash. Then he brought Ben and himself two cold ones from the kitchen.

"That's next week. We should celebrate tonight. I've never been so glad to finish a shoot in my life. If I never work with that ass again, it will be too soon." He lifted his Miller Lite and chugged it.

"I agree. Windsor made it a disaster." Ben stared into his bottle while he swirled it. Then he finished it.

"I swear, if you can't walk again, I won't haul you both in tonight. The last time nearly put my back out. Wherever you land, you stay," Josh said.

Ben glanced at him and pointed at Josh. "Hey, Stretes, why do we hang out with the *buzzkill* over there?"

Josh saluted with his middle finger and laughed aloud.

"How come we haven't made more films together?" Ben asked.

"Because no one can afford our three salaries on the same film unless we each take a cut in pay like we did for this one," Josh said.

"If I'd known Grant made such losers, I'd have demanded triple pay." He took another drink from his brew. Then he picked at the label.

Ben remained silent for several seconds, held his right index finger up, and belched with gusto. "My all-star tribute to the director. May he go down in infamy." He struck his famous pose. The one that always got the girl at the end of each movie. "Men, shall we move this shindig to the proper place for parties? The Reel Shack."

That sounded great to Tony. Anything to put Grant Windsor and this probable flop out of mind for the night. He stood. "We shall."

"Damn it. Here we go again." Josh followed them out.

*Present*

PAIGE STARTED the engine and looked behind her before she backed the Crown Vic out of the parking space. "Will we start the hotel search to find her room once we confirm her identity? Sam or the techs should have it by now."

"I already handed it off to Harley and his partner. Since they want to work homicide, they might as well do a little leg work. Besides, they were vocal about your promotion, so grunt work is what they deserve." He grinned. "Harley couldn't contain his displeasure for the assignment."

"Do you trust them to do a good job without disclosure about Heather?"

"I don't know. I laughed in his face after he showed his ass at my suggestion. Then I made it an order. His pissy attitude better improve, or Captain will give him more of the same. You don't want to get on Underwood's bad side."

"I hope I never do."

"Smart idea." Hank pulled the ViCAP printout from the papers in his hand and reread it. They rode in silence for several miles until they arrived. She parked their car in the lot outside the ME's office. Hank still studied the report in his lap.

"Did you find something? What is it?" she asked.

"It's interesting they found another victim strangled in LA about a year before our first probable match. The primary body from this list may mark the anniversary of Donna Barnett's death. The MO appears a little different, but the initial kill for a psychopath doesn't always go match with their later ones." Hank glanced up and rubbed his stubble. "Probably not connected, but it's a possibility. The FBI will make the determination, so we'll see what they think."

"I figured they'd send someone." She chewed her bottom lip while she walked toward Sam's domain. She didn't want the FBI to horn in on their case.

"It's the way these homicides go." Hank folded the sheets together and stuck them under his arm. "Let's see what Sam has to say about COD and any trace evidence."

He held the door open for her, and they entered the building. Then it hit her. She hadn't been to the morgue since the accident. Crissy rested here in a refrigerated box six months ago, and Bobby did too. She didn't want to remember them here, or the way she'd last seen them. It didn't seem right to think about her best friend and her brother lying here in Sam's cold storage.

She questioned how Hank came here so easily. Of course, this wasn't his first time. He'd been here a dozen times since, and Hank made for a tough read. He'd been a detective for over two decades. She wondered if the years would make her as self-contained. Then she debated if she already was by living with Hank for so long.

Sam greeted her with a wolf whistle. The signal warned a female entering his territory. He meant no disrespect. This audible sign told the guys to clean up their mouths. Sam never had a complaint. The only women she'd talked to said they hated to hear the foul language. If the FBI sent a man, she figured it might work better. It should save a lawsuit for poor old Sam.

She grinned like she generally did when the ME came around. He instilled harmless fun into the day. Certain days he provided the only humor in sight. As tired as she felt, she needed a lift. Besides, she wanted to lose the morbid thoughts.

"So what did you find, big boy?" she said. If he could give it out, she would too.

"COD, strangulation. He carved the eyes post-mortem. The perp played with her a little before he strangled her. He bound her for several hours." Sam lifted the victim's arm and examined the ligature marks on her wrist with a magnifying glass. "I think he used duct tape, but he scrubbed the adhesive off."

"Time of death?" Hank asked.

"TOD at least two hours before the officer found her body. I'll get a better estimate before I'm through." Sam lowered the victim's hand to the table and laid the magnifier back with his other tools.

"Rape kit?" Hank asked.

Sam paused.

Hank gazed up from the body at him.

Sam shrugged. "She had intercourse. More than one time from the way it looks, but at least one time was non-consensual. I found bruising and tearing."

"Any trace?" Hank bent over and examined the victim's wrists and hands.

"I've got tests processing for DNA, but it would surprise me if anything turns up. She appears clean. I'm sure he bathed her. He didn't kill her on site. He dumped her." Sam turned on a brighter light beside the autopsy table.

"I figured the same, but we needed the official report. What showed up on the tox screen?"

"Trace Rohypnol, but he gave it to her earlier because she fought back when he raped her."

"Did you get a confirmation on her ID? Is it Heather Balentine? How long can we hold back the information?" Hank asked.

"Her print confirmed it. California DMV had her index fingerprint on file. I saw an article online that mentioned she would return to set Monday morning. Her family or friends might miss her before then." Sam laid a clean scalpel back on the tray beside the body.

"It may give us a little time before the press gets involved. Sam, keep the body covered if possible. I know others worked the scene last night, but the fewer who recognize her, the better. After the press finds out, the problem becomes how to get any real work done. We need to discover why she came to Tulsa. I heard the media follow her everywhere. Wonder where anyone last spotted her, and how she got away?" Hank turned to leave, but Sam stopped him.

"We're not through. I saved the best part for last."

"What else did you find?" Hank asked.

"You didn't ask about the heart. It turns out the carving hid details."

"How so?" Hank walked back over to the autopsy table.

"Let me show you." Sam took the forceps from his tray of tools and gently lifted the heart-shaped skin from her chest area and revealed what lay beneath. At first, she didn't understand what she saw. Sam put the fleshy chunk into a stainless steel bowl on the side table.

Then he lifted a chain with the same pickups, and a heart-shaped locket danced at the end. Blood and reflections from the bright lights made the gold piece appear alive. It seemed to move by itself.

"Paige, put on gloves and open it. Show it to Hank." Sam nodded toward the body.

She donned gloves and took the blood-soaked jewelry, slippery through the latex. When she finally got the piece between her fingers, she still had trouble opening the locket. In a few moments, she wished she hadn't opened it at all. There, staring up at her, lay the heart-shaped cutout from an iris. But the color didn't match Heather's other eye. If it didn't belong to Miss Balentine, who did the missing eye part belong to?

On the locket's opposite side: a perfect fingerprint. It probably wouldn't belong to Heather either. She gazed up at Sam and then at Hank. She couldn't fathom such perversion. Why would anyone go to such trouble?

"Amazingly strange, isn't it?" Sam's comment broke the silence that lingered between the three.

"He's toying with us. Thinks he's smarter than the cops who chase him, but it might cause him to make a mistake. I hope it's sooner than later." Hank's voice sounded gruff while his eyes stayed fixed on the gold piece.

She looked into the cavity where the necklace had been. The killer cut away a portion from her ribs and exposed Heather Balentine's heart. The locket rested right on the life-pumping muscle. It must mean something important, but what? Did he try to see into her heart, or was this another ploy to get their attention? The SOB got her attention.

"Come on, Paige. We need to find a psycho." This time Hank didn't stop until he reached the door.

His words returned her from her introspection. She gave Sam a hollow smile and followed Hank.

"Tell me what you find out. Let me know if you need someone to take a trip to LA. I got my swimsuit on standby." Sam grinned at her and lightened the moment.

"If anyone goes to LA, I get to go." She rejoined the conversation.

"I volunteer to help you try on your bikini." Sam moved over the corpse and picked up the scalpel again.

"You old lecher, you have naked women in front of you most of the time."

"Yeah, but they're always dead. Now and again, I enjoy a live one."

"Gross." She scrunched her face at him.

"You started it."

"Okay, you two. We've got work to do." Hank gave his attention to Sam. "How long until you finish, and we get a copy for our murder book?"

"I should write the autopsy up sometime tomorrow. I'll send you a copy ASAP."

Hank nodded, then turned to leave. "Come on. Let's go."

As they left the morgue and drove across the Arkansas River back to their office, Hank reasoned aloud. "If she needed to get back to work on Monday, she probably flew in. We'll check for her flight information. She may not fly under *her* name, if it's not her birth name. We need to get techs on the security footage from the airport. We could get lucky and see who met her if anyone did. If no one did, we could still start a timeline from there and try to fill in what we can before the media finds out about Heather. It will make a short timeline.

We might also see what she brought with her. We didn't find any purse or clothes at the body dump."

By the time they reached their station, she'd recorded his words on her phone. Like most people, she carried it everywhere she went. She sat down at her desk to call Bill Graywolf, the best computer tech on the force, but decided she should talk to him in person.

She got back up and told Hank where she intended to go, then left the office. Her mind filled with different scenarios that would put Heather Balentine in Tulsa without the press. Her best guess, the one that felt right to her, included a clandestine meeting with her killer. Of course, Heather wouldn't have known he strangled women. She wondered if Hank would agree with her assessment.

After she drove to the University of Tulsa campus, she parked outside the building where the police placed their Cyber Crime Unit. When she entered the room, Bill sat engrossed behind a monitor she only dreamed about owning one day. The screen measured forty-two inches.

"Hey, Bill, you working on anything critical? I got something I need you to do. It's important. I'll stay in your debt forever if you can squeeze me in." She stared at his black crewcut until he turned to look at her.

"In my debt forever? I like the sound of that. What's up?" Bill finally gave her his attention.

"I need you to help me search the cameras from Tulsa International. I've already run her through the passenger list. Her name didn't appear on it. The person in question is a movie star who probably arrived Friday evening, but to make sure, let's start from Thursday. Most likely, she came from Los Angeles or a connecting flight from there under an assumed name. I figure it will take a while, but we need to discover the time she arrived.

We also need to see if anyone met her and what she brought with her. Before I tell you who, you can't divulge this information to anyone, and I mean anyone. If I don't kill you, Hank will." She had her hand raised like she swore an oath.

"Sounds mysterious. I'm in. Who do I search for?" Bill said.

She lowered her voice. "Heather Balentine, as in *Far from Alabama*. Big box office star. Sam confirmed her identity this morning. You know how news stories can get out of proportion on cases like this. We want to buy a little time to get a head start on the media."

"You're kidding. She's dead?"

"A patrolman found her last night. Luckily, someone with a cell phone didn't find her. Otherwise, her photo would have flooded the Internet by now." She stood by his desk and watched the monitor. She wasn't sure what she'd interrupted.

"What was she doing in Tulsa?" Bill's tanned fingers hit a few more keys.

"That's what we'd like to know. Can you get me the footage? If we both work on it, it should cut the time in half." She tapped his shoulder and stole his attention from his computer screen.

"Sure, but remember, you will owe me big time, forever."

"Okay, Starbucks for one month."

"I thought you said forever." Bill's brown eyes gave her a pointed look.

"Yeah, so does everyone who gets married, but you see how that turns out."

"You're a hard woman, Paige Stone."

"My last name's Stone for a reason." She turned to leave the room.

Bill seemed hesitant, but his voice turned more confident when he continued. "You know, it's all right to discuss what happened Christmas Eve. If you do, you won't break. The rest of us loved them too."

No one had dared to mention the subject before, but he was wrong. Six months and the pain remained as raw as that night. She didn't answer him or peek his way. Tears fought their way too close to the surface, and an eruption forced a path upward in her chest.

"I don't mean to hurt you, but you need to talk about it. You can't hold it inside forever."

"I know, but not yet. I'm not ready." She pushed the door open and hurried away.

**3**

———————

*Three years earlier*

Tony Strete grinned and walked into The Reel Shack. He loved to hang with Ben and Josh. When the three entered a bar, a hush followed. To carry such power in this town meant a lot. Hollywood fed on it. He'd clawed his way up in the movie business, which took real effort, but to stay on top took even more work than getting there. He intended to enjoy the elevated position as long as possible. At least he lived his dream. Most people never got that far.

They took their seats around a glass table that rested on an oversized chrome movie reel. Ben nudged him in the side. "Why do you look so serious? We came to party."

"I plan to start right now. Let's kick it up a notch. Give me a Wild Turkey straight up. Make it a double." He surveyed the club. It resembled a throwback to the thirties and offered every decadent item any young Hollywood star could desire. Sometimes he wanted to pinch himself to see if it was real, if he was truly here in the land built on dreams.

"I'll have the same." Ben winked at the attractive server.

"Bring me a Bud Light," Josh said.

The hazel-eyed, blonde waitress left with their order. He appreciated the view her swaying hips displayed once she departed. Less than a minute later a brunette with a nice rack wanted their autograph. A redhead followed right behind. They asked each one to join them. Before the server returned with their drinks, gorgeous females surrounded their booth and penned them in with extra chairs.

The night wore on, and many A-listers stopped by their table to swap stories. Each guy escorted the girls onto the floor several times and made sure the females felt included. After Tony downed a few drinks, he enjoyed this portion more. He loved to hold and cuddle them while they sashayed around the floor. It's why he only danced to slow songs. You could see how a woman felt in your arms before the situation got down and interesting.

He'd finished his third double with a water chaser when he spotted Grant Windsor across the room. If the windbag started talking, they'd never escape. He poured the fourth double down his throat and swallowed. He didn't take time for the chaser. He wanted away from here. Grant was the most boring person on the face of the planet.

He searched for Ben and Josh, but his eyes wouldn't focus. He knew the way to the bathroom blindfolded and turned toward his goal. Halfway there a fantastic redhead grabbed him and attached her mouth to his. By this time, his lips were numb, and he no longer trusted his vision. She swirled him around in an attempt to dance. The dizziness in his brain increased. Josh appeared and pulled him away. The woman stuck a key card in his front pants pocket, pushed it to the bottom, and rubbed his junk on the way back up.

"Life's hard at the top, but I can handle it." He noticed

Josh's head leaned back. His breath must put off enough fumes to make bystanders high.

"Yeah, I can see that." Josh steadied him as he stumbled.

They took several steps together in the same direction until he got his balance back. Then he pushed past Josh toward the bathroom. The fourth double kicked in, and he had to feel his way.

～

*The Monday before*

BETTY GREENWAY SAT in her Lincoln, staring at the perfect solution. This place should make her a tidy sum. Before long, she could advertise she'd found the ideal place for a major star. The business she'd worked hard to establish could skyrocket into prominence.

Secluded and primitive, the log house offered enough amenities but sat out in the boonies of Rogers County. No one would recognize him here. He'd mentioned an attached garage and a basement. The cabin included both.

For three years, she'd listed this property with no interest. The owner would gladly rent it out for a month or two at the longest. If she could please her client in this transaction, he could recommend her to his other Hollywood friends. The only requirement he demanded was to keep the visit a secret and guard his identity with her life.

She might make more if she cleaned the place herself. Then she wouldn't need to explain or answer questions. Besides, no one else would make it sparkle like she would. Yes, this idea would work best. Keep everything secret, and nobody else would know anything about it. She wouldn't register the money on the books. This way no one would find out. She needed the twenty-five-thousand-dollar bonus money.

She got out of the red Lincoln and walked to the porch. The place remained in good shape. The owner repainted last year. He hoped to bring more interest. Until now, the effort remained wasted, but the partially furnished cabin matched her new client's search. She believed she could sell him on the idea.

She circled the log cabin and decided to shoot her pictures from the southeast toward the front porch. It would give a perfect view. You could see the scenic valley fall away from the small hill on which the cabin sat. The photos would show the cabin's remoteness. He'd been specific about that detail, and trees covered the acreage here.

Then she would work on a few indoor shots. Her new client didn't seem to care so much about each room's condition. The men she'd known wouldn't want to do without sex for two months, but women needed more civilized surroundings.

She wished he'd given his name. Curiosity remained one of her weaknesses. The various stars brought endless possibilities to her mind.

Many different ones could have tried to hire her: Bradley Cooper, Leonardo DiCaprio, or Anthony Strete. For a second, she thought about the last candidate and remembered his bronze muscles, black hair the sun tinted with mahogany, and Paul-Newman-colored eyes. He looked so delicious she secretly wished it was him.

She couldn't help but wonder how the mystery actor got her name, and why he'd chosen her. Oh well, the real estate deal brought money, and her business could surely use an influx immediately.

She took several outdoor shots and went inside. Everything appeared in good shape. She didn't see any dust, but she would make certain before she let her client move in. The whole place needed to shine to perfection, so he'd want to repeat his stays with her, and, better yet, tell his wealthy friends.

After she'd taken about twenty different photos, she headed back to her car to download them. Her fingers manipulated the SD chip from her camera and inserted it in her laptop. She typed a quick message to ascertain if this spot filled his needs. The pictures finally finished. She attached them and sent the information.

She sat back, adjusted her position, and waited for several minutes. She was about to give up and close the computer when an IM popped up.

*Secure it for me. I plan to arrive in three days. Can you set up a laptop with high-speed internet? I'll need a prepaid cell during my visit. Two hundred minutes should get me through. You should receive a package in the mail with cash to purchase these items plus pay the rent. If it's not enough, I will reimburse you once I arrive. Set up the laptop and accounts. Make a file with all the passwords and account numbers. Then label it "Tweet." Password protect the computer using the words "Tweet Tweet." More info later.*

*Tweet Tweet*

She read the words twice before she could believe her good fortune. She could complete each request—no problem. She lifted the laptop and quickly typed the words: *Consider it done.* Then she sent the reply.

The smile lingered until she reached the Tulsa city limit sign. To convince the owner to lease it out for two months remained the main item left to accomplish. If she had to strangle the man, she would get him to agree. She could already see herself counting out the bonus money. A sigh of relief escaped her lips while she concentrated on driving in the rush-hour traffic.

~

*Three years earlier*

HE AWOKE WITH A START. Day-old whiskey fumes attacked his nose. He didn't know what brought him from a deep sleep. He grabbed his head. His brain felt like it would explode. He peered around and saw her. A woman slept beside him. Her name wouldn't come to him, but he did remember she touted herself as the new shampoo girl.

Her blonde hair spilled out over the pillow in a fan shape. She looked dead to the world, but she didn't snore. The sound turned him off. It usually meant no morning-after sex.

His mouth was dry, his tongue felt thick, and his head still pounded. He gently nudged her. She felt cold, and he attempted to cover her until a flash of memory assaulted his hung-over mind. She'd been into rough sex—sexual appetites he'd never experimented with before. She demanded he choke her once he'd entered her. She'd been insistent. He'd been hesitant, but she'd pleaded with him to squeeze tighter.

He grabbed her arm and pushed her. She didn't wake up. He lifted her eyelid and saw scarlet in her eye's white portion. Frantic, he shook her harder. No response. Did he kill her? Oh my god. He vaguely remembered the night before, but only in flickers—fragmented moments before he passed out. "Son of a bitch," he whispered and gripped his head again.

Panic filled his brain. He wanted to flee. He needed to leave here, but his hair and DNA had to be everywhere in this room. It would ruin him. What the hell could he do?

He sat on the bed's edge and attempted to think. How could he remove himself and the evidence without someone seeing? Hell, he didn't know where he'd landed.

Slowly he got up and moved to the window. His head still

felt heavy and dull from the alcohol soaking his brain. He tugged the curtains to the side and gazed out. It looked like a small motel—and not a good one. A red cactus flashed its neon lights.

He thought he remembered she went in to rent the room. She was an aggressive woman and picked him up when he'd gone out to take a leak. The men's room at The Reel Shack overflowed with drunks, and he couldn't wait.

The idea struck his mind then as a grandfather clock did on the hour. No one saw them together. They'd been in her car. If he could figure out a way to get the body into her trunk and away from here, he might get clear from this predicament. He took the bedding with him, wiped every surface clean, and hoped he would come out okay.

He watched to make sure no one could see him and backed her car into the parking space by the front door. To eradicate his presence, he scrubbed the bedroom and bath until his fingers were raw. Satisfied he'd removed all trace of himself from the room, he waited until three in the morning to bundle her body tightly inside the linens. He lifted the old drapes enough to search the darkness outside for anyone who might see him. Then he loaded the blonde into her car's open trunk.

He drove straight to his home in Malibu, obeyed every traffic law, and pulled the car into the garage. The door closed, and he took the bedding and what it contained up to his guest bathroom. He left her body behind in the tub. Then he brought the sheets back down and ran them through the wash. He added bleach in liberal amounts.

He used the rubber gloves his housekeeper kept under the kitchen sink and thoroughly scrubbed her body. Then for a reason he couldn't explain, he blow-dried her hair. With such a lovely strawberry shade of blonde, it seemed the least he could do. After all, she represented Sizzle Shampoo.

Once the linens dried, he carefully re-wrapped her scrubbed body and put it back in her trunk. In the Hollywood Hills, he let the body roll to its final resting place. Then he drove her car to a parking lot next to a Walmart about five miles from his home, adjusted the seat forward to a shorter position, and walked into the store. He didn't want to act suspicious. At the time he came back out, he no longer sported the clothes he'd worn inside. He looked like an early morning jogger ready for the five-mile run to his house.

He arrived home, showered, ate a sandwich, and went to bed. Surprisingly, he slept for ten solid hours.

The next day, he gathered her slinky clothes, oversized purse, and red cell phone. He burned them in his home's fireplace. Not a trace remained of the shampoo girl. He hoped it stayed that way.

Daily, he searched the news for the body's discovery. Someone reported her corpse on the sixth day. Her murder details stayed in the headlines for several weeks before mudslides buried the story.

Her death didn't completely disappear from his sight. In the dark, while his eyes remained closed, he could still see the instant life departed from her blue eyes. The remembrance came to him each night, called to him, aroused him, and incited a need in him he'd never known existed. A whole year passed before he answered the call.

**4**

---

Paige saw the stranger stand dark and brooding beside Hank's desk while she approached her own. His haircut and the way he wore his black suit screamed FBI. Hank had predicted right as usual.

She didn't want the interloper to take their case away from them. They didn't need the Fed's help. It made her wonder if their captain, Bob Underwood, called the Bureau, but the Feeb wouldn't get here this quickly. No. The time read ten past noon. If Underwood called, the agent shouldn't arrive until tomorrow or late this evening at the earliest.

She walked up to her desk, opened the drawer, and ignored him. She'd get her batteries and leave. Hank could put up with him. She still had to help Bill go through the rest of the film from Tulsa International. She'd go back to the campus after a late lunch.

When she turned back around, his hand stuck out in greeting.

"I'm Special Agent Jordan Trinity. I presume you're Detective Stone."

His smile carried the correct allure to ensure cooperation. He'd probably used it on women for years, but she refused to let him persuade her. He didn't belong here, and she intended to make sure he understood her opinion on the matter. She observed his outstretched hand and attempted to move around him without speaking, but Hank appeared from the hallway.

Finally, she accepted his offered greeting and shook it once, but she let it drop quickly. "Yes. I'm Detective Stone."

She glanced up at Hank, who signaled for him to come on. The Special Agent would want to talk with him. As lead detective, he had the most experience, while she showed zero on her record. No doubt, he would look it up.

"Hank." She nodded toward the other man. "Special Agent Jordan Trinity. I think he's here about *our* case." She moved to walk off, but Hank motioned for her to stay.

"You must be Hank Gettering. Everyone calls me Trin. I don't see any reason to be formal." The man's smile oozed charm, but she didn't trust him.

Hank shook his hand and then got down to business. "What do you know about our killer? I'm sure he's done his work elsewhere. No hesitation with the carving."

"No. We believe the unknown subject killed first in LA. Did you find any evidence? We've found nothing useful at the other locations. Of course, the unsub dumped each body. So far, we've not found any actual crime scenes."

Hank shook his head and pulled a chair up close to their desks for the special agent. "Take a seat."

The hopeful expression on Trin's face faded. "This guy remains a ghost. Bodies appear at public sites. I understand he left yours by a statue. He has displayed several similarly." Trin hesitated before he sat down.

Hank nodded.

"I believed the timing worked for this weekend. I've been

watching for a new body to appear on ViCAP." Trin settled into his seat and pulled his briefcase close to him. Then he continued. "I worked with your captain once before. After I talked to him by phone, he welcomed me and asked me to come. I caught the first available flight. I hope you don't mind my imposing, but Bob seemed pleased I came."

She sat at her desk and watched closely for the intruder to make a mistake. Her partner would recognize it immediately. Hank always closed his case. The FBI would take the credit. When the media learned the victim was a big celebrity, an uproar would break loose. The credit should go to Hank, but the Feds would score the big coup. Of course, they were a long way from solving anything yet.

Trin opened his attaché. He searched through his files and drew them out one by one. As he pulled out the third folder, another raised enough for her to see it. He quickly shoved the offending packet back down, but she'd read the name and tucked it into her memory. *How odd.*

Hank rubbed his leg and watched the pile grow in number. She waited for Hank to pounce. He was a no-nonsense detective. She figured he would set the intruder straight at any moment. Hank grabbed one up from the stack and opened it. During his glance through it, the Special Agent interrupted him.

"What evidence did you gather so far? Did you identify the body?"

Hank kept his nose buried in the report, so she answered. "The victim is a problem. We've confirmed her identity. It's Heather Balentine, the movie star. We want to keep the information under wraps for a while. If the press finds out, the situation will bring chaos, but you know how these things go. The information might pop at any time."

Trin nodded.

"We haven't confirmed how she got to Tulsa without the paparazzi trailing behind. An officer discovered the body, and it's the first we heard about her presence." A scowl never left her face.

"I see. What time did the patrolman find her?" Trin took a recorder from his briefcase and switched it on.

"One this morning by a black and white. Otherwise, I'm sure her photos would appear on the internet by now." Hank joined the conversation again. "We had a short night on sleep, but we attempted to check the security cameras from the airport. It's the most probable means of transportation since she is due back Monday morning on a film set in LA. Bill and Paige hope to get lucky and see if anyone met her and what luggage she picked up. We found none on or near the body."

"So far, everything falls in line with the previous victims, except those women came from local areas. They were minor celebrities. Heather is by far the most famous one. You're right about one issue. When the press finds out, it'll make for a god-awful mess," Trin said.

"Well, unless you need me, I'm anxious to get back to the airport footage. You're welcome to join us. Bill needs extra eyes on it if he can get them." She attempted to get up.

Hank motioned for her to sit. "What can you tell us about our guy? Since you already know the particulars from the other cases, you're bound to stay ahead on useful information. I'd appreciate it if you would tell us what you have and catch us up."

"With the public display from his body dumps, he leans toward an exhibitionist killer. He wants people to see what he's done. From this, we can deduce he aims to strike terror in the public. It's where he receives further gratification."

"This type reads the paper, watches the news, and searches the internet for information and updates on the investigation.

In a sense, it's a way to keep score. He'll save clippings or videos about the case for masturbation purposes. In his mind, he has thrown down a challenge. He thinks he's clever and smarter than the authorities. He says catch me if you can and sees himself as dueling with you in the public arena. They often escalate the nature of their crimes, and he will repeatedly kill until you stop him."

"I've read up on serial killers, but this one is the only one I've worked," Hank said.

"His first victim might have been an accident. After he killed once, I suspect the act opened the door to a compulsion inside him. Something about the eyes remains important to him. That's why he carves the one eye and stabs the other with a scalpel. He leaves virtually no clues. Each victim has been a minor celebrity. Your actress has the biggest name by far, and he's more than likely hunting his next victim." Trin paused for a moment. "Strangulation during sex gets his juices flowing and is what gets him off. It wouldn't surprise me if he got his initial experience with erotic asphyxiation during the Donna Barnett kill."

Hank nodded. "I had the same idea. I worked a few that involved perpetrators who choked their partners during sex, so the thought crossed my mind. How many are we talking? I noticed four listed that I figured were our guy, and another that might be his primary."

"So far, our counts agree. This one is the sixth. If we're correct, the unsub started around the LA area three years ago. He dumped Donna Barnett in the Hollywood Hills. She'd recently finished a series of Sizzle Shampoo commercials. They've stopped running them, but they played them a lot for a year or two," Trin said.

"So far we've got little or no evidence. The ME believes he scrubbed the body. Sam sent samples for DNA testing, but he doesn't expect we'll have anything show up. From a glance at your other cases, it seems about right with the rest," Hank said.

"It's true. The unsub left nothing for us at the other crime scenes. No hairs. No prints. No DNA. They finally found Donna Barnett's car, but it'd been wiped clean, and the seat moved back into place. Either that, or he doesn't have long legs." Trin leaned back in the chair.

"What do you make from the heart carving and what resided under it?" Hank rubbed his leg and stretched it out before him.

"What heart carving?"

"The one on Heather," Hank answered.

"The unsub's been adding new steps to his perversion. There've been heart-shaped lockets around the neck, but no carvings on the body except for the left eye."

"This time he left a heart carved in her chest. When Sam lifted the chunky flesh out, the perp had removed two pieces from her ribs and laid the locket on her heart muscle. I'm sure you know what the perp put inside the locket."

"A heart-shaped iris that didn't belong to the victim and a fingerprint that doesn't match hers either."

"Looks like it. Tests are still running, but . . ." Hank shrugged.

"The last two wore lockets, but they hung around the neck, and were positioned to lay between her breasts over her heart. The unsub may evolve a little more with each kill, or more likely, he wants to start a game with the cops. Either way, he qualifies for the one sick bastard award." Trin peeked at her. "Sorry."

Before she had time to respond, her cell phone rang. She walked several steps away from the men and took the call. After she returned, they both stared at her expectantly. "Bill found her at Tulsa International. He's ready to show us what he has."

"We're on borrowed time with the press. Let's go." Hank moved toward the door.

"This might give us the break we've needed. We haven't confirmed how the unsub contacted his victims. We could get lucky if the airport has enough cameras," Trin said while he cleared the door right before it closed.

They reached the technology lab on the TU campus where she introduced Bill to Trin. Then they got into a more comfortable position to view the monitor.

"I first picked her up on a Southwest flight from LA before six Friday evening. The flight stopped at Vegas for about half an hour." Bill started the film on his monitor.

By this time, they'd pulled up chairs, and their eyes examined his big computer screen. In less than five seconds, Heather Balentine's image appeared on the monitor. With a pink backpack already over her shoulder, she walked directly to the baggage terminal and grabbed a rectangular black bag with wheels and a pull-up handle off the turnstile. She only carried the two items. Bill found another camera which showed her leaving the front of the airport in a taxi. From the film, they got the cab number.

"Great job, Bill. You got us the best information we possess on the victim. At least we know how she got here. If we can find out where she went and why she came here, the case could change quickly." Excitement raced through her veins, and she got up to leave.

~

*Three years earlier*

Tony Strete's cell phone woke him from a deep sleep. After the third ring, he picked up.

"Streets, my man, what have you been up to?" He hadn't seen Ben McCall in a week.

"Sleeping, until you woke me up." He laid his head back down on his pillow and wished Ben's voice would go away.

"Hey, you can catch z's anytime. A discussion about my idea requires your presence." Ben sounded much too energetic for his peace of mind.

"Can't you handle it by yourself, McCall? I've been prowling for two days straight. I'm beat, man." His body ached with fatigue—nothing about going interested him.

"I said it requires your presence."

"Can't you use Josh? Go wake him up." He remained determined not to leave his bed.

"He's already here. We're waiting for you."

"Where are you?" He forced his groggy brain to wake up and focus. When Ben wanted something, he was persistent.

"My place in Malibu. Hurry. I got a cold one here with your name on it."

"I'll get there in a few." He closed his cell phone and tossed it on the table next to his bed. He glanced at the clock beside it —2:45. Since he'd closed the blackout shades before he collapsed into bed, he didn't know for sure if the time was day or night. With Ben, it might go either way.

After another thirty seconds in bed, he threw off the covers and made his way to the shower. The hot water did nothing to revive him, so he turned it briefly to cold. That got his attention.

Within half an hour, he rang his friend's doorbell.

"Look who finally showed up," Ben greeted him.

Ben's chipper tone made him want to turn and go home, back to the bed where he belonged. "Cut the BS. I told you I'm worn out."

"Whoa. The boy's all business." Ben laughed.

He didn't wait for an invitation and went around him into the house. Josh sat on the black leather sofa and held a beer. He threw himself down on the loveseat opposite Josh and ignored them both for a moment. "I'm having this conversation horizontally. What's so important?"

"You know what I like about you? You always get straight to the point," Josh said.

Ben moved over to the sofa where Josh sat, but he remained standing. "I had a genius idea. After the film we finished, we need to put something together to redeem our reputations. We can't afford to wait too long. Think about *The Man Who Shot Liberty Valance*. We could do a remake. The script calls for three male leads, each with a great part, and I count three of us. This time let's get the best director we can afford. Steven Spielberg, Ronnie Howard, or Ridley Scott. Somebody great."

"How will the studios afford them plus us in one movie? They'll never go for it." He got up to get a beer from the kitchen.

"We would put the deal together ourselves," Josh said.

"Yeah, if we own the movie, we'd retain total control over it. I don't want any more directors who will ruin the movie with their interpretative bullshit." Ben finally sat down at the opposite end of the couch from Josh.

Tony closed his eyes for several seconds and deliberated. Then he took his first drink and swallowed. "Do you two have any idea what it takes to produce a project like this? I certainly don't. I mean, I some knowledge about making movies, but not enough to produce one. The specific details like catering, stunt crews, assistants for the gaffer, or whatever, I don't know shit about those. We stay in our trailers between takes. What can we learn about the other essentials? Most importantly, who to use for the rewrite. Should we update it, or do we leave it intact? The particulars. We need to find out about those."

"Hey, I used to work on a stunt crew, so I can do the heavy lifting on those. I'll admit, I don't know much about gaffers and catering, but still," Josh said.

"We're each scheduled to work on separate projects soon. Mine starts in a week. Let's take the opportunity to learn. When we get the chance, we need to pay attention to the details. Ask tons of questions. If this last picture we made flops, we could revitalize our careers plus make a load on this project." Ben watched them for their answer.

He figured what his friend wanted. Ben expected total agreement with his plan as usual.

"It's a good idea, but we do need to do extra work and research." Josh looked introspective for a moment, then tipped his beer up.

"I'll think about it. Who gets to play John Wayne?" He assumed this issue would be the biggest problem. With egos like theirs, reaching an agreement might take a special touch. The room stayed silent while they stared at each other. He figured he'd got it right.

"The script doesn't contain a character named John Wayne," Josh said.

"You know what I asked, Josh. John Wayne played Tom, the rancher who doesn't get the girl. It's still a fantastic part, and who hasn't wanted to play John Wayne?" He watched the other two and figured they had discussed a lot before he arrived.

Ben glared at Josh and him like they were crazy. "It's my idea. I'm the obvious choice. Josh seems the perfect one to play Ransom Stoddard, and today, your attitude *is* Liberty Valance, the title role. What more do you need? Problem solved."

"See. I'll need to weigh my decision for this reason. Lee Marvin mostly played the heavy after his performance. I don't want to be typecast for the rest of my career. I would do an awesome job, but then every time someone needed a nasty villain, they would naturally hire me. It might ruin me." He sat up, stretched, and took a long drink from his beer. Then he grinned.

"Hey, they already do. I called you first thing," Ben said.

But Tony saw past the joke. Seriousness flashed in Ben's expression. "Ha, ha." He sat up, put his feet on the floor, and grabbed his beer. The label caught his attention, and he picked at it.

"I'll have the most screen time because I get to tell the story. Tony will work steadily since every movie needs a really good bad guy, and Ben gets to play John Wayne. This way we each win," Josh said.

"I never said I'd play Liberty. I said I'd think about it. If we do this, you can't do it like John Wayne. We must make it our own. We don't do a knockoff. I won't participate if we don't get it rewritten." He figured his adamant attitude would ruin the idea for sure.

"I've deliberated about the script, too. I don't want to do it like the Duke. Besides, movie tastes change. We would need to keep the integrity from the original, but make it appeal to the modern movie-goer." Ben got up to go to the fridge and tossed his previous bottle in the garbage.

"Yeah, the film worked great in black and white, but I don't think you could sell it that way anymore. The 3D pictures have made a mark too. It would take creative insight on how to approach the remake." Josh paused. "Hey, bring me one," he called to Ben.

"I say table it for the present. Let's make our movies. Stay in touch. Learn what we can. Then we'll see if it's doable. It'll give me time to decide on the part. Liberty might give me a good challenge. I'm not sure. The script has to be exceptional before I touch it." He punched the pillow, laid back down, and got more comfortable.

"Yeah, the last chick you dated said the same about your sex life." Ben always had to get the last word.

PAIGE WALKED behind the men when they descended upon the Yellow Checker Cab Company on Twenty-First Street near Sheridan. Hank asked to speak to the dispatcher. After a short discussion, Hank received the name and pertinent information for Carl Solomon, the driver who'd picked up the victim at the airport.

She glanced at his notes, then dialed Carl's number. She handed the phone to Hank, and he stepped a short distance away.

She saw the strange look on Trin's face. "What?"

Trin didn't say anything.

"Hank doesn't like to admit he can't see the numbers on his cell phone like he used to. So, I help him out with small issues, and he teaches me what I need to know. It works for us."

Trin nodded and smiled as if he understood.

"He raised me. My father was his partner for a long time before drug dealers killed him on the job. Hank took me under his wing. He's like a father to me ever since." She hated that she felt obligated to explain herself to the outsider.

"No answer," Hank said then moved closer to them.

"Shall we?" She motioned to the vehicle, and they got in.

They reached the apartment complex near Admiral and Mingo, then searched for the correct apartment number. Hank pounded his fist on the door. After they waited a few seconds, he called out, "Carl Solomon, we need to talk to you," and knocked loudly again.

It took several more minutes for Carl to peek his eyes out the slit he opened with the door. "Yeah."

"We are detectives with homicide at Tulsa PD and Special Agent Trinity from the FBI. We want to talk to you about the passenger you picked up at the airport yesterday around six. She had red hair, very attractive. Do you remember her?" Hank flashed his badge.

Carl ran his hand through his disheveled hair while he opened the door completely. "Let me think. I'm still half asleep. I didn't get off last night until three." He paused and scratched his day-old beard. "She looked hot. I remember her. She swore she wasn't anyone famous, but she reminded me of someone. Couldn't remember who."

"Where did you take her?" Hank clipped his badge back to his belt.

"She gave me a humongous tip to forget." Carl shrugged. He hesitated and looked uncertain.

"Here's a great tip. She won't care. She's dead. Where did you leave her?" Hank scowled and waited for the answer.

Shock flashed across Carl's expression during the time he processed what Hank said. "Man, what a waste. Gorgeous female. I took her to Woodward Park. Up in the part where you can drive through. She got out and walked toward the shelter with the toilets."

"Did you see anyone waiting for her? Any cars parked near-by?" Hank asked.

"I got a call to pick up another ride about the same time. I'm sure a few cars sat in the lot, but I didn't pay any attention to them. I don't remember much about it." Carl shook his head and bit his lower lip.

Hank stared at Trin. "Do you want to ask something?"

"What did you talk about? Did she say where she planned to go? Anything that could help us?" Trin asked.

"I remember I assumed she had a hot date. She primped a little, stared in her mirror, put on lipstick, and fixed her hair. I tried to talk to her, but she didn't show any interest, so I finally shut up and took her where she wanted to go. She seemed so familiar, but she assured me we'd never met."

"Did she mention her plans for the weekend? Where she would stay?" Trin rephrased the question.

"No. I don't remember if she said anything like that. I pulled up, and she gave me a fifty-dollar tip to forget I saw her. Then she got out, took her suitcase and her backpack, and went back toward the shelter and toilets. I got a call to go pick up another fare, so I left." Carl shook his head. "Nothing comes to mind. She didn't seem friendly. Wouldn't talk much."

"What time did you let her off?" Trin asked.

"Around six thirty, I think. I'm not sure, but somewhere around there." Carl scratched at his beard. Then he glanced up, uncertain.

"Okay." Trin nodded his head. He'd finished.

Hank took a card from his jacket pocket and handed it to Carl. "If you remember any little detail, call me day or night. You can never tell what might be important. Call me."

Carl nodded and closed the door.

"Someone picked her up. I can't believe she spent her whole time here in the park. People would have heard her scream. Besides, we know he dumped her body," she said while they walked back to their car.

"Do you mean they found her body in the same park?" Trin asked.

"Yeah, the victim was placed down the hill, in front of a statue. The way her body was laid out, she looked like a sacrifice. Crime techs took pictures if you want to study them, and I took my own," Hank said when they reached their vehicle.

"Does it make a difference that they found her in the same

park? I mean, were any previous ones?" She stopped and stared over the Crown Vic at Trin.

"I'm not sure. The unsub could have evolved more, or maybe we know more about this victim's movements on the day she died. It's difficult to say without extra information," Trin answered as they loaded up and Hank drove away.

# 5

*Two and a half years earlier*

Tony sat and nursed a beer at The Reel Shack. He glanced at the oversized clock on the wall. Quarter past noon and the place was dead. He enjoyed his drink without putting on an act for a change. In Hollywood, he always felt pressured to look and act a certain way when he left his residence. The only real home he'd known waited fifteen hundred miles east at his parents in Tulsa.

The Eagles' "Tequila Sunrise" played softly in the background. His plan to run out for a quick ride along the coast brought him here. Restlessness plagued him the last few days. Lost in thought, he didn't notice the group who'd entered the club. Since they served food from eleven on, most customers came here to eat an expensive lunch and to be seen.

The atmosphere changed. The skin on the back of his neck tingled. He sensed someone watched him. He couldn't wait to leave. He threw several twenties on the glass table and got up. As he turned to go, Grant Windsor walked up to him and blocked his way out. He'd forgotten how huge the man was. Though the director stood only three inches taller, his build intimidated.

"I haven't seen you in a while. Staying busy?" Grant had a young, hot blonde on his arm.

She didn't interest him, so he didn't bother to flirt. He wanted to get out of this funk. If he talked to Grant for long, it would make his mood worse.

"I'm on my way out. It's good to see you again. We can talk later." He attempted to leave.

"I heard a rumor. You can tell me if it's true."

"What's that?" He didn't know why Grant irritated him. Something about the man seemed off.

"Someone said you, Josh, and Ben want to put a picture together. We worked great on our last project. I figured you might need me to direct it for you. After all, this step up is a big one for the three of you. You'll want someone with good experience to guide you."

"Where did you hear that? Who told you?" he asked.

"Oh, you know. Rumors float around this town most of the time. I can't remember who told me." His smile resembled a sneer, like the man understood more than he said.

He shrugged. "First time I've heard anything about it." He moved to walk off.

"Don't forget my offer, in case you hear the same buzz I did."

He nodded. Then he forgot about his mood and walked out the door. He got into his silver Ferrari convertible and turned the ignition over. *Son of a bitch. How did Windsor know about their tentative plans?*

~

PAIGE LISTENED to Hank and Trin's discussion while they drove to Woodward Park. Once they examined the body dump site, the group moved up the hill to the place where Carl Solomon let Heather Balentine out. Nothing appeared out of place. Four cars sat parked in the area near the shelter when the three arrived. The restroom revealed nothing helpful. Each fanned out and took different trails back down through the enormous trees to the area that surrounded the horse and Indian statue. They didn't find any evidence tied to Heather Balentine.

Following their return to the station, Hank and Trin drove down to the morgue to see Sam. Trin wanted to examine the new carving on the body. She entered the station to collect everything they had from the various officers who canvassed the area. No new leads turned up.

After the other two got back, they brought the contact information Sam received when he ran Heather Balentine's fingerprints.

Hank looked at Trin and her. "I think we need to release her death to the public. We can get her private cell phone number and email accounts from her contacts in LA. I'll call them, or you can." He nodded toward Trin. "The news will surface quickly. You know how the media operates. With the internet, it only takes seconds. Unless you come up with a better idea."

"We'll notify the family before, if possible. The time factor is critical. Let's do it. We've been lucky to keep it quiet this long. Put the call through. I'll contact the FBI databases to see what I can get from them," Trin said.

Hank nodded and sat down at his desk to place the call. She pointed at hers for Trin to use. She leaned her hip against a file cabinet while she waited until they each finished. Hopefully, something broke soon on the case. Right now, they had nothing.

A few seconds later, she remembered something that should help. Several traffic cameras ran along Twenty-First Street, but she wasn't sure how many. Bill Graywolf could find out for sure. She would visit her favorite tech and see. They'd been so busy with other details that she figured they didn't check the traffic cameras yet.

She got Hank's attention and motioned she would come right back. She drove the three and a half miles to the TU campus and found Bill in the tech room busy staring at his monitor.

"Hey, good looking, I need your help. How many traffic cameras are in and around Woodward Park? Would you check them to find what faces we caught on film? Who went to and from the park on Friday evening around six thirty? We placed our victim in the park around that time. I know several cameras run along Twenty-First Street, but I'm not sure how many others work in the general area."

"Boy, you seem determined to make my job secure, don't you?"

She grinned then made a mock-pleading face with her hands folded in a prayer-like manner. "Pleeease."

"No begging allowed." Bill attempted to hold out. Then he laughed.

"But we're stuck. No leads. Going nowhere. We need help."

"Damn it, Paige. You know I can't say no when you do the pitiful act."

She continued to smile but stayed silent. Since she'd traded on the unwritten code more than once, she knew he would cave.

"Okay, but other cases need my attention, too. And you

understand, these cameras are a long shot. Do you have any idea how many cameras are in the area?"

"I know, but the officer found her dead by one in the morning so the time lapse shouldn't take long. Someone had to pick her up close to six thirty. The killer needed time to play with her, clean her up, and get her back to the statue before one. The kill zone was probably in a rural area. I mean people would hear her scream or see him move the body if he used a populated area. It's a guess, but the idea sounds logical to me. So I'd check the hour following the time she got out of the taxi at the park. If you don't find anything with those parameters, then search a longer time frame."

Bill nodded and deliberated for a minute. "Okay, but you will owe me for life on this one, and you need to promise me you'll consider what I mentioned earlier. I know you were in love with Bobby."

Her face turned white. "Did everyone know?"

"I"—he hesitated—"don't know."

"Did everyone know?" She emphasized the question this time. "Did Hank know?"

Bill didn't look at her.

"Oh my God. The whole force knows, and you didn't mention it to me." She stared at Bill for a moment, then turned to leave the room behind. She wanted to exit without running from the humiliation that followed close behind her.

She ducked into the first restroom she found. Tears formed. By the time she reached the last stall and locked the door, the drops spilled onto her cheeks. She felt ten years old again.

PAIGE WATCHED *Crissy lay the doll down on her bed. The white-satin dress glistened in the afternoon sun.*

*"I don't want to play with dolls. Mom always thinks I*

should play with dolls like a girly girl, but I love the animals in the barn more. I sneak off and ride Buckshot every time I get a chance. Do you ride horses?"

"No. I never lived where people owned horses. We always lived in the city." She still held her doll, which wore a wedding dress. She glanced at the toy, but Crissy's idea got her attention.

"Let's go see the kittens. Mama Kitty has three she keeps in the barn. They're so cute. You've got to see them."

They left her room behind and moved silently through the back door. Once outside, the sun felt hot on her back. But she sensed freedom in the air as they half-walked, half-skipped their way to the barn.

"Come on up. The mama usually has them on the third row."

"Is Mama Kitty mean?"

"No. She likes to rub against your legs a lot. Mama Kitty has tripped my mother so many times that she always yells at the cat. We finally moved Mama Kitty to live in the barn."

The structure held so many distinctive smells she'd never sniffed before. She scrunched her nose. Crissy giggled and climbed up the next row of bales. The hay felt stiff and scratchy, but then she saw a black furry mass peep out from between two hay bales. She grabbed the kitten and pressed it to her neck. The softness and warmth felt like heaven in her hands while she cuddled the small pet.

"We call him Preacher Sam since he doesn't have a white hair on him anywhere." Crissy picked up a yellow tabby. "Morris chases mice if he's not too lazy. The young gray and white one we call Jezebel. She's the only girl in the bunch. Mom said we couldn't keep her. We don't need any more cats underfoot."

"How do you ever go inside and leave them? They're so cute and fluffy."

"Mom says I should leave them alone part-time because they need to eat, and babies sleep a lot."

"Oh."

"I sneak out here a bunch, and they always play and bite each other. So, I'm not so sure Mom is right. I think she doesn't want me to get too attached so she can give them away. But I got Daddy to say I can have one. He always keeps his word."

She smiled and remembered her father for a moment before she heard a vehicle back its way toward the barn's opposite end. The truck stopped next to the other side of the hay pile. She stared at Crissy. "Will we get in trouble for being here?" She worried about trouble a lot. She wanted to live with Hank forever. She would die if she had to go back to Children's Services again.

"No. Dad's cool with me and the kittens. He thinks Mom fusses too much."

She peeked up toward the top bales. When she saw Bobby, the most handsome young man she'd ever seen, he stole her breath away. She saw his powerful shoulders and arms, and for the first time, she recognized muscles looked beautiful. She wanted to run her fingers over their smoothness. The feeling wasn't sexual like people would think, but she felt an awareness, a sense she finally fit. One gaze into his dark eyes and her adoration belonged to him.

He'd helped his dad and Hank haul hay. Sweat beaded above his lip. With his shirt off, his tan back rippled with the weight of each bale he lifted into place. She'd never witnessed such a sight before, and she didn't want Bobby ever to quit stacking the hay.

A few minutes passed before Hank introduced her to Bobby and his father, Glen. Their father asked her if she enjoyed the day. She nodded, too shy to say a word.

Nervousness always left her quiet during the time Bobby

*hung around. His four advanced years made the young man treat her like a kid sister. Over the years, it kept her up more nights than she could count. But until nine months ago, she couldn't say a word around him.*

PAIGE DRIED HER LAST TEARS, blew her nose, and splashed water on her face from the tap. She inspected herself in the mirror and blotted her face dry. Once she felt certain no one would know she'd been crying, she left the bathroom and walked out of the building.

She arrived back at her desk to find the guys finished with their phone conversations. They both stared at her with questioning eyes.

"Hey, I only left for a minute."

They glanced at their watches in unison.

She grinned. "Okay, so I disappeared for more than a minute. I did a little ass-kissing. I wanted Bill to check for cameras in and around the Woodward Park area for our time-frame on Friday evening. You never know."

Hank nodded. "It might lead somewhere, but let's not hold our breath. I wonder if we shouldn't hold a press conference and see if anyone who was in the park Friday evening witnessed anything. I hate to do it. It always brings out the nut jobs, but we need a break in the worst way."

Trin looked them both in the eye and frowned. "We don't have anything to go on, but I hate to think about dealing with the half-wits that usually call us. Let Bill work on the camera angle for a time at least, until we notify her family. By then, we can obtain her cell phone records and email accounts. Something could break on one of those. If not, then we'll check into the press conference angle."

"Sounds like a good plan to me. Before long, the media will

force us to hold a press conference to announce her death. You and the captain can handle that matter." Hank motioned toward Trin.

She couldn't figure Hank out. He never acted this docile. She'd never seen him take to another law enforcement member like this except for Glen Youngblood, his last partner. Of all the people to befriend, Trin and the FBI were not the ones to trust. Something seemed amiss with Hank, but she didn't know what. Her whole life she'd heard him complain about the Feds. Still, he cooperated with them without resistance. It didn't make sense.

TOM MCCALL SLUGGED *Ben's mother and slammed her head against the wall. Her eyes rolled back in her head. Ben understood she couldn't take another hit. He moved up close behind his father to trip him while his father backed away from the blow he'd just delivered.*

*Tom staggered and turned around. Ben scrambled to roll away from the old man, but his dad caught him by his shirt and dragged him back into range. "You stupid son of a bitch," his father yelled as the old man put his fist squarely into his young ribs.*

*"I'm sorry. I didn't mean to trip you. I promise," he lied and scooted away from his father's range. Tom stepped forward and grabbed him again. The next blow split his lip against his teeth. He tasted blood. Tom continued to beat him until the hatred that flowed freely through the bastard's veins abated. The night his mother died remained the last time he'd ever begged his father for anything.*

Ben tossed and turned for the umpteenth time and got up

from his bed. He wandered into his study. Why he owned one, he hadn't a clue, other than it came with the house.

He switched on the lamp and stared at the gold image. It sat beside the light on the massive mahogany desk. He'd earned the award for the best actor in a leading role, but he'd performed his whole life. Early on for women, then to reenact his father.

The first time he read the script for *Deserted Dreams*, he knew he could play the main character better than any other person. He chased the lead vigorously and finally landed the part. The excitement lasted for days. Later, the enchantment wore off.

During his younger years, he'd watched his father turn into the same bastard. Once shooting started, he'd had to climb back into his worst nightmare. He received accolades for his performance but felt like a sham. He didn't need to act. The script resided in his soul. His real existence. The one that disappeared following that murderous night.

He pulled out the cushioned chair and sat. The Oscar haunted him until he picked it up and a tear wet his cheek. He examined the award and remembered how much he believed it would change his life. Gently, he rested his head on his outstretched arm, which still held the golden replica. The figure dangled out over the edge of the desk. His upper body softly relaxed across the teak wood top, darkness pulled him back into his disturbing dreams, and the iconic statue dropped quietly to the thick carpet below.

## 6

Paige sat and listened while Hank announced the LA Police Department made the notification an hour ago. Terry Balentine realized her sister was dead. She dialed the number for the young woman and handed the phone to Hank. She hit the button to put the phone on speaker. It rang five times before a female answered.

"Is this Terry Balentine?" Hank's tone sounded respectful.

"May I ask who is calling?"

"I'm Detective Hank Gettering from the Tulsa Police Department. We need to speak to Miss Terry Balentine regarding her sister, Heather."

"I'm her sister. I'm Terry Balentine. The police said you'd call."

"Are you okay, Miss Balentine?" Hank waited for a few more seconds. Sounds of crying still came through the speaker. "If you feel up to it, we would like to ask you a few questions that concern your sister. You think you're able to do that?" Hank rubbed at his knee.

"I guess so."

"What did your sister plan to do in Tulsa? What was the purpose of her visit?" Hank asked.

"I didn't know she went to Tulsa." Her voice steadied. "She never said anything to me about it."

"Did she mention to you what she planned to do this weekend?"

"No. Heather mentioned something like she would see me Sunday night and grinned, but I'd assumed she had a hot date for the weekend. If she did, the guy was someone new. I didn't hear her mention anyone specific for a while." Terry abruptly stopped speaking as if she'd said too much.

"Is there a reason she didn't indicate anyone new? It would help us considerably to find out the specifics concerning her personal life. We're not the press, Miss Balentine, but we need to catch a killer," Hank said.

"She took the breakup from her relationship with Anthony Strete hard. Since then, she hasn't dated much. She's been seen out with different guys for publicity reasons, but none meant anything. Lately, she's been quiet. I've seen her on her computer a lot and her phone. I don't know who her chat partners were. She's mysterious when she wants to be."

"Do you have the number for that phone or her online account name?"

"I have her main numbers, but not her private ones. I don't think anyone got those. At least, not to my knowledge. My sister kept one computer with her wherever she happened to go. She used it exclusively, and I saw her pull up Google on it once. She didn't let anyone near the information on her laptop. Even Jill didn't get to mess with that. Heather owned at least one cell phone she managed herself. My sister never gave me the number for the private one either. She claimed that private electronics gave her a lifeline to the real world. During the time she talked on it, she didn't have to act like the Hollywood Heather Balentine. I attempted to tell her it might lead to trouble, but she was three years older. I'm the little sister. She never listened to me."

Paige never had a sister. But she knew she would have given Crissy access to anything. Why wouldn't Heather give Terry her number? It didn't make sense.

Hank wrote the name on his pad. "Who is this Jill you mentioned?"

"She's Heather's personal assistant. She managed her other online accounts. Everyone has to open an account on Facebook, Twitter, and all the socials, then build a website. Jill handled those plus ran errands for her and generally did whatever she needed. Heather kept Jill plenty busy."

Hank absently rubbed his leg again. "Can you give the last name and number for Jill?"

"Sure. Jill Caywood. The studio lists her info, but I have it right here." She gave him the number.

"So, you're saying you know for sure your sister owned a set of private accounts, but she kept a regular set for the public to contact her. Did Miss Caywood get access to the private accounts?" Hank asked.

"I don't think so, but you should ask her. I'm not a hundred percent sure. Heather had issues about her private life, especially since Tony dumped her."

"You mean he dumped her? She didn't dump him?"

"Of course he dumped her. The affair broke her heart. No one ever left her before. She was so beautiful and could get anyone she wanted, but he waltzed in and stole her heart. Then he left. It pissed her off. You've probably met his type before. He's one slimy bastard."

"Yes, I know his kind. How long ago did they break up?" Hank asked.

"I'm not sure. A year ago or more. Somewhere around then."

"Did your sister get over this broken romance, or did she still love Mr. Strete?"

"I'm not sure. I assumed my sister was still nuts about Tony until this weekend. It surprised me when she said what she did. Something about she'd see me on Sunday evening. I'm not sure if she met Tony again or someone new. She never did share private information with me. Heather probably wanted me to assume she didn't participate in cheap Hollywood affairs. In this town, what else do you get? It's a crazy business. It's difficult to explain, but sometimes she seemed so isolated and lonely for real friends. The kind you can't buy. Those are impossible to find out here."

Paige heard the sound of Terry blowing her nose.

"Yes, I'm sure." Hank glanced over at Trin and nodded.

"Miss Balentine, I'm Special Agent Trinity. Did your sister take her separate laptop and cell phone with her on her trip?"

"I'm sure she did. She always kept them in her pink backpack. I remember she took it with her. I saw the bag over her shoulder as she stuck her head in the door to tell me she would see me on Sunday evening. Oh my God. She has to resume filming on Monday. What will they do? We need to call them immediately."

"It's all right, Miss Balentine. We understand your concern. The situation is unexpected. It's caught you off guard. Did your sister mention anyone in her life lately whom she hasn't talked about previously? Not necessarily a new boyfriend, but someone she's remarked on in casual conversation several times? Someone you've not noticed her talk about until recently? It probably wouldn't stick out in your mind. Can you think of anyone who'd qualify?" Trin asked.

"No one comes to mind. Sometimes we talk about everything. Then other times we get busy and hardly talk for weeks. I'm a resident, so I'm always pushed for time. She got into acting since I wanted to go to med school. She started in the business to pay for my education. She never dreamed she'd make so much money, but I always felt guilty after she gave up her normal life. It's a huge trade-off to live out here in la-la land."

"You've never been tempted to try your hand at acting?"

"No. That's Heather's world. I kept out completely. Heather didn't want me in it, either. That might be why she kept secrets about her computer and phone. She still attempted to find a life separate from the Hollywood crowd. Now, she'll never find it."

Terry's voice cracked with emotion.

"Miss Balentine, you've been helpful. I know you need more time to grieve your sister's death, but keep in mind our question about her revealing anyone new in her life. Someone she normally didn't talk about in conversation. If you think of a person similar to what I've described, no matter how little you assume it matters, please give us a call. It might help us a lot." Trin gave his and Hank's numbers and ended the call.

*Two and a half years earlier*

Tony walked into Ben's kitchen to get another beer. He barely noticed the exquisite view of the sunset displayed over the Pacific Ocean that the sliding glass doors revealed. His target lay in the refrigerator.

"We could shoot in Oklahoma for pennies compared to most other locations. Have you ever been to the western part? I went to a funeral several years ago in the area. The mesas run for twenty miles or so with flatlands in between. To the north near Waynoka, The Little Sahara State Park runs sixteen hundred acres with nothing but dunes. The park should work for another perfect location to shoot. We'd probably pay the ranchers a little for rental." He sat back down.

"What is there to do out there in nowheresville?" Josh settled into the sofa.

"Act, but I'll tell you what else they have in Oklahoma. Native American Casinos. They opened a Hard Rock right outside of Tulsa, which takes three hours or so by turnpike from where we'd shoot *Liberty*. Besides, my parents live in Tulsa. I can't stay so close for two months and not visit them."

"So who died out in the sticks, and you attended the funeral?" Ben liked to get details.

"An old maid aunt. She owned a farm out near Cleo Springs. I hadn't been near there for years. There isn't anything out in the area worth talking about but the scenery. The setting would work perfect for a western, especially in August or late July, after everything gets parched from the hot, dry summers."

"You sound like you know the place." Ben drank freely from his beer.

"I do. I got into a little trouble with gangs in Tulsa back in the day. My parents sent me out there to stay for my senior year. I figured I'd go nuts. Talk about nothing to do. But I survived. I was young." He shrugged.

"We could get the tax laws checked out for the state. I don't suppose your aunt left you the farm. You said she was an old maid." Josh always hunted for a way to save a buck.

"Yes, she did, but the house hasn't been lived in since she died. The home seemed ancient when I lived there." He regretted mentioning it. H wasn't sure he wanted them out there tromping on his memories.

"Does the inheritance property include enough land to

build a street scene on it? If the structure looks old enough, we might use it and build Shinbone. We need to either find an old town to use or build a modest one somewhere." Josh glanced at Tony.

"Probably. We've got room enough. The two-bedroom is an old clapboard and would look appropriate for the period. It sits on a hundred and sixty acres. If nothing else, we could probably use it for Tom's cabin. His character plays a rancher." He watched Ben to get a read on his viewpoint.

"So the residence is not in use?" Josh asked.

"I didn't say it wasn't in use. I rent it out. A guy runs cattle on it and keeps the fence up. I might get him to leave the cattle there while we film." He settled back in his seat.

Ben ran his hand through his hair and gripped the back of his neck. "Let me get my lawyer to check out the specifics. I hadn't considered Oklahoma, but I suppose it could work. We should figure out a time we can schedule the shoot. I'm booked solid for another year and a half. We'll start with our calendars. We should get our agents to synchronize our time."

"We have to get a script written first. Who do we want to do the honors?" Josh asked.

"A script will involve spending real money. Up to this point, the most we've done is talk. Are you ready to sink money into this? It's chump change for my lawyer to check out the tax benefits for the state. If we hire a screenwriter, it will cost, but it's the next step to take. I think it's time to put up or shut up." Ben nodded toward the other two.

"Are we in this for real?" he said.

"If we hire a writer, we better be." Ben took another drink. "So how much do we put in on the deal? We might produce a huge money maker, or we could crap out."

"I can afford ten million to start. How about if we each put in ten million? We put it in an escrow account where it would draw interest before we need it. By then we can figure out how much it will cost to complete this movie. Money goes fast for a movie these days, but we won't draw a salary. The farmers and ranchers in the area surely won't cost much. It should go a long way on a western." Josh got up to put his empty bottle in the kitchen trash.

"Let's make it at least fifteen million apiece. If we're too cheap on the movie, it will show. It has to be top quality. We each make close to that amount on one movie." He absently rubbed the label on his beer loose.

"I agree. Let's not scrimp on this. We may have to add more at a later date if we want to continue to own it," Ben said.

"By the way, how did Grant Windsor find out about it? He sniffed me out at The Reel Shack last week. Hinted he wanted to direct it for us. I didn't tell anybody." He took a drink from his tepid beer and made a disgusted expression as he stared at his bottle.

"You didn't give anything away, did you?" Josh frowned.

"No. Of course not, but I got to thinking. He might fill John Carradine's role. Grant was a good actor before he ruined his life with directing. I can see him playing Major Cassius Star-buckle. He's the perfect blowhard, and by the way, the charac-ter's name has got to go. No one in this century would take that name seriously," he said.

"You're right about that. The name's crap. I don't care how hard Windsor sniffs. We won't let him direct. That's the one place we spend serious cash, but not on him," Josh said.

"I'm sure we agree. No problem there, but before we can get a director, we need a script. Derek Haas worked on *Three Ten to Yuma*. What about him? We should do more research on writers. We want the best one who knows how to make west-erns appeal to this generation." Ben swallowed the last drink from his beer. "At this quarter's end, let's get the escrow account started. Can you both get your money together by then?" The two guys nodded at Ben while he got up for a fresh round.

~

*The Thursday before*

BETTY GREENWAY HAD COMPLETED everything on the list. The cabin stood ready. Because he'd requested, she password protected the computer and cell phone. The inside shined like new. Surely, she'd impress him. The house appeared as near perfect as a cabin in the woods could get. The key hung on a nail in the tree out front. The last detail left was to let him show up.

If she kept her mouth shut for two months, her worries would disappear for a long time. For her, it remained the most challenging part, but she would do it. The bonus made curbing her instincts worth it. She didn't use the full ten grand he'd sent to pay for the list of requests he'd made. If he didn't specifically ask for it back, she'd keep the leftover.

With no late appointments, she left her Tulsa office a little before six. Though she didn't live far, traffic tangled in a mess on the way, but her small home near Thirty-First and Harvard appeared cheerful when she arrived. She could hardly wait to kick off her heels and let the soft carpet cushion her complaining toes. Once the car was parked, she picked up her laptop and the bag containing her burger and fries that sat on the seat beside it. Another few steps and she would be in her comfort zone.

She unlocked the door and gave it a hefty shove. It usually stuck a little. One pesky problem she hadn't gotten fixed yet. The chore was on her list for next Friday. She smelled a faint odor in the front room that seemed unfamiliar. Men's cologne? That couldn't be. No man had been in her home for years. She must have imagined it since she'd been thinking about those hot actors today.

Her pumps quickly hit the floor. She was too excited at the moment to put them away. Once she ate and rested a short while, she would return them to her bedroom closet.

She closed the door and laid her purse, keys, and laptop on the table nearby. She moved toward the kitchen and opened the refrigerator door then examined her beverage choices.

The blow of the knife penetrated between her ribs and drove upward into her heart. She barely felt pain before life rushed from her body. One sharp sting and Betty Greenway departed this earth.

THE KILLER WRAPPED her in a plastic sheet. He would return later that night to move the body. No one would miss her for days or longer. The house made no sound as he walked through and found her laptop on the table by the front door. He opened her scarlet purse and dug through it until he found her cell phone. With his gloved hand, he replaced the red bag to its former location. Then he grabbed both items and carried them with him.

He reentered the kitchen, picked up her hamburger with fries, and left by the back door. The food inside the greasy bag smelled delicious. He smiled. Betty Greenway had already provided many useful items for him, and now she'd brought him his evening meal.

## 7

_______

Paige turned off the speaker and disconnected the phone. Holding her tongue wasn't easy, but she forced herself to sit still and read the files in front of her. Hank wouldn't welcome her ideas on the matter.

The perp must know Heather's private information. He had her computer and phone. They should count on it. If they couldn't find anyone who knew the account names and numbers, it would remain impossible to track Heather's movements through them. They needed to get in touch with Jill Caywood.

"Do you think our guy uses the internet to get access to his targets?" Hank got up from his desk chair.

She knew his legs ached if he stayed in the same position too long. The symptom reminded her again about the issue neither wanted to address.

"It's a good guess. If the other women owned private accounts, we never discovered them. I always figured he picked the earliest victim up by accident, but we never figured out for sure how he chose or contacted the rest. The celebrity factor gave them a detail in common. Each held at least one claim to fame," Trin said.

"So, the asshole has her backpack. We're sure it contained Heather's private laptop and cell phone. Do you suppose he keeps them or destroys them?" Hank stretched and sat back down.

"At this point, it's difficult to tell. If our unsub's a collector, he might consider them a trophy. He's a silent, cunning predator who's come to love the killing game." Trin got up from his leaning position and paced by their two desks. Then he stopped and glanced at Hank.

"Tulsa doesn't fit his pattern either. If we're correct about Donna Barnett, he strangled in LA first, then in New York City, New Orleans, Chicago, and Las Vegas. Somehow, Tulsa feels like an odd next choice. It's a bit smaller, less likely known for a sin city type. I figure you deal with problems here like any city, but the unsub wouldn't necessarily think Tulsa ranked in the same league with the previous cities he chose. You know what I mean?" Trin said.

"Yeah. I see what you mean. People come here to visit Oral Roberts University or religious meetings in the area. The city boasts two world-class museums. Of course, the Indian Casinos attract a large crowd. They get action, but it might only tie you to Las Vegas if he gambled. I didn't think about it before, but New Orleans has gambling places, too. I'm not sure about Chicago or New York." Hank looked excited, like they'd uncovered a lead.

"I'm not sure it's the tie-in, but we will keep it in mind. Since we've uncovered a few differences about this victim, we might find more about the others. It should give us more places to explore in each situation. Sometimes a single lead can break the case loose." Trin leaned against Hank's desk this time while he settled back down.

She felt antsy. She wanted to suggest a call to Jill Caywood, but Hank was in charge. He'd been explicit about keeping her mouth shut. She would do what he said.

"We agree his original kill was probably Donna Barnett. She did the hair product commercials. You've studied the specifics more than we did. Is there any way what we've learned here could help with her death?" Hank asked.

Trin remained quiet for a moment. "I'm not sure it fits in his profile. His original more than likely happened by accident. If he contacted them through the internet, how can he know for sure they are celebrities? Terry Balentine stated her sister never gave the account names to anyone. She hinted Heather used the account under an assumed name. So how would he know she boasted any claim to fame?" Trin got her attention back with the question. He called it right. Then she watched him yank a stack of files from his briefcase. He pulled several photos out for each target.

"I see what you mean. Did all of them have special online accounts, and you didn't find listings for those? Or did you know to even check for unlisted accounts for the rest?" Hank got back up and moved to Paige's desk.

She'd studied the printout from early this morning. Mona Lansing from New York City did a radio talk show. She maintained an aggressive manner with her callers. She'd often been called the female Howard Stern.

"Paige, did you fall asleep?" Hank brought her back to the scene at hand.

"I examined the jackets on the individuals again. You told me to keep my mouth shut and learn. I've worked hard to do what you said, Hank." She shoved the papers away from her. The printouts slid across the desktop and stopped near the edge.

"I guess I'm used to your constant questions. It helps me think." Hank sounded as if he hated to admit she had merit.

"Oh sure, blame it on me," she said.

He smiled this time, and she knew she landed back in the game.

"You seemed engrossed a minute ago. What grabbed your attention?" Trin watched her.

"I read about Mona Lansing, the woman from New York. She appeared to have a tough personality. It made me curious if it carried over into her personal life. Was she strong, independent something along those lines. Did our victims share any secondary traits besides their celebrity status? Do we know the *private* lives they enjoyed? You know what I mean." She arched both eyebrows while her cheeks burned. Guys were so obtuse when they wanted to be. She never felt comfortable talking about sexual matters in front of Hank.

"I don't know if they ever found out for sure on every individual. Most times, family and friends try to cover for their loved ones. They want them considered snowy white and picture perfect. New York PD pursued it thoroughly, but never confirmed the sexual preference for Mona Lansing. People don't like to admit to that appetite, but we do know Donna Barnett enjoyed it big time. We never proved it with any of the others." Trin placed the photos on the white magnetic board. The pictures displayed before and after shots for each female.

"As you can see, he doesn't keep to a particular physical type. Mona was brunette. A couple had blonde hair. Heather was a redhead. Their physical size varied, too. Eye color ranged from blue to hazel to brown. They all rose to fame in the cities or regional areas in which they lived. They know yours internationally." Trin stepped to the side so they could view the photos better.

"You can see the way his handiwork progressed. He's

added more perverse details to the later victims. With yours, he went all out. It appears he enjoys playing games with the police. He thinks we can't stop him since he considers himself above us mentally. We can only hope this attitude will cause him to make a mistake soon. It's our best chance to catch him." Trin leaned against Paige's desk, and they studied the photographs. Then he yawned.

Hank stood and stretched his legs.

"I can't believe how late I've kept you. We've used up this whole day without much progress. Bob will want to give a press briefing soon, and we still don't know squat. At the conference, you need to stand there with the captain, and Paige and I will try to watch the crowd. It'll be a crapshoot if our killer shows up, but we need to try at least to check for anyone suspicious or unusual."

"How long until you think he'll insist on it?" She didn't look forward to the press after they found out. Everything would get crazy then. She'd never worked a murder case before, let alone a high profile one.

"I would guess it will hit the ten o'clock news here. The nationals will pick it up immediately. After that, all hell will break loose, and so far, we've got nothing," Hank said.

"Don't give up. We got a few new bits of information on Heather. It's way more than we have on the others. We can push harder on their past lovers to see if the victims had any similar sexual proclivity, and the casinos could lead to something. It means mega legwork and phone calls. If Ms. Balentine kept a separate computer and phone, the others probably did too. We have plenty to work on, but the information doesn't stand solidly at this point. We need to accomplish a lot before Bob pulls the trigger and holds the press conference." Trin sounded more encouraged than his expression showed. He paced several steps. "I'll call and get agents started on legwork. We'll do what we can from here on the rest."

∾

TRIN WALKED out to the platform beside Captain Underwood.

For a split second, he saw a flash from the press conference over thirty years ago. His memories carried him back to that day, his parents' faces lined with grief. During the time he'd stood and waited for the sheriff to speak, it felt like he missed half of himself. When the official had finally spoken, the horror from the situation turned real for him. His brother might never come home again.

The reporters had examined their faces and searched for any little detail to make their story unique. To him, they were vultures who picked at the remains from his family's life. So he'd gazed toward the green cornfields on his father's farm. In his mind, he pictured Jared as he hurried through the stalks closest to their home. His brother would run and hide to get away from him, but he'd been Jordan then. Long before his arguments with his father about leaving the farm to join the FBI.

He closed his eyes for several seconds and returned to Tulsa, the night hot and muggy while Captain Underwood introduced him.

∾

PAIGE SEARCHED the group gathered from the many news channels and local papers. The people present overall seemed like the usual crowd from various affiliates. Since she'd lived in Tulsa her whole life, she could recognize most reporters and their names. She didn't notice anyone questionable. Were they wasting their time policing the crowd?

The podium stood with multiple microphones placed strategically by City Hall. Captain Underwood and Trin would come out in less than two minutes to announce a Hollywood superstar's death. From her view, no one in the crowd had a clue what was about to happen. Somehow, they'd managed to get this part right. Which appeared to be the only miracle slated for the evening's event.

Hank nodded at her. From his expression, he didn't find anything suspicious either. She ventured a little farther afield. Everything checked out normal. Everyone here belonged.

She turned around to examine the gathering again and bumped into someone. She glanced up and saw the malicious grin on Harley Judd's face. "Don't get too comfortable in the new job. You won't stay there long."

"You could get Artie into big trouble if I pressed charges with your nasty joke, but I like him too much to take out your failures on him, even if he used poor judgment."

"You've confused me with someone else. I don't know what you're talking about." His breath reeked of alcohol. From the shadows, the sneer made his handsome face ugly.

"You lie as poorly as every other job you do. Your problem is you blame everyone else for your own stupid choices."

"At least I got where I am on my own. I didn't suck up to the captain."

"Maybe, but you'll never get any further, you creep." She pushed away from him and returned to inspect the crowd. The sorry excuse for a man made her cheeks burn. She wanted to belt him one. Most men on the force felt the same way about her promotion. They might not think she deserved it, but they didn't try to push it the way he did.

Hank did help her get the promotion. They were right. But

Hank needed her. She couldn't let him down—not after everything he'd done for her.

The general noise from the small throng quieted once the two men came out of City Hall side by side. The captain walked up to the microphones. He cleared his voice to ensure the amplifiers worked. The speakers seemed ready to go. She still felt unsettled from her confrontation with Harley. Her edginess grew with the beginning words that came from the captain's mouth.

"Early this morning a police officer found Heather Balentine's body here in Tulsa. The death was a great surprise to the people involved. We will work the leads with the FBI's help. Special Agent Jordan Trinity has agreed to assist us. We will use every source available to track and find the answers. Due to COD, we must withhold certain facts. I convened this conference primarily to announce her discovery and death. We will work the case hard and use all available resources to get the job done. At this time, I would like to turn the press conference over to Special Agent Trinity to allow him the opportunity to say a few words." Bob Underwood moved back to let Trin take his place behind the microphones.

A hush fell across the gathering. It lasted for only a few moments. You could see the confusion and the questions form in each reporter's face. Then the noise level raised several decibels. Her pulse pounded in her ears. With the adrenaline rush that flowed through her veins, she felt sure nothing would ever be the same.

"First of all, let me say how glad I am to assist your competent police department. This event came as a complete shock to Heather's family and friends. We've kept the details tonight to a minimum. Since Ms. Balentine is a celebrity, we must use discretion. Your patrolman found her body this morning shortly after one. We will give more details at the appropriate time. I know I gave you little information, but the investigation is ongoing. We cannot comment further at this time. Thank you for your attention and consideration." Trin turned and left the podium. With his departure, the crowd became alive with activity.

It surprised her they'd given so little information to the press. The media would get pissed, but at least they didn't tell them the detectives had nothing to go on. If the captain could keep the reporters off their backs, they could manage to get a little work done.

They still needed to call Jill Caywood and check into the personal lives of the other victims a little more carefully. Do something. She felt frustrated they had no significant leads to chase.

She studied the group again and saw cell phones light up and camera feeds go directly to the stations across Tulsa. She felt sure if she checked the internet, the story would already appear there.

Before ten minutes elapsed, the lot cleared. Only a single reporter remained. He looked older and talked to Hank. Their conversation seemed more animated than normal. Not fighting exactly, but the situation didn't feel right between them. Hank got cranky at times, but he wouldn't start anything with a reporter. They both were acquainted with the personalities around Tulsa. This guy she didn't recognize. She didn't think he was local. Sometimes Oklahoma City sent their reporters to cover big stories in Tulsa, but no one should have known this press conference would give out information about the death of a superstar unless someone warned them.

She watched them talk for several minutes before she wandered closer. They didn't notice until she got nearby since their discussion remained intense. Hank peeked up first and stopped mid-sentence. Strange. She smiled to cover her uneasiness.

"I don't believe I know your friend." She presented her hand for shaking.

"Peter Faulkner. He used to work the police beat in Tulsa a long time ago. I haven't seen him in years. He now works out in LA."

After Hank's introduction, Peter took her hand and shook it like an old friend. "So this beauty is Martin's daughter all grown up."

The stranger knew her father, which startled her. Not many on the force still remembered him. Why would an outsider? She peered at Hank, her eyes searching his for answers. Then she stepped back and waited for their conversation to end.

"Peter, I hate to cut it short, but we need to get back on the job. You can tell, we're swamped. It's good to see you again. Next time you're in town look me up. We'll go drink a beer together." Hank went to move away, but Peter grabbed his arm.

"Can't we make it a fast one tonight? I want an update on old friends, and I'd like to catch up with you." Peter's expression hinted at important secrets between them.

She felt as if she'd been dropped into the middle of a melodrama without a script. Something wasn't in sync with these two.

"Not tonight. I can't," Hank said.

"It's your loss." Peter shrugged and walked away toward a lone rental car.

She stared expectantly toward Hank, but he didn't say a word.

≈

Paige dialed Jill Caywood's phone number and put the phone on speaker. The phone rang three times before a drowsy voice answered.

"Hello?"

"This is Detective Hank Gettering from the Tulsa Police Department. Are you Miss Jill Caywood? The personal assistant who works for Heather Ballentine?" Hank sat down at his desk and leaned back in his chair.

"Hold on. I'm half asleep. Who did you say you are?" An odd sound on the other end came through the line for several moments.

"I'm Detective Hank Gettering with the Tulsa Police Department. We're trying to find a Miss Jill Caywood. They told us she works for Heather Balentine. Are you the person I need?" Hank leaned his face closer to the speaker on the phone.

"I work for Heather. Why would you call me from Tulsa?" The voice yawned.

"We'd like to ask you a few questions about Heather Balen—"

"I have a nondisclosure agreement. I'm not allowed to talk about Heather to anyone." She disconnected the call.

Paige hit redial. This time the phone rang twice before the same voice came on the line.

"Miss Caywood, I'm Paige Stone. Before you hang up again, we need to tell you Heather Balentine is dead. I'm also a detective with the Tulsa Police Department. We're sorry to inform you this way, but we must get information about why we found Ms. Balentine's body in Tulsa, Oklahoma. NDA aside, we need your help. Do you know the reason Ms. Balentine came to Tulsa this weekend?" She sat forward, leaning toward the phone to make sure Jill heard her.

"No." Jill hesitated. "You said she's dead? God, I can't

believe . . ." Her voice trailed off. "She indicated she'd planned a big weekend, but she stayed quiet about the details. I didn't know she left town. You say you found her in Tulsa? Huh. I can't imagine why." She heard more movement from Jill's line. The bed squeaked.

Paige thought she heard sniffles. She nodded at Hank to take over.

"Miss Caywood, her sister told us you handle Heather's online accounts. You keep them up to date. Did she receive any hate mail or anything along those lines?"

"She got letters from avid fans, but not much hate mail. She received marriage proposals every month and propositions not so legal. Men sent pictures to try to get themselves a date. You know, the regular crazies, but no one seemed to hate her."

"What about her private accounts? Her sister indicated she owned a laptop she kept for her personal use and a cell phone. Do you know the account names or the phone number for those?" Hank stood up and stretched his legs.

"No. Heather called me last year from her phone once, but I'm sure she bought a different one. She dropped her old mobile about a month ago and broke it. She mentioned needing to contact someone important and sounded worried he wouldn't answer his phone if he didn't recognize the number. It upset her a great deal. I'd never seen her so flustered in all the time I worked for her." Jill's voice caught several times as she spoke.

"You're sure this person was a guy she wanted to contact?" Hank sat back down.

"Yes, I'm sure. She—"

Paige cut Jill off. "Did Heather call this number we are using with her other phone, or do you have a different phone number Heather called you on?" She looked directly at Hank and motioned she had a reason.

"This one." Jill sounded curious.

"Do you remember the exact day and time she called you?" Paige held up a hand when Hank scowled at her.

"The night the Oscars were on TV, about seven in the evening our time. She broke a zipper on her gown. I brought her another backstage. She presented in white silk and danced later in pink sequins." Jill answered with more details than necessary.

"Yes, I remember. Miss Balentine wore both perfectly. Listen, your information has helped me to come up with a possible solution. I will let Detective Gettering finish his questions, but later I may ask more. Thanks so much. Hank still has further questions." She motioned for Hank to take over the conversation and got up from her perch on her desk. She took off down the hallway while Hank's eyes glared after her.

**8**

———————

Paige walked up to Bill Graywolf's desk. He didn't glance up.

"Are you ignoring me or what?" she said.

"Yeah, I'm concerned you'll find more work for me to do." Bill turned his dark brown eyes toward her and grinned.

"You're right. I've got a telephone number for you." She leaned in and wrote the number on his notepad.

"I was afraid of that."

"I always like to provide job security where I can." She sat down at the computer station beside him.

"You don't need to help this much. What about the number?" Bill watched her as she logged on at the desk.

"We think Heather called this number from a burn phone the night of the Oscars around seven Pacific Time. We need to find the phone number and get a list for every call made and received on it in the last few months. It could lead us to her killer, I hope. I'll search for the Oscar date if you do the rest." She typed in the name and hit enter.

"Your deals seem so one-sided," Bill said after she got back up and approached his desk.

"I know. Sorry, but it could be important. Did you get time to search the traffic cameras?" She wrote the date down on the pad beside the telephone number.

"I've spent a half hour on it. No luck so far," Bill said.

"I figured, or you would have called me. Thanks. If you get more time, would you check the rest? The telephone number seems more important. I feel it's a more solid lead. The traffic cameras are an outside chance." She turned to leave and glanced back at him. "Thank you again, Bill. I appreciate it. Thanks for your concern, too, but I'm fine."

"Are you sure? You look gorgeous as always, but you seem more tired than normal."

"I don't always get enough rest. The job calls Hank and me out late at night a lot. The crazy hours make me tired. It helps to know you watch out for me."

"Anytime."

She figured she didn't convince him, but she refused to tell him about the dreams that tormented her. They troubled her nights enough that she hated to go to bed.

As PAIGE WALKED toward her desk, she could tell by Hank's conversation he talked to someone else. They'd finished with Jill Caywood.

"He's asked for the studio president," Trin said. "They went to locate him. My guess, the guy already knows. It's probably why they can't find him."

"I got Bill started on the telephone number. If we can locate the last people Heather talked to from the old phone, we might get the number for the new one. It's a reach, but a lead could pop." She stretched and lifted a mug from her desk. The effort gave her something to do. She felt nervous while she waited with Trin. He still felt like the enemy. It didn't seem the same with an outsider along, and he could find out about Hank.

"I'm Detective Hank Gettering, from the Tulsa Police Department. We need to notify someone about Heather Balentine's death. I understand she worked on a movie for your studio. Can I talk with someone who's in charge of her film? We need to get a few specific details for our investigation." Hank waited for a response, but it was long in coming.

"I'm Seth Cooper, and I'm not officially attached to Ms. Balentine's movie, but most everyone from her set left until Monday morning. We heard they're scheduled to restart filming at that time. I must say, it will cause a big stir to finish without her." The voice sounded high pitched and nasal.

"I can imagine. Do you know if the studio carried life insurance on her in case she couldn't finish the film?" Hank asked.

"They do. I'm not sure about Heather's policy. I don't know about her situation since I don't work on her film." Strange noises came from his line as if people randomly wandered through the place.

"Do you know if she had any clause where she reported her whereabouts? Would she need to notify anyone if she left town?" Hank said.

"I can't specifically say, but normally it's not required." Hammers pounded in the background.

"I need to talk to people she worked with on her crew. Any close friends. Can you get me a list? The sooner, the better." Hank spoke over the new noise level.

"I'm sure it will take until Monday. I don't see anyone on the lot who works on her film, but I will check to see ASAP." The hammer continued to bang.

"Mr. Cooper, I need a number where I can reach you. I don't want to start this whole process over with someone new every time I call. I don't need further complications. Do you understand?" Hank's stern voice accompanied his vicious frown.

"Yes, sir. I understand." He gave Hank his number.

"I will call you back on Monday morning, ten o'clock your time. By then I expect answers, and I'll need numbers to go with the names on the list. Numbers where I can reach them. If they had her insured, I want to know how much and where the money goes. Who receives it? I assume the studio, but sometimes you get fooled by assumptions," Hank said.

"Yes, I'll see to it." The racket ceased.

"Good. I'll talk to you then." Hank disconnected the phone. "Where was the man? It sounded like they were framing houses."

"He might build sets. Who knows?" She finally sat down at her desk.

"Paige went to get someone who could track down the old phone number for Heather. At least, we hope it's for Heather. She could have borrowed someone's phone, but we need to check it out. It's worth a shot." Trin leaned over to stretch. "This sitting business makes me stiff."

PAIGE STOPPED on the way home to grab takeout. Tiredness weighed on her like a cloak. She thought sleep might fix her attitude.

When she parked and opened the car door, the heat blasted her face. She hoped the broiling temperatures didn't last forever and climbed the stairs to her apartment. She entered, kicked off her shoes, and put everything she carried on her coffee table. Then she walked over and switched on her computer.

She promised herself only half an hour and then bed before she went to the kitchen for water. Her feet ached as she came back into her living room, picked up her Mexican food, and sat down in front of her desktop. She keyed in Jared Trinity on her search engine and hit enter. The name wasn't much to go on.

While she waited for the results, she unwrapped her taco, added hot sauce, and took a bite. God, the spicy food tasted good. She hadn't realize how empty her stomach felt until now. After she finished her taco, she took a huge drink and scrolled through the results the computer listed.

Trin's folder she saw earlier was labeled Jared Trinity. Jordan's relative she'd bet. Why else would he carry the information with him? Then he'd hurried to put the file away. She had suspicions he hid significant information about a relative, and she intended to find out what. It paid to know the people who had your back.

The first results from her search turned up more information than she wanted to wade through, but she continued to check the various items listed that looked promising. She clicked on an article. It told about a Jared Trinity who'd disappeared from a small town in Indiana. His brother's name matched. Jordan. Bingo. This piece could show her what he hid.

The boy, only nine years old, played in his yard when he vanished. No sighting reported since. They never found the body if one existed. She read several articles on the subject, but no new information showed up.

So much intrigue. Jordan's brother disappeared, and he didn't mention it. Not just any brother, but an identical twin. Many reports and articles existed about the close ties between such pairs. So the FBI's man carried secrets that trailed back thirty years.

She grabbed up the rest of her food and moved to the couch. She unwrapped another taco and took a bite from the cold food. The flavor had vanished with the temperature. She jammed the remainder in the brown bag and wadded it up for the trash. The agent might have charmed Hank, which was not easy to accomplish, but she still had her doubts about Special Agent Jordan Trinity.

**9**

———————

Trin parked his rental in the nondescript motel parking lot. He couldn't count the many generic places he'd stayed. His mind meandered to Paige as he exited his car, while the hot night air brought sweat to his brow.

She looked more like a teenager than a detective but seemed capable at her job. He'd never seen a relationship between partners like the one she and Hank had, but it seemed to work. Her eyes didn't miss a detail. He figured she'd seen the file on his brother. She'd probably researched his name on the internet. He smiled. It's what he would do. Always know your back up.

Paige's loveliness attracted in an unassuming way. She didn't seem at all aware of how beautiful she was. Her smile alone made him want to engage in entanglements he shouldn't. He shook his head to clear it. She was way the hell too young. Besides, they needed to stop a killer.

He unlocked his room, entered, and switched on the lights. He dropped his black suitcase to the floor while he laid his briefcase on the bed. The night stretched before him with only work in sight. He intended to get familiar with everything related to Heather Balentine and her murder.

After a quick shower, he got comfortable in his bed. He pulled the briefcase closer, removed the laptop, and turned it on, laying the folders beside him. Then he saw Tim Jennings' picture, which lay near his brother's file. The photo slipped out from Jared's folder. He'd forgotten he put the picture inside.

The kid's innocent face stopped his reach for the Balentine folder. The child favored Jared so much. They were close to the same age at the time each vanished. He didn't want to think about this, but he was tired and couldn't control his mind. The young boy's memories crept in and flooded his soul with regret. If only he'd arrived a few minutes sooner, Tim would still live today.

He didn't need a shrink to tell him he'd spent his whole career with the FBI and chased down missing children because his brother disappeared. The fact seemed clear to everyone. He didn't care what his colleagues thought. He could do with his life as he pleased, and he wanted to find for other people what someone denied him.

No one understood how deserted he felt when Jared disappeared. Thirty years later he still longed for him unbearably. They'd raced through the cornfield and played tag the morning someone took him. Their father chased them from the rows each time he caught them, but they always sneaked back. Jared wouldn't leave the tall stalks alone.

He loved to run through the bright green tips that blew in the wind against the light blue sky. The corn grew tall enough to hide two ornery boys with a full life ahead. He questioned so many times whether Jared remained alive. What was his personality like if he did? If not, how did he die? Questions, always unanswered questions.

He wanted to search for lost children, but his superiors wouldn't let him any longer. Tim took too big a toll on him. He'd gotten personally involved. Now he chased after a serial killer who figured he had the right to play God. No one possessed that right: not this monster, nor the one who took his brother.

He turned off the bedside lamp and quit for the night. Evenings like this, his he couldn't focus on the case at hand. Better to acknowledge the fact and get some rest.

*Late Thursday Night*

AFTER THE DARKNESS deepened the shadows, he backed his black SUV up the alley to Betty's drive. He angled the vehicle to her home's rear door. Since he'd taken her keys, entry presented no problem. After he stepped into her kitchen, his gloved hands picked up the plastic-encased body off the kitchen floor. He sniffed the air for decomposition but found only the normal staleness from a shut-up home.

With a small flashlight in his mouth lighting the way, he quickly put her body in the back of his vehicle and covered it with a dark blanket. Then he closed the SUV's door quietly and walked back into the house.

He pulled the light from his mouth and diligently checked the two rooms he used during her murder. He refused to be sloppy. She must go missing like the others. Completely vanish into the night. No one should notice her absence for days. If fate held, it would take longer.

He obeyed every traffic law when he drove to the log cabin. He passed the house and continued up the slight hill to the stand of trees. Betty Greenway would spend eternity under the thicket. An ideal spot, he dumped her body in the hole and let the insects and worms do their job.

He worked hard and filled in the space he'd dug this afternoon. Then he replanted the thorny blackberry plants he'd dug up, which provided the finishing touch. The undergrowth appeared like new by the time he got back inside his Escalade. With the lights off, he drove down the hill into the garage and closed the door behind him.

He removed his clothes and rolled them into a lump. Putting them into the back of his vehicle, he walked naked into the bathroom. The shower cleansed the sweat and dirt from his hands. Fresh clothes soothed his tired muscles as he climbed into the bedroll. His slumber came undisturbed and dreamless.

When Paige arrived at work the next morning, she saw Peter Faulkner talking with Hank beside her mentor's Silverado. The detective's whole demeanor screamed anger. She knew how much pressure it took to get Hank worked up like that.

She wondered what they discussed. Probably Heather Balentine and the case. Before long the press would demand answers. Reporters could tell if the police withheld more information than usual, and to keep the murder details under wraps seemed an impossible task.

She stood beside her Cavalier and watched the interchange between them. Hank's fury increased to boiling point. She hesitated to interrupt, but Hank's blood pressure presented an issue. She wouldn't let him stand there until he had a heart attack or stroke. She owed him her life.

Decision made, she approached. "You two seem intense for this early hour. Your face has turned a little red, Hank. Can you take it down a notch or two?" She pasted on her most charming smile and waited for a response.

"It's all right. Mr. Faulkner is leaving." Hank gestured for Peter to go.

"Actually, I'm not." The reporter didn't budge. Belligerence oozed from him in waves.

"All right, I attempted politeness. What the hell is going on here? Hank has issues with his blood pressure, so back off." She lifted her hand to turn Hank toward her. She wanted to make sure his health passed her scrutiny.

"Or what? You'll go Rambo like your old man? Hank can tell you about it. The raid almost cost him his life. He caught a bullet for your father's actions." Faulkner stood his ground, confident about his information. It startled her. She knew he lied.

"You don't know what you're saying. My father died a hero in the line of duty, for God's sake. It's time for you to leave. Get your ass away from here." She glance at Hank's face, then looked more closely. And recognized the truth. Her universe tilted. Something wasn't right. Hank wouldn't look at her. He didn't say a word to defend her father. The reporter's ramblings couldn't be true.

Peter laughed. He seemed to relish watching her world collapse around her.

She stared back up at Faulkner, face filled with confusion. Hank remained silent.

"You can pretend if you want, but it's true. Your father wouldn't wait for backup. He wouldn't follow procedure. It cost him his life and put Hank in the hospital near death. I can't believe you didn't find out. It ran in the papers for weeks, and they didn't get the bad guys. Your dad's killer got away clean." Peter shrugged as if the details were standard information, but she'd been ten years old. Newspapers meant nothing to her at the time. She'd been a little girl consumed with fear in a world filled with strangers.

"Come on, Hank. We're going inside. I won't put up with his bullshit. If he won't leave, we will." She took Hank's arm and attempted to move him away from the man who said he reported the news. She needed to get Hank inside the department. Whatever went on between them, Hank's health was more important.

"This won't go away. I'll fill the news with stories about Martin Stone and his wannabe police daughter who works with the lead detective on the century's most prominent murder case. I can stir up more trouble than you can imagine. I need answers. I want them now. How did Heather die?" Peter stayed adamant.

"Let me get this straight. You expect me to roll over to blackmail? Are you crazy? Get out of my way. Hank and I are going inside." She attempted to move around him, but Peter grabbed her arm to stop her.

She didn't think. She took Peter down and held him in a chokehold before either realized what happened. "You don't know anything about me, but an assault on a police officer is against the law. So is extortion. Get the hell out of here before I arrest you for both."

She stood slowly and released the man. He twisted around with fury in his eyes. "I'm sure Heather came here to meet a new lover. It's why I'm here. I took a second plane. I missed her flight."

"That would be your problem, not mine. How did you get this information?" She figured she should get what she could from the idiot. She hadn't been this angry in ages.

"I'd followed her for weeks. I figured something was up, but I wasn't certain what. Heather met someone here for a quiet little getaway. Now she turns up dead. It seems a little too pat for me. You won't tell the press any details. It's like she met a serial killer or something and no one will talk."

She gasped when he spoke about a serial killer. Why would he mention such a detail? Faulkner instantly recognized he'd hit on the truth. "I think you're full of it. I didn't hear my captain say anything about her death to warrant such a leap. You've been in Hollywood too long."

"I don't think so. I think I got the facts right. Thanks, Paige. I figured you would give me what I needed." Peter turned to leave.

She grabbed him by the shirt collar. "You scum bag. You breathe another word about my father, and you'll see the world from an eight-by-ten cage." When she let him loose, she turned back to Hank. He leaned on the car next to them with his head down. She made Hank move toward the department. His face looked pasty, and his breathing sounded uneven. She wanted to scream in frustration, but it wouldn't do any good.

Peter would get a headline in print by the time he got back to his car. The information would travel around the world in the time it took to text the message. She understood she was in deep trouble, but she needed Hank to calm down. She reached into Hank's jacket pocket and pulled out a tablet, then stuck it in his mouth. He swallowed. In a minute or two, his color came back a little.

**10**

———

Paige strode down the hall and attempted to check the internet on her phone. She saw Trin turn the corner and moved in Hank's direction. He must not confront Hank for at least another twenty minutes. It would take a while for Hank to get up on his feet. She made him lie down on the sofa they kept in the corner of the detective's department. In her childhood, she'd slept there many times waiting on Hank.

"Hi. You're here bright and early." The cheerful words poured from her lips. She recognized her foolishness the second they came out from her mouth. "You want to join me? I want to go check with Bill. He might have information on our telephone number." She casually took his arm and led him in the direction she wanted him to go.

"Okay." Trin walked beside her, an odd expression on his face.

She felt sure he recognized she had an agenda, but she couldn't help it. This crisis needed to vanish. One disaster at a time seemed more than enough to handle. She would worry about the next one later.

"Where are you staying? Were you comfortable?" She understood her rambling didn't help. The mundane chitchat only made her situation more superficial. Especially after yesterday's attitude, but she didn't possess any other ideas to delay Trin. Her mind went blank for dealing with him.

She tucked her blonde-streaked hair behind her ear. Once the story hit the news and the internet, her life as a detective would cease to exist. She rolled her bottom lip between her teeth and envisioned Captain Underwood's fury. Another good reason not to visit Bill, but it was the only idea her mind delivered. Hank needed time to recover. They would force him to retire if the captain found out. He wouldn't make it without this job.

"I slept fine. What's going on this morning?" Trin asked.

"I wanted to check in with Bill first. I figured you might take an interest." She attempted to return the eye contact, but she'd never been the best liar except during interviews with suspects. Trin's expression looked unconvinced.

As they weaved their way through morning traffic to the university, both remained silent. She couldn't come up with a single item that wouldn't make matters worse. They arrived at the door to Bill's tech lab, and she turned the knob, then gave Trin space to enter.

"How's your morning?" she asked while Bill ignored her cheerful countenance for a moment.

He sat in his regular space and finished whatever strokes he required. Finally, he glanced up and acknowledged them. "I figured I'd see you before long. The number came back a prepaid cell phone. I'm still tracking down the phone calls both to and from it. Give me another hour or so. I should put names to most."

"I'm glad to hear about the progress. It's the only detail we've found useful so far. I brought you Starbucks, but I'm sorry to say I accidentally dropped it in the parking lot. I promise I'll bring something extra special tomorrow." She bit on the corner of her bottom lip.

"I had my taste buds keyed up and ready for it. What happened in the parking lot, anyway?" Bill stopped typing and gazed up at her.

"Oh, nothing. I attempted to carry too many items at once." She figured he might have seen something on the cameras mounted around the lot outside the main headquarters. Her expression told him not to go any further with the twenty questions.

"I'll expect something great tomorrow. And no lame excuses." Bill punched the keys on the computer as if nothing had happened.

She sat herself down at the other computer next to Bill and logged on. With several strokes, she found the headline she dreaded to read. The news came out already. Peter Faulkner got his wish. The caption read, *Heather Balentine Slain by Serial Killer*. She logged off.

She turned around. Trin stood right behind her. He watched over her shoulder. Her pulse quickened, and her cheeks flushed. The only action she could take to protect Hank was to cover up the parking lot incident. No one would listen if she pleaded she'd done nothing wrong. Her downfall went precisely the way Harley Judd wanted. *Shit.*

She decided to face her dragon and conversed with Bill in nonproductive gossip for a minute, then left him behind. After they exited the tech room, she walked about ten feet down the hall and spun around to face Trin. No surprise showed in his expression, only frustrated betrayal.

"You saw. It's not what you think, but the information got out there. I wanted to make sure before I said anything." She didn't breathe while her whole world crumbled about her.

"How is it not, Paige? This is your first homicide." He snapped his fingers. "The whole world knows a serial killer murdered the most famous film star in the world. You're the only one who knew the story leaked. What am I missing?" He glared at her with disappointment and disgust. Then he pulled up his cell phone and keyed in the necessary information. The longer he studied the screen, the more his expression turned grim.

"I swear I didn't tell him." She moved away, and her wounded dignity followed with her.

Once they got back and reached her desk, Hank sat behind his. The color in his cheeks looked normal.

"Good morning, Hank. I'm afraid I brought bad news. The press knows about the serial killer angle with Heather Balentine." She needed to warn him or Trin would. Her explanation seemed the less unpleasant of the two. With the horrible shape he'd been in, she didn't know for sure if Hank understood what happened out there in the parking lot.

"I figured it wouldn't take long. Since Bob said so little last night, the reporters figured something was up." Hank stared directly at her while he spoke, but she couldn't discern what he believed. If he remembered what happened, she didn't know. He was always a difficult read.

"You don't appear too surprised." Trin's piercing eyes examined Hank's.

"We figured we couldn't keep it silent forever. I'm disappointed the press found out so soon. Who let it slip?" Hank asked. Trin's eyes only stared and accused her.

Hank glanced back and forth between the two several times. "Paige blabbed to the press."

"You surely don't believe that. I've always done exactly what you told me, Hank. Always. How can you consider such an idea?" Her eyes searched his but didn't find what she hoped to see. "First, my father. Now this. What a day to find out truths." She pulled her desk drawer open until it jerked to a stop, grabbed her small backpack, and kicked the drawer closed with enough force the desk scooted back a foot. Her cheeks burned as she left the room, walked down the hall, and out from the department. She had no idea where she would go. Away. She needed to get away.

PAIGE PARKED her silver Cavalier near the OneOk Building and stared across the street. The Mayo Hotel sat sturdy and tall. Tears trailed down her cheeks. The building brought many emotions to her, but the sense of loss always prevailed. Martin Stone died there over fourteen years ago.

He remained her father, her hero, her complete orbit in life. If everything she thought true turned into a lie, what did it say about the existence she'd constructed? Hank, though she loved him, stood by and watched her erect the perfect image of her father so carefully and with such devotion. How could he let her build on a false premise? Her whole life created on lies.

She started the car and pulled into traffic. The time spent seemed meaningless—the hours and hours she'd studied, the nights she'd helped Hank work each case just like a grown-up. She gave up a massive chunk from her childhood. What did any of it mean? Nothing. It meant nothing.

She followed the Broken Arrow Expressway to Garnett, exited, and drove to her apartment nearby. The stillness greeted her when she stepped inside the small, plain space. She moved directly to the desktop, switched on the unit, and sat down at her desk. Her fingers drummed, and the computer hummed. An eternity passed until she entered her password. She'd never needed to research her father's death for details.

The lies the police told her during that nightmare were easy enough for a ten-year-old to believe. It remained easier to go with the status quo. God knows, she'd done everything possible to please Hank.

She typed in her father's name followed by death. A minute later the results displayed. She waded through a long list and read one news report after another. Eventually, the picture emerged. Her father endangered Hank's life and gave his own in an abrupt judgment call. He didn't wait for backup. He wouldn't bother. His mistake left her alone. If Hank hadn't take her to raise, she would have been put into the system forever.

Anger screamed in her brain. *Her father didn't care.* No family existed to come and get her. Why did he take such reckless chances with his only child? Thank God, Hank came for her. Where would she be without him? Still, it hurt Hank didn't trust her.

She remembered each detail the day her father died. The pale blue sky filled with crisp morning air promised a glorious day ahead. She spent school recess with Anna McCreedy. They raced to see who could make their swing go higher. Paige attained a slight advantage before Mrs. Bond walked up and asked her to come with her.

She didn't have a clue when her teacher took her back to their classroom. Though she saw a police officer there, it didn't dawn on her the two things might be related. Then her whole world collapsed. With her mother the year before, they'd known for months cancer would take her life, but her father seemed invincible. The police officer informed her he wasn't. He died in the line of duty. Her father would never come pick her up again.

They removed her from her home, and she didn't return. She got to take her clothes and one doll, but the house she'd always loved disappeared forever from her life. Only strangers gave her necessities.

The Child Welfare Department, part of DHS, enrolled her in a different school system. She lost her friends and faced isolation in a strange new universe.

They placed her in one foster home for three days. The father figure at the residence molested a young girl her same age. Then the system put her back at the Family and Children's Services for another week. They shifted her two more times in the thirty days she remained in the state's care. She'd mourned her mother's death for more than a year, but this was so much worse. At least then she still had her home and her father.

The day that changed everything was ordinary until Mrs. Bond came to get her from the playground. The day Hank came, they turned the sun on again.

She stared out the window at the rain that day and sensed God cried with her. Her tears flowed every day since the policeman told her about her father's death. She believed the waterworks would run out, but so far, that hadn't happened. Miss Holly, the social worker for her case, knocked at the door. She couldn't figure out why. The door always stayed open.

"Paige, you have a visitor." Miss Holly came into the room.

When she turned around, Hank stood there. She recognized her dad's partner but wondered why he would come to visit her. She never thought he liked kids.

"Hi, Paige. I brought a surprise for you." Hank took a few steps in her direction.

She wiped at the tears in her eyes and peeked up at him. He was so tall but seemed uncertain. She'd never seen him hesitant. When Hank talked with her father, they always acted important, like everything they did changed the world. To see him unsure of himself confused her.

"Hi, Hank," she offered and attempted to hide how much

she'd cried. He would think she acted like a baby. Police officers didn't understand girls who weep a lot. The idea rang true in her young mind. Her father always hated for her to cry.

"I'm sorry I didn't get here sooner. I got injured and have been in the hospital. Then it took me a while to find where you were. But I'm finally here." He attempted a big grin. On Hank, the expression didn't work. It looked fake.

She watched him and didn't know what to say. Nothing made sense. She only wanted to go home, but she could never go there again.

"I hope you'll like the surprise, Paige. I promised your mother if anything ever happened to your dad, I would take over your care. I'm sorry it took me so long to get here, but I got here. I felt horrible about your situation. You can come home with me to live. That work okay?" Hank took several steps closer. His timid eyes found hers.

She stared at Hank like he spoke a foreign language for a moment. Then she ran into his arms and wouldn't let go. She clung to him like a lifeline.

She determined never to make Hank sorry he rescued her. She studied hard and learned to like the interests he enjoyed. To become a cop was the only idea that ever made sense to her. She wanted to be like her father and Hank. Until this morning, she'd never seen disappointment in Hank's eyes concerning her actions.

She put on her bravest face, walked back out to her car, and took the journey that started earlier this morning. She must go back and face Captain Underwood. He would demote her. The worst would happen, but she'd told the asshole reporter nothing. If he hadn't blindsided her with the news about her father, her face wouldn't have given her away.

The situation wouldn't change, but she would go on. She remained a police officer. The job was all she knew. She wanted to stay a detective. This time for herself, not to honor her dad's memory or even to please Hank.

❦

Paige entered Bob's sterile glass office before he called for her. He glanced up, and surprise flashed in his expression. "I gather we got you to thank for the wild speculation that's floating around the world's information highway." Bob stared at her, his expression now furious.

"Not exactly, sir." She stood militarily correct.

"What does 'not exactly' mean?" Bob's shrug didn't appear to disperse his anger.

"What I said, sir. Nothing more."

"Do you expect me to make sense of your cryptic remark? Did you cause what happened today?" Menace seemed a tame description for the captain's countenance as he inspected her.

"Only partially at most, but I don't believe—"

"Explain what happened today and don't waste my time. Your big mouth brought a nightmare situation to my office. Do you understand?" His eyes pierced hers. His whole face turned red.

"Yes, sir. I do understand." She fell silent.

They both stood in the quiet room for several moments. She didn't dare look at him. She would lose it any second. His expression remained deadly and calm. It only happened right before he exploded in a rage.

She heard the ticking clock on his desk and understood she was finished. She saw her promotion slip away, but she would not betray Hank. Besides, she couldn't find fault with Hank, either. No explanation would resolve this situation to anyone's satisfaction. It was the only truth she came up with, and it stunk.

"Since you refuse to give me any answers, I can make your life difficult until you do. I've already told Hank. You are off the Heather Balentine case. You will report to me until further notice. Do you understand?"

She nodded.

"Pissed does not come close to my anger over this mess. After I gave you this opportunity." He shook his head in disgust. "I put another case on your desk this morning once I heard. A missing person case. I expect that to be your only focus until further notice."

The sick feeling hit the pit in her gut and overwhelmed her. She failed her first test as a detective, but a missing person? Homicide unit didn't typically handle those. Did it mean she would never work murder cases again? She'd probably never get to work with Hank either, and she didn't think he would make it without her. Her cheeks flamed, but she didn't care. The life she'd known landed in the outhouse.

"Yes, sir." She managed an about-face and moved to the door.

"And Paige, I won't change my mind. Keep your nose on your new case only." He motioned for her to leave, and she nodded her agreement.

Everyone in the department stared when she walked back to her desk. She placed her black backpack in her drawer, closed it, and opened the file folder. Head down, she didn't look up for anyone.

She attempted to read the folder's contents, but her eyes wouldn't focus. She sat there for ten minutes and shuffled the pages. Her attempt to appear normal failed. Finally, she took her bag out from the desk drawer and left the room. Her nerves were shot. She could only take so much. She had to go home and calm down.

She hesitated at the white marker board with Heather

Balentine's timeline. The white panel mocked her. She'd wanted to add a few lines to the board. It would never happen. Her life was not over. She would live through this. Though at this moment, she didn't know how.

She strode toward the front door, and Harley Judd approached. He stuck out his hand like he wanted to shake hers. "Congratulations. You screwed up in record time. Way to go."

She pushed around him and stalked through the group that crowded in to watch her downfall.

## 11

Trin watched while the action took place in the main squad room. Paige covered for someone, but who or about what, he didn't know. From the beginning, something didn't seem right about her relationship with Hank. This morning, the former quiet shadow of Hank took him off the old man's hands long enough to accomplish something. He wasn't completely sure what.

He recognized when he'd been had. At the expense of a rough dress down, Paige held her ground. She didn't cry and didn't attempt to flirt her way out as she did with Bill. She took her punishment and moved on.

At this point, he didn't think it was a good idea to throw her off the case. She seemed to have the right instincts. She understood how to handle the various players to get the job done. That quality was invaluable in cases where different groups were at cross-purposes.

Hank interrupted his thoughts. "You need any coffee? I could use another quart."

"No, I'm good." He watched Hank slip away and wondered

if he went to catch up with Paige. He sensed she could do with a shoulder.

After he waited a few seconds, he decided to follow. Sure enough, Hank walked toward the parking lot. From the doorway, he could see Paige leave. Her silver car's rear end pulled onto the street. He hurried back to Hank's desk.

A minute and a half later, Hank returned with coffee in hand.

He gave the detective a few minutes to settle. "So what's the deal with Paige?"

"She's the one responsible for letting the information out. The captain is outraged. I don't know what happened. Paige doesn't usually disobey a direct order." Hank stared down at his hands.

He watched him fret. He could tell the old man felt worried or guilty about Paige. "Did you talk to her? Attempt to call her?"

"No." The older man's spent eyes looked up at him.

"Do you think you should?" He could see Hank struggle with the decision.

"No. We got work to do. She's fine." Hank picked up the file and offered it to him.

∿

*A year earlier*

THE SURF POUNDED THE BEACH. The relaxing sound tempted Tony with sleep, a beer safely tucked in his right hand.

"I finally got the information I needed yesterday from Paramount to do the remake. I signed a waiver to do two movies for them, but they agreed to pay me my normal price for each one.

It wound up a lucrative deal." Ben sat down next to him and reclined on his lounger.

"Good." The conversation didn't interest him. A five-minute nap took priority.

"You didn't promise I'd do any, did you?" Josh set his beer down with a thump.

"Nope," Ben said.

"Thank God. Last time I worked with them, they used me to do a Disney wannabe. It stunk. I think they enjoyed ruining my career." Josh leaned back, and his chair squeaked.

"So who will we hire to play Hallie? You know, Heather Balentine would work great if Tony hadn't pissed her off so badly." Ben took a long drink.

His eyes flew open, and he glared at Ben.

"We can't use the redheaded witch. I won't deal with her. It takes too long to shoot a movie. Shit, Ben. What are you thinking? She hates me." Sleep completely left his mind.

"If you used a little more finesse with the girls, we wouldn't have a problem. No woman in Hollywood wants to work with you." Ben winked and glanced toward Josh for agreement.

"He's right. I've already heard comments about your carousing. More than one woman wants no part with you on the same set." Josh grinned and nodded.

"You both act like you've never screwed anyone and left them behind. Neither of you can claim you're any better than I at delicate relationships. Your lists run longer than mine. Besides, you were both with Miss Balentine before I got there. Her words about you two were not kind. I seem to recall curse words involved." He took a big swig and set his bottle down with a clink.

"I only drank from that well a few times, but you went back for several months as I recall," Josh said.

"I didn't know we kept a tally. Besides, I wanted Heather to finish the movie without hysterics. It worked, too. We made a great film together. *Far From Alabama* got several Oscar nominations." He worked to peel the label from his beer.

"It's your exit line that needs work, Streets. You have to let them believe they don't deserve your dishonorable ways. Let them down tenderly, like you're heartbroken to let them go." Ben's instruction hit a sour note with him though he understood they meant it in fun.

"I'll think about it once they pay me to act. I only perform for fifteen million a picture, or when it suits me to do otherwise. Hell, I'd need to pretend I care what women think. It's not like I force them to crawl in bed with me." He took another drink and still felt exhausted from his late night the previous evening. This topic remained sensitive. He had this same discussion with his agent last week.

"See, it's your attitude that hurts women. You tatter their pride. How will we ever find a decent Hallie for our movie?" Ben's smile lingered.

"Offer them enough money, or better yet, mention the Oscar buzz they'll generate. Then we could get them for free." His fingers worked harder to dislodge the label from his bottle.

"You are in fine form today. I'd hate to see you if you were in a pissy mood." Josh rejoined the conversation.

"I don't like to beat around the bush. Women like to screw around like we do, but after it's over, they're so surprised I don't want to marry them. I, for one, don't believe in that trap. Damn. Can you imagine the same woman day after day after day? Forever? I think I'd rather get shot." He picked up his beer to take a drink but set it back down without a sip.

"It's so good to hear you're a romantic at heart. Women everywhere will fall at your feet." Ben finished his beer and tossed it into the trashcan nearby.

"At least I don't lie to them. I never tell anyone I love them.

I don't give fake promises to get in their panties. They always know the truth before we start. It's not my fault if they ignore the rules. So back to the point. Who do we offer Hallie's role?" He got up and retrieved a fresh beer for himself and Ben.

"Thanks." Ben took the cold beer he offered.

"What about Cameron Diaz or Katherine Heigl? Oh! You know who would be perfect? Gwyneth Paltrow. I vote for her if we can get her," Josh said.

"If we did her makeup right, she would work. I think we found the one." Ben nodded.

"I agree, if she's not too expensive. We need to put our money into the places that count, but she would make a great Hallie." Ben and Josh stared at him. He wasn't usually so serious.

"So we agree. We'll contact her agent to find out her price. If it's reasonable, we offer her the part." Ben turned to him. "No screwing the leading lady. She's got kids, for God's sake."

"What the hell do her kids have to do with anything?" he asked.

Ben rolled his eyes, held his hands up in surrender, and shook his head.

He flipped through the channels and saw her for the first time on the portable television he used when he traveled. She looked perfect. He realized the instant he saw her he would take her for his own. Her radiant hair reflected the light. She brightened the television screen with her smile, and her brown eyes sparkled with life. Those eyes would bring him such pleasure.

Her lips enticed him while she spoke. He must possess them. Burnished red hair flowed smoothly like satin. He longed to wash away the blood and blow it dry as he brushed it. He visualized the scalpel. The instrument moved tenderly and carved her lovely eye.

He couldn't court her online the way he usually did. He needed to get away from the Tulsa area before anyone figured out he'd been here, but this once, he would take two in a single city. His excitement more potent than he'd realized, he'd rushed his performance with Heather. The spark of life in her eyes had faded too soon.

He needed to do a little research to learn where this angel lived and worked. Then he would figure a way to take her. A smile formed on his face, so gentle and sweet no one would imagine the darkness that lay hidden beneath. He knew he fooled them all.

He turned his computer on and brought up the internet to begin his quest. He typed in the name Caroline Montgomery and waited for the answers that would help him capture his new star.

*Two in Tulsa* made such an excellent title. It would stay *the* headline around the world for weeks to come.

**12**

––––––

Paige arrived back at her apartment, unaware of how she got there. The file folder rested in the seat beside her. She still reeled over being taken off Heather Balentine's case. Her first homicide as a detective, and someone else would solve it. Someone else would piece together the clues she should have found. "Shit." She slammed her fist down on the offensive folder. "Damn it."

A missing person case. Who gave a rat's ass? This case hardly seemed in the same league with the previous one, a case which might keep Hank busy for years. He needed her to watch over him. She wanted him to mentor her—to learn from the best homicide detective on the force. The plan should have worked great. How did she screw up so badly? She hadn't seen Captain Bob that mad ever.

She picked up the folder and left the car. While she used her keys to open the door, her phone rang. She glanced at her caller ID. She didn't want to talk to anyone right now, especially not Bill. Her betrayal would travel over the department.

She decided not to defend herself. She'd stick with it. The time to explain had passed.

After she stepped inside, she walked to her desk and placed the folder there. She forgot today was Sunday. She would put her pajamas on and retake control of her life. Her phone rang again.

This time she didn't recognize the number but witnesses often called her. She pressed the connect icon. "Hello."

"Hi. This is Officer Danny Baker. I found Heather Balentine's body."

"Sure, I remember who you are. Did you recall something else?" He'd probably called to gloat, the ass.

She walked into the kitchen and opened the cupboard doors. She had nothing to eat in the apartment and decided to have a pizza delivered later.

"No. I heard about today." He paused for a moment. "I wanted to say. I, uh, I'm sorry for my attitude the other night. It stunk. I felt like everything was just so easy for you, just fell in your lap. But I didn't want something like this to happen. I promise I didn't."

She stopped and listened more intently. "Thank you for your kind words. I'm not sure what was said, but the information did get out there."

"I wanted to say I know you're a good cop. You work hard at it. Hank has helped you a lot, but it's only natural. He raised you." His voice sounded sincere. Did no one put him up to this? She questioned whether to trust his call. The guys at work loved to give her hell, especially since her promotion.

"Thank you for saying so. Sometimes I'm sure it does seem I might have received preferential treatment, but I try to work hard to make up for it." She opened the refrigerator and took out a Pepsi. She unscrewed the top and took a drink.

He paused as if he couldn't think what to say. "I wanted to comfort you a little. I figure it's been a tough day."

"Thanks. It's not been the best day. I appreciate your thoughtfulness."

She stepped back into the living room and sat on the couch, then picked up the remote, hit mute, and flipped through channels. Nothing got her attention until she landed on the classic movie channel. *Laura* with Dana Andrews played.

"If I can do anything to help, let me know. I can come over and keep you company or help with whatever comes up." Hopefulness infused his words.

"It's not necessary. I've lost so much sleep since this whole case started, I'll probably take a nap, but thanks for the offer. I do appreciate your call. I just want to rest a little." They both said their goodbyes and disconnected. She got comfortable on the sofa and dozed off while she watched the movie.

Later she awoke, and the movie was over. She was more rested with this nap than any sleep since that early morning she'd gotten the call about Heather. The star remained her favorite. She felt like she'd let Heather down. To get thrown off the case was the worst possible outcome.

Who was she kidding? They didn't need her help. Hank knew more about how to solve cases than she ever would, but still, she'd wanted to be involved with the investigation. Not for the glory so much, but to close the case as a gift for someone who brought her laughter.

Joy seemed a rare treat in her life. Since Hank dealt in murder, amusement didn't come often around their home. She remembered the antics Heather and Anthony Strete had performed in *Far From Alabama*. They'd made a great pair. It seemed a shame they would never do another movie together. She smiled again. Before this instant, she didn't think she would ever wear the expression again.

Her stomach growled. She picked up her cell phone and speed-dialed her favorite pizza parlor. Tonight she would indulge her guilty pleasures. After she flipped through two dozen channels, she settled on a romantic comedy. This time, Ben McCall attempted to tame a red-haired beauty. The close-up showed her face, and Heather Balentine appeared.

She'd forgotten they'd made more than one film together. This one, they made early in both their careers. *Stolen Hearts* wasn't their best, but she enjoyed the movie until the doorbell rang.

She muted the sound and went to the door expecting her pizza delivery. Then she stepped back with surprise. Special Agent Trinity stood at her door holding a flat box.

"Do you deliver part-time?" She smiled to cover her amazement. She never dreamed he'd show up at her apartment.

"Only this once, and my timing seemed impeccable." His smile charmed. He shifted the pie, which smelled delicious, and nodded his head toward the door, requesting entrance into her apartment.

She moved aside. She couldn't imagine why he came here—and with her pizza no less.

"I'm told they're the best in Tulsa." Trin set the box down on the coffee table.

"The pizza? Yeah, they're good." Her smile felt stiff. "Can I pay you? I assume he didn't give it to you for free."

"No, but I plan to steal a piece or two. Are you okay?" Trin cut the small talk. His expression revealed his intent.

"I'll survive, but my pride might not." She attempted a smile and sat down on the sofa, then motioned for him to do the same.

"So, what's the real story?"

"What do you mean? You know what happened." She placed her trembling hand on her knee.

"I'm not sure I do. The rumors don't line up with the Paige I saw yesterday. She stayed quiet and followed Hank's every move. Today she sidetracked me for a reason I have yet to determine, and I'm sure she covered her partner's ass. Did he let it slip?"

His question rattled her for a second. "No. You've got it wrong. I didn't cover for anyone. If I explained, neither you nor the captain would understand, anyway. There's no reason to discuss it. He assigned me another case to work. I'll check into it. It's that simple."

"Who will watch Hank's back? I figured that's what you've been doing. Isn't it?"

"No. He's a little older. I try to help out if I can. He trained me as his replacement. In my opinion, he's the best detective on the force. I was fortunate he would work with me. It stinks that I blew it." She opened the pizza box and inhaled to distract Trin. She felt uncomfortable with the current topic. He proved far too adept at reading people and situations.

"So why didn't you defend yourself? Did you screw up?"

"It's a matter of interpretation. I don't think I did, but the information got out there regardless. At this point, it's all that matters." She picked up another slice to keep her hands busy.

"Now it sounds more intriguing. You didn't do anything wrong, but somehow the information magically appeared on the internet for the whole world to read." This time he took a piece from the pizza box.

"See, I knew you'd never understand. Let's agree to disagree on terms and talk about something else." She picked up her tepid Pepsi and took a sip.

"Okay, how do you see our case so far?"

"We've got nothing unless the prepaid cell number pays off. I figure Heather came here for a clandestine meeting with our killer, and he took her life. End of story. If we don't get him this time, he will kill again." Her tone sounded confident, but her jaw quivered slightly.

"So, you still consider yourself a part of Heather's investigation team?"

"No. Of course not, but I thought you meant Heather's case when you asked the question." She put the slice down and stopped her pretense of eating.

"I could get you back on the case." He watched her reaction.

"I don't want you to try. I have to work here once you're gone. Eventually, this mess will blow over. I'll get through it. If you interfere, I would always stay the chick who needed help to get where she is. I don't want to play that game for the rest of my life. The force already thinks along those lines." She got up and went to the kitchen for paper towels. Then she came back a few seconds later and offered him one and a full Pepsi. "It's the only drink I keep around except bottled water. Do you prefer a glass?"

"No."

"So what happened to put you on the serial killer track?" she asked.

"I figured you'd look me up. I'd do the same in your situation."

"It said you were a hot shot with missing children. Seems like a huge jump from there to chasing serial killers." She nibbled the pizza slice she'd picked up.

"I suppose it does, but both include sexual perversion. More than a few missing children cases comprise sexual abuse or pedophiles, and many serial killers display a form of sexual deviance." Trin observed his hands for a moment.

"What triggered the move to the new department?"

"I got too close to a particular case. We found the boy dead.

If we'd been ten minutes sooner, he would've—but we weren't."
He finally glanced at her from his far-away stare.

Neither talked for a time as they ate. After Trin finished his slice, he grinned. "Why plain cheese? It makes me feel about eight years old again."

"I don't need frills," she answered without thought.

"I'll bet not." He grinned.

She returned the grin. She enjoyed a smartass. Apparently, he did, too.

She tried not to stare at him but couldn't help noticing the way a lock of his black hair fell over his forehead. She couldn't deny the attraction stirring within her. If he wasn't a Fed, she might like him, but his take-over of her first case still rankled a little, especially since she got thrown off of it.

Trin left a short time later. A hint of disappointment altered her mood. Not since Bobby's death had she been the least bit interested in a man. She peeked out the window and watched him go to his SUV. Why did she find men she couldn't have attractive?

She stuck the leftover pizza in the fridge and walked over to her desk. The file still laid there. She picked it up, strolled back to the sofa, and sat down. She grabbed the remote, flicked the television off, and placed the control back on the coffee table.

She wondered again if this case meant she didn't work on the homicide unit anymore. She'd never heard about anyone from that department who worked a missing person case. If only she possessed the ability to rewind time and start the day over again. She opened the folder and read the file about the missing real estate agent, Betty Greenway.

~

Paige logged on to her computer at work before six the next morning. The missing person case file rested beside her. She dialed the phone number listed for Betty's cell phone. She let it ring until it went to voicemail. The numbers listed for her landline and business gave no response either.

She called the local hospitals. Admitting didn't find her name listed at any. None had a record for any Jane Doe. She'd given Betty's physical description, but it didn't get her a positive result, either. Too many clinics to phone this early, so she didn't bother.

Next, she searched the website for her real estate office. It gave the business address and ways to contact her. She left a short message and asked her to call Detective Paige Stone since someone reported Ms. Greenway missing. They needed to ascertain if the agent was alive and without harm.

Then she did a quick computer search under Betty's name. Nothing unusual turned up.

Betty Greenway ran an office close to Thirty-First Street and Harvard, located in a small strip mall. The pictures online presented a clean and well kept business. She employed one part-time worker, Stella Benson. Stella reported Betty had disappeared.

She decided to make a trip to the woman's residence to check it out. Besides, she didn't want to get caught here after Hank and Trin arrived.

She left a note on the captain's desk and reported where she'd be. She felt like a thief, sneaking out. People milled about in the department, but no one paid any attention to her. Relieved to escape undisturbed, she climbed in her car to see what the missing woman's home could tell her.

~

Trin listened to Hank phone Seth Cooper at ten o'clock Pacific time. The phone rang eight times before Seth answered. Hank's droll expression darkened with each ring.

"Are you blowing me off?" Hank spoke immediately when the ringing stopped.

"No. Someone was talking to me at the time your call came through. It took me a few seconds to get rid of them."

"So, did you get the names I wanted?"

"Close. I got the ones I could with the time allowed. Most people involved were unavailable for the weekend. Once they arrived this morning, I gathered information until time ran out. Plus, I had to notify the head of the studio this morning. The episode was *most* unpleasant. He threw a fit. He'd been out of town for the weekend and hadn't heard."

"I want you to email me the names and numbers you've compiled. Then keep working on it, complete the list, and send the rest to the same place. Next, did you find anyone she seemed close to?" Hank pulled his note pad from his pocket and grabbed a pen off his desk.

"Not from anyone I asked. Everyone I talked to said she hung around with her personal assistant. I hope she knows something," Seth said.

"We've already talked to her." Hank tapped his pen on his desk several times. "What about her makeup assistant and hair-dresser? Did you put them down?"

"Yes. He's on it. I caught him early this morning." Background noises came through the phone lines.

"What did you find out about the insurance policy?"

"A policy exists. The beneficiary is the studio. The studio president refused to give me the specific amount, but I'm sure it's in the millions." The noises coming through Hank's phone grew louder.

"I hope you took his number down and got his name. I will need to speak to him personally."

"I'll put him at the top of the list when I send it to you." The hammering started again.

"What's the latest scuttlebutt about Heather? What rumors are floating around? I want you to add them no matter how crazy they sound. Sometimes the strangest ones contain an element of truth." Hank's voice grew louder as the construction crew's volume increased.

"I'll put those on the list if I hear any. I don't associate too closely with the film Ms. Balentine worked on. I believe I explained before." The construction sounds remained constant.

"Yes, you did, but I still need answers. I'll expect your email right away and don't take forever on the second one either." Hank yelled to be heard, then disconnected, ending the noise. "Shit. I think I got a set designer."

"It sounded like it." Trin laughed.

Hank shook his head. "God, this case has been one disaster after another. We can't seem to buy a solid lead, and I get my only information from a flunky who doesn't work on her movie. If that don't beat a setting hen a-pecking." Hank got up to stretch his legs.

"Did you talk to Paige yet?" He waited to see the old man's expression, and how it would change.

"No. I thought she'd come by her desk this morning. I planned to talk to her then. So far, I haven't seen her." Hank glanced over at her empty chair.

"I looked her address up yesterday and caught the pizza delivery guy who drove up at my arrival. She wouldn't talk about it. I figured she was covering for someone, but she wouldn't explain." He waited for Hank's response.

"She can be stubborn if she puts her mind to something.

Over the years, I've learned to give her space. Once she's ready, she usually comes around." Hank's expression bore no guilt.

"So how does the relationship between you and Paige play out, anyway?"

"Following her father's death, I took her in to raise. Her mother died the year before, from cancer. I wouldn't let them put her in foster care. Her dad was my partner. Unfortunately, she only knows a cop's life. We worked cases together in the evenings from the time I took her in. I had to work at home in the evenings while she lived with me. We're close. You can probably tell. I let her handle certain details for me because she has since I first took her in. I always believed she did so as a way to say thanks for my taking care of her, but she's prickly too on occasion." The older detective's grin turned sentimental.

"Sure was true yesterday. She handled herself well enough when I attempted to grill her."

"So do we need to make a trip to Tinsel Town? A set designer, who can figure." Hank changed the subject.

He considered a moment. "We might. Phone conversations are a lot more difficult to read."

"True, but you're going to tell Paige if we do. Otherwise, she will never speak to me again."

## 13

Paige drove to Betty's residence. The place, painted a sedate gray, rested in the old addition not far from the Ranch Acres shopping area. The small row house displayed a lawn manicured to perfection, the best-kept on the street.

She pulled up behind a red Lincoln and parked. The model wasn't new, but it appeared in good shape. She got out of her car and walked up to the vehicle, noting how clean it looked both inside and out.

After she knocked loudly on the front door several times, she peeked in the windows. Betty's living room faced the front of the house. A taupe-colored sofa inundated with perfect accent pillows sat beneath the side window and awaited her return. Each one, plumped to fullness, lay in its precise place. Everything she viewed resided in its proper position except the tan pumps kicked off by the front door.

She moved to the window on the right. The kitchen, in red apple décor, revealed nothing out of place—not even a dish in the sink. At least not one she observed from the window. Then she walked around to the other side. The frilly pink bedroom seemed spotless and ready for the crew from *Good House-keeping* to photograph. From its appearance, the house would pass a white glove test. Which was why the shoes by the front room door bothered her.

She went to the house next door on the right side and knocked, then waited for an answer. Several minutes passed, but she heard noises inside, so she waited a little longer. Eventually, a white-haired woman with a walker presented herself at the door.

"I'm Detective Stone with the Tulsa Police Department. I checked on your next-door neighbor, Betty Greenway. Have you seen her lately?" She moved her jacket to the side and showed the badge attached to her slacks' waistline.

The old woman observed her for a moment through the slit. The chain rattled, and the door opened wide. "Why don't you step in? I need to sit most of the time. My legs aren't what they used to be."

"Thank you, ma'am. Do you know Ms. Greenway?" She entered the woman's home and waited for her to sit in a mauve recliner.

"Not well, but we wave at each other occasionally. We've had a few conversations. People are busy these days. Go ahead. Sit down, please. Would you care for something to drink?" The woman's hands indicated the sofa as she spoke and later pointed to the kitchen doorway.

"No, thank you. I'm fine. We received a report that Ms. Greenway might be missing. Do you remember when you last noticed her?" She pulled her note pad from her jacket pocket and sat on the faded gold couch.

"I remember I saw her come home from work the other

night. She carried takeout food with her. I thought to myself people don't eat healthy anymore." The older woman's hands continued to move while she talked.

"Do you remember which evening?" She made a note about the takeout while her conscience nudged her about the way she ate.

"Let me gather my thoughts for a moment. I got the trash ready to take out for pickup the next morning. It was on Thursday. The trash man comes early Friday morning, so I get it ready the night before. Otherwise, I miss him. I'm sure I did it on Thursday." The woman's hands never stopped moving while she spoke.

She nodded and wrote the day on her pad. "Did she leave again, or was her car gone later?"

"No. The car has been here several days. I thought that was strange. She's normally in and out a lot. I figured she was sick since she didn't leave for so many days."

"Did you spot anyone near her home during that time? Someone who didn't belong around her house." She gazed at the woman and waited for the hands to move again.

"No. I didn't notice anyone come by her place. She rarely entertained company. I can't remember the last time anyone visited Betty. You know, I had a weird incident the other night. The sound of a vehicle in the middle of the night woke me. It felt real enough. A car door closed after I woke up, but surely, I only dreamed it. The next morning everything seemed back to normal. I'm certain you've experienced something similar before, so real you assume it happened for the first few minutes after you wake up." The woman's hands stopped moving.

"What night did that happen? Do you remember?" she asked.

"Oh my, several nights ago. Let me think. I thought it was

too early for the trash truck so Thursday night or early Friday morning. I didn't look at the clock," the older woman answered.

She nodded and smiled. She pulled a card from her inside breast pocket and handed it to the woman. "I'll give you my card with my phone number. If you see or hear from Ms. Greenway, please contact me right away. If anyone shows up around her house, or if anyone asks about her, call me. I need to get your name for my records."

"I'm so sorry. My name's Henrietta Clark. I can't imagine I didn't introduce myself." Her hands remained motionless for a moment as she spoke. Then she accepted the card.

"You've helped a lot. I appreciate your agreeing to talk with me." She reached to shake the woman's hand. "You stay seated. I can show myself out."

She left and closed the door behind her. Her mind lingered on the strange dream the old woman had. It wouldn't hold up in court, but did it happen for real? She would still consider it when she looked over her notes.

She needed to get into the house to examine Betty's belongings. The woman's car remained parked at home. She kicked her shoes off after she walked in the door, but Betty kept her house much too neat to leave them there for long.

The next step on her list involved a trip to Betty's office. She could get in there. Stella Benson had a key to the office and planned to show up in half an hour. Plenty of time to grab a Pepsi and still get to the appointment on time.

~

"Someone followed us. I figure it's reporters," Trin said.

"Really?" Hank glanced in the side mirror. "You're right. Everything about this town has been upside-down since the press conference. Did they recognize you when we came out the front of the building?"

"I don't know. I've worked high-profile cases before, but nothing like this."

"How long have you done this job?"

"Too long. I've been with the Feds around fifteen years. My passion for missing children lasted until about a year ago. One case got too personal. Supervisors moved me to this one. You've worked law enforcement long enough. You get the picture of how it goes."

"Yeah, I do." Hank nodded.

"Our coffee run turned into more than we expected. We've been cooped up in the department so long, I needed to get out for fresh air. I never considered the press would latch onto us," he said.

"It sounded good to me, too. You want to stop and give them a sound bite or blow them off?" Hank asked.

"Let's find a drive-thru instead of Starbucks. Then we can lose them."

He saw a McDonald's sign a block up the street and pulled in to place their order. Once it came, he handed the sack to Hank and pulled back into traffic. He drove slowly. After the light at the next intersection stayed yellow, he floored his rental through the red light. No one from the press followed since they tailed law enforcement officers.

At the next block, he turned right and meandered through a residential area and came out from the housing addition, a mile over and a half a mile up.

"Do you think we lost them?" he asked.

"It looks like it. Next time, we'll use more care if we leave the station."

They arrived back at the department about twenty minutes

later, and there the vultures sat. He grinned. He expected the journalists would return to wait for them.

"We got outfoxed," Hank said.

"I can't say I'm surprised. I figured something like this might happen. Let's get it over with." He got out of the car and started for the building in front of him, but the reporters swarmed him and cut him off.

"Didn't you work on the Tim Jennings case? What kept you from getting there a few minutes faster?"

"Was Heather killed by a serial killer?"

"What was Heather doing in Tulsa?

"Do you have any suspects?"

"What caused Heather's death?"

The questions flew around him while the reporters jostled to get their news clip answered for the next broadcast. He attempted to block the noise out as he waded through them toward the safety the building provided. The scene felt like a nightmare. Then he remembered Hank. He scanned the mass of people but didn't spot the detective. Panic crept up his spine. He thought Hank might be down on the ground until he saw him reach for the handle to the station. Relieved, he pushed his way toward Hank. After the department egress closed, he noted Hank's pasty color and abnormal breaths.

"Are you all right?" He watched Hank take something from his pocket and pop it into his mouth.

"I need a minute," Hank wheezed.

He presumed he'd found out why Paige had distracted him yesterday morning. She wanted to keep Hank's secret. *Damn it.* This situation put him in one hell of a position. He never got involved in police politics, but Hank remained his backup for this case. The man wasn't physically ready to do the job.

~

When Stella Benson pulled up at the office, Paige got out of her car. She considered the short, stout woman with graying brown hair and decided the female looked dowdy for a real estate broker. The woman must answer the phone.

"I'm Detective Stone with the Tulsa Police Department. My supervisors want me to investigate your request about Betty Greenway. I assume you still don't know her whereabouts." She offered her hand to shake.

"No. I haven't heard from her, and I'm worried sick. She would never stay away from work like this for so long. The weekends are often our busiest times." Stella took her offered hand and shook it.

"I'd like to ask you a few questions, if I may. It will help me decide how to proceed. Can we go inside?" She moved behind Stella while the woman unlocked the door to the office.

"I'll answer any I can. I'm only around Betty through work. We don't socialize. I come in on Fridays and Saturdays. If we're busy or scheduled, sometimes on Sunday, but what with the market down, I haven't worked the Lord's day in a long time." Stella smiled and rubbed her hands down her pants' legs several times.

"Calm down. My questions shouldn't make you nervous. I'm sure we'll reason out what happened to Ms. Greenway. Has she seemed different lately? Excited about something or wound-up? Has anything changed in her life recently? Could you tell?" She pulled her notepad out from her pocket.

"I don't remember anything that made her seem enthusiastic. I've always been the eager one. My daughter gave birth to a new grandbaby two weeks ago. Of course, I've been excited about it for months. A little boy, Jackson." She picked up a picture from her desk to show off the infant.

"He's adorable, ma'am. Did Ms. Greenway have any plans for the weekend? Does she have a family?" she asked.

"No family. At least, none I know of. She didn't mention she had plans, but we haven't talked since a week ago on Saturday. I suppose something might have come up, but she would call if it did. She was meticulous about everything. She would call," Stella repeated. Her forehead furrowed in concern.

"What did you do for Ms. Greenway?"

"Greeted customers during her time away from the office and answered the phone. But I'm a qualified agent. If the need arises, I can sell a property. I've sold two homes since I've been here, but she did most of the sales." Stella rubbed her thumb across the edge of her grandson's picture. By her expression, she seemed lost in her thoughts.

"How did you come to work for her and how long ago?"

"I've worked here around a year. A friend recommended me to Betty. I'm semi-retired. My health is not as good as it used to be. I help a few days a week with whatever she needs." Stella's thumb stopped for a minute then started up again. "Would you like a cup of coffee? I need one."

"No. Thank you. That's one beverage I don't like. I often catch flack about it at work, but I can't stand the drink." She smiled. Stella got the pot ready to make some.

"Are you familiar with her acquaintances? Did she have many friends?"

"I can't say. We never talked about them if she did. Betty only seemed to care about her business. She said she might get extra cash soon, but she never explained from where. She didn't mention any family. I talked about mine most of the time." Stella pushed the switch to start the machine.

"When she left Thursday, you hadn't communicated with her that day? Nothing by phone or email?"

"No, but it didn't seem unusual. I rarely heard from Betty before I arrived on Friday. This time I came in, she wasn't here, she didn't phone, no message, that was unusual. I called her a bunch, but no answer. I waited around and told myself she got a flat or something, but she never showed up Friday or Saturday. I called the police, and they said they had a waiting period. I'm certain something has happened to her. She might be in a ditch somewhere hurt or dead. I'm not sure what to think, but something is wrong. I know it."

She sensed Stella's tears were sincere and patted the woman's arm.

"I'll do the best I can. I have little information so far. I should check around here before I go. Does Betty have a boyfriend or someone close?" She figured her own life sucked, but Betty had her beat.

"I don't think she dated anyone. She never spoke about someone special. She probably wouldn't like for you to mess around in her stuff. But I tell you, I'm so worried, I don't care. She can fire me. You search whatever you want." Stella pushed a key into her hand.

"What's the key for?"

"Her house. She kept a spare key here, just in case. I got it after I turned on the espresso machine." Stella gazed up at the pot and sniffed the rich aroma. "It smells done."

"Why don't you sit down and enjoy your coffee. I'll look through Betty's desk and see what I can find that might help me. I could sure use more information about her private life. Without it, I can't judge where to investigate next." She moved over to sit behind Betty's desk.

HE TURNED THE COMPUTER ON, entered the password, and waited. He loathed wasting time for anything except to lure his next victim. To entice and capture prey equaled pure pleasure.

Under her name, he found numerous hits. He started with

her website. It gave a short bio about her salvation and a few miracles in her life. She had CDs and DVDs of her preaching for sale. The site offered short messages for free download. He was tempted to order at least one, but they might put his information on a list. He didn't want his internet address to get added to their register. He'd like to use this laptop for a few more days before he trashed it.

He left the website and searched through various articles that mentioned her name. She'd stayed a busy woman for someone so young. The pseudo-saint ran an orphanage in South America and outreach centers in various cities, in addition to preaching salvation on TV. She probably deserved her high-profile status, but it was also what made her ideal for his needs.

After he got up, he paced for several minutes beside the old kitchen table that held his laptop. She appeared flawless, young, and perfect. If she were untried as a woman, he would teach her so many things—evil, delightful things she would enjoy so much. His junk hardened while he visualized what he would do to the beautiful Caroline. Her eyes filled with fear, her naked body writhed during its search for air. He climaxed when her life left her body, and the eyes turned vacant. Then the art to prepare her for viewing began.

He sat down and used skills he'd paid dearly to learn. His expertise made him privy to information his eyes should never see. He hacked into her bank account to check her money. Those same accounts also contained her home address. He checked her calendar and learned her schedule. He found the registration for her car and the plate number. Her life became a book, his to read. He would study them and pick the best time. He didn't have long to steal her away, but take her he would.

As he watched her face on the computer screen, his dreams

for Caroline developed into more—much more. Soon he couldn't distinguish the fantasy from the here and now, but it didn't matter. The foreplay would blend with reality soon enough.

## 14

Paige sat down at Betty Greenway's desk. She spotted a Rolodex first. She'd never used one, but she'd heard about them. This one displayed the brand on the side. Most people used computers and cell phones for such information these days. Apparently, Betty still used hers. "Did you ever see Betty use this?" She pointed to the old system for address and phone information.

"No. I don't think she got everything moved from that gadget to her computer. She often put the new address information on her cell phone, then synced it with her laptop. She kept good records. Anything listed in that antique came from a long time ago." Stella blew on her coffee.

"Okay." She flipped the cards to the G's for anyone with a Greenway name. She thumbed through and glanced past several sections along the way, but nothing stood out.

She opened the top drawer from Betty's desk as Stella sipped her coffee. Then she shuffled through blank page forms about the real estate business. Betty kept ten sheets of the various documents in every folder. Each set was filed numerically by number.

The next one below it held an alphabetical file system. She snooped inside several folders. The contents contained sold property information. Betty kept tabs on what colors the wife favored, the square footage, what style home they preferred, how many bedrooms and baths. Nothing useful found there.

In the bottom drawer sat a blue plastic school box, along with various other personal items. She ran her fingers over a hairbrush, a lipstick tube, and a tampon. She hurried on to the center drawer just under the desktop.

The thin drawer contained pencils, pens, extra staples, and the like. Everything tidy. She noticed Betty's obsessive-compulsive tendencies ruled her business life as well.

She turned on the desktop computer. While she waited, she went through the third drawer again. She pulled the blue school box out from the drawer and snapped it open. A stack of money secured with a rubber band caught her eye. Under the currency lay several receipts. The contents surprised her.

"Do you recognize this blue box and its contents?" She glanced at Stella.

"No. Betty always kept her belongings to herself. She kept forms for me in my desk. I never used hers. Did you find something important?" Stella took another drink from her coffee, then set the cup down.

"I'm not sure. Let's see what I find on Betty's desktop." She remained silent as she searched through the data on the computer. She didn't find much. The folders she searched through were about her real estate business. She opened and closed files systematically and checked for another half hour but didn't find a single item useful. The desktop held nothing personal, which would help direct her next steps.

"Did Betty own another computer she used? This one contains no personal information. Every file I've opened is about her business." She stood and stretched. Then she sat back down.

"She carried a laptop with her and took it home at night. An old Dell, I think. I have no idea what information she kept on it." Stella got up from her seat on the sofa and paced three laps.

"I might find the PC at her house." She continued to check files but found nothing of interest.

After ten more minutes, she returned to the blue box. First, she counted the currency. Just under five thousand dollars. Then she examined a receipt for a prepaid cell phone and a new computer from a big box store. Not a Dell, but the slip included a 4G hookup for several months. She questioned why Betty acquired the items.

She opened a folded piece of paper and found another handwritten note. The sheet contained information for a cabin rental for two months. Betty's receipt listed a telephone number but no name. The signature was illegible. She attempted to find an entry on the computer for the items, but none existed. The woman had too much cash left unprotected. The box's contents seemed out of place for a scrupulous woman like Betty.

"Is there a copy machine here in the office I could use? I need to reprint these register slips. I want to track these down. They might not lead anywhere, but I still need to check. Plus, I have to write out a note to replace the currency. I want the lab to check it out. I'll need to copy the others, too." She watched Stella's expression when she mentioned what she found.

"You mean she had money tucked away in the desk?" Stella pointed at the blue box.

"I counted close to five thousand." She nodded. "Did you know she had that amount stashed here? Know where she got it?" She watched Stella's reaction and felt confident the woman didn't know about its existence.

"No. If she kept money around here, it's a surprise to me. It doesn't sound like Betty to leave so much lying around. She always took the green stuff to the bank, but mostly we dealt with checks from mortgage companies. Those she deposited." Stella dropped back down on the sofa and picked up her coffee cup, but she didn't take a drink. "It's a three-in-one printer. You'll find the machine over there." She pointed to the back wall with lower cherry cabinets.

Paige switched on the equipment and waited several minutes. During her wait, she glanced into the trashcan. The receptacle remained empty.

"What day does the garbage truck run?" She glanced back up at Stella, put the cash in an evidence bag taken from her pocket, and labeled the sample. She tucked the contents back into her jacket pocket.

"Betty collected the trash on Thursdays, I believe. I never took any out, but it's what Betty told me. The cans are always empty on Friday, the first day I come to work. Of course, Betty would empty it every day." Stella sipped from her cup.

After she made her copies, she searched the entire office and spotted extra supplies in a walk-in storage room but found no laptop. She bent over and checked the cabinets along the back wall in the main office but didn't find the new items there. She wondered where the new purchases went. Why would Betty need a prepaid cell phone for the business, and who rented houses for two months? A short-term rental seemed odd.

"I discovered a few receipts here which seem unusual. A new laptop, a prepaid cell phone, and a house rental for two months. Do you recognize any of those items? I'm not in the real estate business, but why would she need them?" She walked back over to the copier, tapped the copies into a nice stack, and glanced up at Stella.

"Goodness, I can't even guess. I never heard Betty mention those things. I have no idea why she would want them. In my years in real estate, I've never had a reason to use a prepaid cell phone. Sometimes people rent places for a few weeks to vacation, but otherwise, I can't imagine about the house rental either. Usually, you get those short-term rentals in places like the coast or Hawaii. Vacation spots. Places like that." Stella finished her coffee and took the mug to the small sink and rinsed the cup.

"I see. I didn't find the computer or cell phone here in the office. Do you have any idea where she might keep them?" She picked up the copies, folded them, and put them in her other jacket pocket.

"No. I'm sure I haven't see them anywhere. I hope you find them at her house." Stella watched as she put the receipts back into the blue box and returned the container to the proper drawer.

"I plan to look for them. Thank you. I appreciate the effort it took from you to come in today. Your kindness helped. Hopefully, we will find Ms. Greenway soon." She shook her hand again and left.

～

*Two months earlier*

TONY STARED at the three black Escalades that sat in Ben's driveway. What the hell did they do? How in the world did he let them talk him into buying matching black Escalades? He remembered they stepped out to celebrate the crew's departure the previous night. He'd gotten higher than he intended before the night ended. The rest remained a blur.

"I don't know what the hell we were thinking last night. Those farmers will figure we're pimps from the south side of LA. Whose idea was this, anyway?" His head ached like a bitch.

"Yours I think." Josh laughed and moved toward the driver's seat.

"You're my buddies. You should have talked me out of it. What the hell will I do with a black Cadillac from the hood? And we got three?" He placed his dark glasses on his nose and pushed them into place.

"You promised if we bought four-wheel-drive vehicles, we could take them to ride the dunes in the Little Sahara Park. We think that's a great idea." Ben walked up to the group and joined the exchange.

"You're supposed to use four-wheelers, not full-blown Cadillacs." He strolled around the cars and felt like an idiot.

"We've got to leave in a few minutes, so get over it. I asked the crew to pack our belongings in Tony's and my Cads. Then Buzzkill can drive us in his. We'll enjoy the trip more if we travel together. The crew can drive the other two out to the big OK for us." Ben smirked at him.

"We should stop by the Grand Canyon on the way out. I've never seen the place. Have either one of you seen it?" Josh waved the key fob to his Escalade.

"Yeah, I've stopped by several times. Are you the tour guide or what? We'll never get to our shoot if we stop for every one-horse place along the way." He moved to the back passenger door and got inside. He planned to sleep for the first half of the trip.

"Cheer up, Tony. I've never seen the canyon. We'll only make a short detour to please Buzzkill. He gave us a lift. Once you sober up, your attitude will improve." Ben hopped in shotgun and motioned Josh to take off.

"How long will it take to get there?" he asked and worked to make himself more comfortable.

"Who knows? It depends how many times we stop and let you puke." Ben smiled and glanced back at him.

"I never vomit during a hangover. If only I could, my head might feel better." He closed his eyes.

"GPS says about nine hours if the traffic stays good." Josh kept his eyes on the road.

"When is the traffic ever good in LA?" He groaned as they hit a chug hole.

"No whining allowed." Ben pushed his dark glasses up and reclined his seat.

"You two are certainly entertaining. I could have traveled alone." Josh switched on the radio.

"Always glad to help." Ben gazed out the window for a minute or two before he started snoring.

The two passengers drifted off to the sound from the Eagles singing *Somebody*.

Paige put the key in the lock and turned it. She pushed the door extra hard and stepped inside Betty Greenway's home. The tan pumps still lay beside the front door. She picked up her sample kit and placed it inside the door. Since a good deal of the force besides patrol was working Heather's case, she'd brought hers along. With the spotless house, she didn't think she would need it, but she liked to be prepared.

A large red shoulder bag sat on a table next to the front door. She opened the satchel with gloved hands and peered inside. Another tube of Brandywine Red lipstick, a wallet that contained thirty-two dollars, and three peppermint breath mints rested in the bottom. She checked the wallet for a driver's license. Betty Greenway. No surprise there, but most women didn't go far without their handbag and all their personal items. She searched for an address book or cell phone. Betty's purse included neither. No information on next of kin to notify.

Two details bothered her. Something must have happened right after Betty arrived home Thursday evening. Otherwise, her shoes would be in her closet, and no woman takes off without her handbag for long. She walked around the living room—not much to see. The place remained immaculate except for the fine dust layer she wiped with her gloved finger.

From the front room, she moved into the kitchen. It seemed perfect too. She opened a few cabinets. Everything appeared in textbook order inside and out. She pulled drawers open, but nothing grabbed her attention.

She opened the refrigerator door and glanced inside—a few soft drinks, not much food. When she closed the door, she spotted a small reddish-brown spot on the floor not far from the fridge. The compacted, dried powder looked like blood.

She moved back into the front room to grab her sample kit and brought it into the kitchen. From the case, she placed a yellow marker beside the spot on the floor. Then she took her cell phone from her jacket pocket and snapped three photos. Next, she bent down and scratched a little loose from the spot and put the scrapings in a small evidence bag from her kit. Without testing, she couldn't know for sure, but she felt certain it was blood.

Either Betty didn't see the small stain, or something prevented her from cleaning up the mess. She continued her journey through the house. Betty was not alive. She continued opening doors and even peeked under beds, but she was sure.

She didn't detect the smell of decomposition though. Where was her body?

This time when she went back through the house, she examined every detail. She searched every cabinet, closet, and drawer for the new computer or cell phone. She found nothing out of place. She also didn't find the items she wanted.

After she checked her notes, she remembered Henrietta Clark observed Betty with takeout. She checked in the various trashcans throughout the house. She found two receipts: one for Chinese food, dated Tuesday, and another for pasta from a pizza franchise, dated Monday. She didn't find any fast food from Thursday.

If the woman carried in her evening meal the night before the trash pickup on Friday, where did the wrappers go? It didn't remain in her wastebaskets, but several previous food sacks did.

The shoes in the wrong place, the blood on the kitchen floor, her purse still at home, and missing fast food wrappers. Not a lot to go on, but something didn't seem right. So what did she do with the new computer and phone? She couldn't find Betty's old laptop or her cell either.

Besides, what about the trash? If the trash truck came on Friday, why would the fast food wrappers from Monday and Tuesday remain here? A meticulous woman like Betty Greenway would take her garbage out for pickup on Friday morning, but several waste cans contained trash. This brought her back to the same obvious conclusion. Something happened to Betty Greenway after she returned home Thursday evening. But *what* happened?

She found Betty's keys by the red shoulder bag on the table close to the front door. One key had "Lincoln" embossed on both sides. She needed to check everything and stay at it until she finished. Her body could be in the trunk, but she doubted it. She didn't smell decomp when she'd pulled up. In this heat, a body in a car trunk would produce odor quickly.

After she unlocked the door and the trunk, she set to work. Dust covered the car. Otherwise, the vehicle remained spotless. Still no laptop, not even Betty's old Dell. She would love to discuss the case with Hank, but she wasn't sure he would talk to her. He might believe she'd let him down.

At least this case required legwork. It would keep her busy for a day or two. She had receipts to check out, a house to find, and she'd only talked to one neighbor. Others might know the real estate agent better.

She returned to the house to close up and took a hairbrush from Betty's bedroom. The lab could use the hair to DNA match the blood from the kitchen floor. She locked the door behind her and returned to the forensic lab to log in her evidence. With the high priority for Heather's case, she wouldn't get results on the blood work for a week or probably a lot longer.

~

*Two months earlier*

Tony awoke, and the Eagles still sang *Somebody*. He felt like he'd slept for a long time, but the radio played the same song.

"What time is it? I fell asleep to that song." His mouth felt like one huge cotton ball.

"You've been out several hours. I switched stations many times since then. Ben's out, too." Josh nodded over at the shotgun seat.

"At least my head has quit screaming at the noise, but my bladder needs relief. Can we stop and take a leak? I could use something to drink. My mouth's parched." He sat up and gazed at his surroundings: desert, desert, and more desert.

"The sign advertised a rest stop in two miles. We can take a short break there. My stiff ass wants up from sitting so long." Josh played with the radio again after the song finished.

"Sounds like a plan. So why haven't you been to the Grand Canyon? I assumed everyone stopped at the landmark." Except for the urge to take a whiz, the day looked better.

"I've never been in this part of the country before. I've flown over several times, but I've never driven it." Josh tapped the steering wheel with his thumb and matched the beat from the song on the radio.

"I've got to say the canyon is impressive. You should see it. We can stop. Last night's party caught up to me earlier." It was as close as he got to an apology.

"I figured. You ever consider slowing down a little? I don't want to see you get hooked on that shit. My old lady lived for her next drink. Alcohol never did my brother and me any good." Josh glanced in the rearview mirror at him. His friend's stare remained earnest.

"I guess I do get carried away a little, but I intend to enjoy myself while the party lasts. I figure in a few years, someone else will make the next-big-deal list, and we'll fade into the background. Everyone always says that's how Hollywood treats you. I don't plan for a surprise to kick me in the ass when it does," he said.

"A number have lasted. Look at Eastwood and Denzel. They've been A-list for a long time. Others managed it, too. You're a natural in front of the camera and in their league. Don't screw around and drown in the bottle. It would ruin everything for you." Josh kept his eyes on the road for a few minutes. "Do me a favor. After we get to the set, don't touch any alcohol until we finish the shoot. I won't say a word to Ben.

Prove to yourself you *can* leave the hard stuff alone. I worry about you sometimes." Josh stopped talking, but his eyes remained focused on the road.

He never answered Josh. His drinking wasn't such a problem. But if his friend was worried, what the hell did that say? He stared out the window at the barren landscape. The whole area appeared bleak and traveled on forever, like his life. Josh was right, damn it. He craved a drink.

## 15

Paige knocked on the door of the home on the other side of Betty Greenway's. She attempted several more times and gave up. No one answered. She walked across the street. Lady Gaga blared from the upstairs of the house directly across from Betty's.

Over the loud music, she hammered the door with a fist. After a few seconds, she pounded again. It took more than a minute for anyone to answer. The door cracked open, and the scent of marijuana wafted out.

"Police." She placed her foot in the crack and gave it a good shove.

The kid backed up two feet. Her blonde ponytail bobbed for several moments. The girl, in her early teens, put her hand over her mouth.

"Why do I smell pot on the premises?" She stepped inside.

Her young expression turned ashen. She attempted to fan the scent away with her skinny arms.

"A little late for that isn't it? What's your name?" She moved her jacket to the side, revealing her badge.

"Sonya. Sonya Busby." She moved back even more. The girl might stand five foot two.

"Today is your lucky day, Sonya. I won't bust you on the marijuana charges, but you will give me your stash. Then we need to talk to your parents about what you do when you're not supervised. I hope you'll take this seriously. You should. Do you understand?" She stared the young girl down and waited for her response.

A pale Sonya nodded.

"Where do you keep it? Let's go."

"It's upstairs in my bedroom." Sonya climbed the oak steps. She followed.

She followed Sonya into a bedroom with posters of Justin Bieber hung around the room. "What were you thinking? Think your friends will offer to do your stint in detention for you? I doubt it."

Sonya shook her head.

"I'm here on another matter. I don't have time for this, but I would shirk my duty not to get your parents involved. Someone needs to care about you enough to force you to examine your choices. Sometimes decisions can ruin our whole lives. Ever think about the consequences?"

Sonya shook her head again.

"You need to. This crap doesn't do you any good, and it usually means you run with the wrong crowd." She calmed down a little. She'd seen so much of it during her time on patrol. Kids and dope always riled her anger.

"I need your help with something else. What do you know about Betty Greenway, the lady who lives across the street?" She nodded in the direction of the real estate agent's house. She took the small baggie of weed from Sonya and stuffed it in her jacket pocket.

"Nothing." Sonya couldn't say the word fast enough.

"Have you moved here recently?" She took her notepad out of her inner jacket pocket and a pen.

"When I was three. I don't remember, but Mom says we've been here since then." Sonya looked down at her feet.

"You've lived here that long, and you don't know anything about her. I bet you observed a lot more than you think. I need help with this." She continued her grim expression.

"I don't know. She doesn't do much. Leaves for work in the morning. Comes home and stays in for the evening. It's the same every day." The young girl shrugged.

"Who are her friends? You spot anybody come and go from her place?"

"Nope." Sonya crossed her arms over her flat chest.

"Do you talk to her? Say hey or wave as she drives away?" She looked back up at the girl.

"Not really. I see her late in the afternoon. She usually brings takeout home with her. Her life seems pretty boring." Sonya looked down at her finger nails like they were the most interesting thing in the world.

"What about people watching her or following her? Any strange cars in the neighborhood?" She'd hoped to take notes, but none of the information was worth writing down so far.

"Nah, but Mom and I used to joke about the guy down the street. He always watches her house when he walks by. The guy exercises every night right before dark. It's been hot this summer, so he leaves in the morning after sunup. I notice him from my bedroom window sometimes if I wake up early enough, but my mother says he's harmless. He never bothers anyone."

"You've seen him stare at Betty's home while he goes by her place?" Now they were getting somewhere.

"Mom figured he might have a crush on her. I can't say why. She's old." The kid rolled her eyes.

"Crushes are a relative thing. How old is he?"

"I don't know. Johnson's old, too."

"See what I mean? You think they're both old. He could believe they're right for each other. Do you remember the last time you saw him?" She used her pen to jot the info down and shifted her weight to the other foot.

"Several days ago. I'm not sure." Sonya shrugged.

"Which house is his? Point the place out to me."

They both moved back down to the front door. Sonya motioned to a yellow tract about three doors down from Betty's.

The little ranch seemed cheerful, but she'd been an officer long enough to learn monsters often lurked inside houses that appeared innocent.

"What's the man's name?"

"I think it's Frank. I'm sure about his last one, Johnson. I read it on his mail once. The postal guy mixed his letter in with ours. Mom made me put it in his box. That's the only detail I have. Honest."

She pulled her cell phone from her pocket. "Give me your mom's number. I want to talk to her." Another trip to the lab to book the stash into evidence. Not what she needed.

While the line rang, she gazed at the young girl beside her. "You ever run any track?"

"No."

"You're going to start. I go several times a week. I've chosen you for my new partner. I hope you own decent running shoes." She grinned, and Sonya's mouth fell open. Her mother answered the phone.

TRIN WATCHED Hank read the list in his hand. Charles Frost headed the studio. At least, Seth Cooper listed him that way.

The detective dialed the number and put the mobile on speaker. He would much prefer they spoke to the man in person, but the economy in Tulsa had turned down like everywhere else. Money for a trip to LA was out, if the department could avoid it.

After the fifth ring, a woman's voice came on the line. "Mr. Frost's office. How may I help you?"

"This is Detective Gettering from the Tulsa Police Department. I need to speak with Charles Frost concerning Heather Balentine's death. It's urgent I get in contact with him." Hank glanced up at him and shook his head in disgust.

"I'll tell him you are waiting. One moment, please." Her connection went dead, and the theme from *Gone With the Wind* filled the room.

In a few minutes, a baritone voice came back on. "I'm Charles Frost. Seth said you might call. How may I help you?"

"Detective Gettering from Tulsa Police Department. We need to ask a few questions about Heather Balentine. We learned you bought a life insurance policy on the star. Could you tell us how much and who receives the money?"

"I checked on it. We normally retain a contract to reimburse the initial salary for our star. In her case, it would run eight million dollars. However, once we get further along in the movie, other costs are involved. At a certain stage, if you have to reshoot around the star, it's more expensive. We reached that point. So we increased the policy to seventy-five. The studio itself will receive the money to re-film with a replacement. I'm afraid the situation is complicated." This time, Hank heard no background noises.

"So, do you have a new actor in mind?" Hank asked.

"Not yet. We didn't prepare for this. I don't believe it has happened before," Charles said.

"No. I suppose not. Did you know anything about Ms. Balentine's personal life? Who she dated or any of her close friends?" His older partner stood up, moved a few steps, and shook his leg.

"No. She kept her private business quiet, except on one of her last movies. I understand she took up with Tony Strete at the time. The rumor is they broke up once the movie finished, but I'm not sure about the facts on it. I always say, rumors rarely run true." He imagined Mr. Frost as a small man who acted important because he held self-esteem issues. Charles' bored tone hinted at panic.

"Did she give you a cell number to communicate with her or a private email account? Someone told us she used one." Hank sat back down.

"Heather filled out a personnel sheet. My personal assistant will find it for you."

Hank nodded at him. "You got any questions?"

He shook his head no. The contact information the PA repeated through the phone matched what they already had. The detective finished the conversation.

"That discussion wasted our time. The amount on the insurance seemed astronomical, but I guess films cost a lot these days," Hank said.

"I thoroughly agree. We found nothing there. You want to call the hairdresser next? Or we could go see if Bill got anywhere." Hank's expression picked up after he suggested the latter.

"Let's visit the tech." He rose from his seat.

Hank followed him out of the department.

~

Weariness enveloped Paige when she left the station, but she wanted to get a feel for the man who had potentially stalked Betty. When she ran his name through the system, his record came back clean. Most stalker reports turned out harmless, but Ms. Greenway disappeared. Traffic snarled in several spots along her return to the Ranch Acres area.

She parked down one from the yellow house where Frank Johnson lived. His yard appeared in decent shape but not up to Betty's standards. The mowed lawn looked good, but the edging seemed a little sloppy. The flowerbeds needed attention. A green hose laid out of place on the grass.

She got out of the car and walked to the front entry. She observed the immediate area during her stroll. Often in older neighborhoods, the houses ranged in various stages of repair. Johnson's home fit in the middle.

She knocked loudly. Several minutes passed before the door opened to reveal a tall, well-proportioned man in his mid to late fifties. She bet he turned the ladies' heads in his youthful days. He didn't seem the type to take an interest in a nondescript middle-aged woman like Betty.

"Mr. Johnson, I'm Detective Stone with Tulsa PD." She moved her jacket and let her badge show. "I want to ask you a few questions."

"What about?" He looked genuinely baffled.

"A neighbor of yours went missing. I'm canvassing the neighborhood to find any information I can about the lady. Are you acquainted with Betty Greenway?" She watched for a tell and didn't discern any.

"I don't know who you mean." His right shoulder hiked up.

"She lives three doors down. The residence with the red Lincoln in the drive."

"Oh, yeah. I go by there when I exercise. I've had heart problems in the last several years. My doctor wants me to walk two miles a day." His hand extended toward Betty's house.

"Did you see anyone who hung around the neighborhood and doesn't belong?"

"No. I don't always pay attention. I try to get my goal in and go home."

"Someone said you seem to watch her place while you pass by. Can you explain?" She kept her eyes on his reaction.

"I do?" He rubbed his chin. "I suppose I do a little. I used to own a red Lincoln like hers before I retired. My lifestyle isn't what it used to be. I miss what was. Can't help but admire that Lincoln. No more mini-mansions and fancy cars for me." His rueful grin didn't last long.

"I can understand why you might. Did you ever notice if Betty entertained guests or anything odd that happened in the neighborhood lately?"

"No. I don't socialize much anymore. For years, meeting people was a job requirement, and I did it a lot. I'm happy not to bother now." His body relaxed against the doorframe.

She reached for her business card, but Frank seemed hesitant. She waited for a few seconds longer. "Is there something you want to add?"

He shrugged. Hesitation became uncertainty in the way he stood. His hands smoothed his slacks twice. "The guy who lives behind me is into voyeurism. I walk at various times during the day and evening because of the heat we've experienced this summer. I mean the temperature was over a hundred degrees how many days? Anyway, the man across from my back yard has a telescope that never points at the sky." He lifted his eyebrows and looked at her intently.

"So does it ever land in Betty's direction? Or can you tell?"

"It's hard to say, but he's not watching the planets rotate. That's for sure."

"I'll give him a visit. Thank you for your time. Here's my card. If you should think of anything else, please call me at once. Thanks again." She left, confident he wasn't their man. But if this continued, she should lower the crime rate in this neighborhood before the case was closed.

## 16

Paige booked the money and marijuana into evidence, which took forever. She always hated the tedious parts of police work. Then she drove to the TU campus.

She opened the door to Bill's office and found Hank and Trin already there. She wanted to back out and leave, but she wasn't a coward and refused to act spineless. She smiled instead and entered like she always did.

She walked over to Bill's desk and wrote a telephone number on his note pad that she spent half the day to obtain. She couldn't help but notice the last one she'd written remained posted there. When Bill finished with a request, he habitually removed it.

"Hi." She included everyone in her greeting.

"I assumed you'd come by your desk. What happened to you this morning?" Hank said.

"I got an early start. My missing person case kept me busy. How's your case coming along?" She attempted to keep her voice even. It would kill her if anyone figured out how much her removal from the case hurt.

"Like a hamster on a wheel. We're going in circles. You doing any better on yours?" Hank glanced her way.

She didn't know what his expression conveyed. Did Hank think she was still angry with him? She wasn't sure her mentor remembered the events from the morning before. Yesterday, she'd felt certain she should take him to the emergency room, but he refused to go.

"I'm not clear how it's going. The woman is so anal with her organizational skills it's ridiculous, but then I find a blue box with receipts she kept separate and five thousand dollars in cash. I have several details to chase down from the blue box. Her car and purse are at her house with no sign of the woman. It seems a strange situation, but so far nothing has turned up. It's odd but doesn't tell you much. You know what I mean?" She shrugged, but her expression showed concern.

"Ours isn't any better if it helps." Trin smiled at her, and her stomach fluttered. He was one gorgeous man, but he'd taken her place with Hank. That was difficult to get past. She knew he didn't cause the problem, but she didn't want him to figure out Hank's health issue. What he would do with the information she couldn't know.

"Bill, you seem quiet. I added another number to your list. I know you're busy with Heather's case, but if you get a chance, I'd like what you can find on this number, especially its location. I can't find it, and she only purchased the phone this past week. I don't think it has a GPS, but I'm not positive. Anyway, like I said, if you get a chance to squeeze it in, I'd appreciate it." She recognized she rattled on, but she couldn't seem to stop her mouth from moving.

"I'll work it in. You know I always help you out." Bill pushed ten keys. Then pushed more. "Are you certain it's the right number? I don't show any activity on it. No one has used it to dial out. Nothing received. I don't think anyone turned it on so I can't tell you where it's located." He looked puzzled.

She stepped closer and double-checked the number. It matched the one she wrote on her notepad. "It's the same. See what I mean about this case? It's got these odd little elements, but nothing you can define one way or the other." She shook her head.

"We know how you feel." Trin nodded.

"What other receipts were in the blue box?" Hank asked.

"A computer with a 4G hookup and a house rental for several months. See what I mean? Odd details, but not illegal," she said.

"You said she had five thousand cash with it? Hmm," Hank said.

"Just under five grand. I need to run. I still have items on my list to check." She sounded cheerful as she left the guys behind. She figured Hank would roll it around in his mind for a good while. If he came up with anything, he'd tell her.

After she left the room, the knot in Trin's stomach lessened. She was too young. He'd told himself the same words more than once since he first laid eyes on her, but somehow his stomach didn't get the message, let alone his genitals.

"Bill, since the princess has gone, can we concentrate on the Balentine case?" It seemed harsh, even for the sensible Hank. He still wondered what the two of them weren't telling him. Hank seemed fine until Paige turned up.

"Sorry, Hank, you know it's difficult for me to tell her no. You've never complained before." Bill paused. "I made a list of the other numbers dialed and received from your victim's phone. The one Paige asked me to find on Oscar night. I reversed the digits to get names to go with them. I'm glad you came by. I was about find you. The people I've contacted from the list who answered didn't have a newer number for Heather. I've marked the ones off I completed. You can try the rest of them. It shouldn't take you very long to finish."

"Okay. Sorry I grumped. I didn't rest much last night. Sleep has evaded me since I got this case. We've got more calls to make. Keep at it. Let me know the minute you've got something." Hank turned to leave.

"Will do," Bill said.

Trin and Hank walked out the door.

PAIGE DROVE around the block two times to see if she could accurately tell which place had the telescope. The house directly behind Frank's contained the instrument in question. From the street, the window gave her a good view of the device.

She parked in the drive, got out, and walked up the steps. After she knocked loudly, she noticed the curtains move near the window. A few moments later, the door opened. A brown-haired man in his fifties stuck his head out.

She flashed her badge. "Do you own this residence?"

He nodded.

"I'm Detective Stone from the Tulsa Police Department. I'm canvassing the neighborhood. We've had someone reported missing in the area. Did you see anything suspicious?"

"No, ma'am."

"Did you see any strangers around? Anything unusual?"

"No, ma'am."

"I see you own an awesome telescope. I love them. I bought a small one for myself, but it's not this nice. Could I look at it up close? You wouldn't mind, would you?"

His eyes glanced anywhere but at her. He swallowed several times. Finally, he nodded for her to enter the house.

"I didn't catch your name. My friends call me Paige. Why don't you do the same?"

"Oookay." The sound seemed to drag out forever.

"Are you all right? You're not sick or anything, are you?"

He cleared his throat. "Ah, no."

By this time, she stood right behind the telescope. She put her eye to it and waited for her vision to adjust. She saw a woman bent over exercising in a skin-tight outfit that barely covered her backside. She brought her head up without a word, folded her arms across her chest, and stared at the man.

"My name is Homer Sutton." His voice cracked mid-sentence.

"You spend your free time this way? You watch other people?"

"I can explain. I recently moved the telescope in from my back patio. I guess it landed in that position." For the first time, he became animated.

"That's not what I hear. A neighbor reported you as a voyeur. You know, a Peeping Tom." Her raised eyebrows demanded an answer.

"I—I don't know what you're talking about." He gulped down a gallon of air. His hand jingled the change in his pocket.

"I mean you engage in a nasty habit and watch other people live their lives in a way they wouldn't want you to see. You're caught in the act with the woman exercising. What do you know about Betty Greenway? Don't think about lying to me."

"Who's Betty Greenway?"

"The woman who disappeared Thursday night or Friday morning."

"I don't know any woman named Betty Greenway."

"She lives down the alley from you. Drives a red Lincoln."

"I don't know her. I think I've seen her around."

"You watch the neighborhood with your telescope. You've surely seen something. Betty vanished. I want to know what you know about her. The smallest detail could help."

He hesitated a moment. "Thursday night?" He rubbed his bristly chin. "A dark SUV drove up the alley and stopped by her place. Her lights never did turn on though. I think that was Thursday night. A few minutes later, it drove away. I swear, it's the only detail I can remember about her. I don't watch her much. She lives like a monk."

"What time was that?"

"I don't know. It had been dark a long time. I never pay any attention to time. Hurt my back years ago. Been on disability ever since."

"Now, let's talk about this Peeping Tom situation."

Trin waited while Hank dialed the phone number for the hairdresser and switched the phone to speaker. It'd been a nonproductive day so far. The phone rang six times before a male voice answered.

"This is Detective Gettering from the Tulsa Police Department. I want to ask you a few questions about Heather Balentine. You did her hair and makeup? Or her hair only?" Hank got his notepad out and laid it on his desk.

"Seth said you might phone me. I did both. She was a pleasure to work with. She always looked so pretty even before I applied her makeup. I can't believe she's gone. I keep thinking she will waltz in the door, and I will get the chance to make her beautiful one more time." He gushed with a nasal twang as he rambled on.

"Your name is Brad Tyson?" Hank hesitated.

"Yeah."

"Mr. Tyson, did you and Heather maintain a friendly relationship? I understand women often tell hairdressers details they might not tell everyone else. Who they date, what they plan for the weekend. Anything like that?" Hank picked up his pen.

"She chatted with me a bit. We discussed her love life often. Especially in the first months of the movie. She still loved Tony Strete then. Several times she cried, and we had to retouch her makeup, but the last month or so she seemed to get over him."

"How do you know?" Hank asked.

"She stopped crying every time someone mentioned his name. Then she carried her special phone everywhere. If it rang, she would stop everything to answer it, but she never let on who it was. The caller remained a huge secret. I attempted to ask her once about the big deal she made, and she got upset with me. I knew not to ask again." Brad's voice took on a dramatic flair for secrecy.

"Did she mention anything about this past weekend? What she planned to do?" Hank got up to stretch his legs.

"She never said a word, but I could tell by her actions something of interest would happen. She asked me questions by the dozen about what color worked well with her skin tone. Was her figure still good enough for a nude scene? The film she's shooting doesn't include her naked. So I figured she met a new guy and planned to heat up the sheets with him. I assured her she looked perfect. We talked about clothes. She wanted my approval. Of course, she had excellent taste, so she worried for nothing." He figured if Brad answered every question at this rambling pace, they might wind up on the phone until the day's end.

"Did she mention where she planned to go? What she

wanted to do over the weekend?" Hank seated himself behind his desk again.

"She mostly wanted advice on lingerie, so I assumed they arranged a weekend of wild sex, but she never said so directly."

"I see. Who did you think Heather went off to meet? Did you get a clue by anything she let slip? We need to find this guy. He might know important information about what happened to her." Hank rubbed his legs again.

"You think he's the killer?" Brad's salacious attitude showed plain enough.

"Not necessarily, but the guy might have witnessed something. He might know where Heather went. What she planned to do. Why she came to Tulsa." Hank finally stood up again.

"I'm sure she thought him famous. I felt he was probably a married actor or something. I can't remember exactly how she worded it, but I got the impression he worked in the film industry. Someone important. From what she said, it's the idea I got."

"You never did figure out who?" Hank asked.

"No. Heather always stayed too cagey about him." Brad stopped for a moment. "You know, I do remember she said something about Twitter. I'm positive Heather said she would tweet him when she got home. They must have used the internet. You should find him from her computer."

Trin wanted to strangle the man. Like they hadn't already thought about that.

"Yeah. We'll give it a shot. Do you know any other close friends she might talk to about her love life?" Hank sat and threw his pen down on his notepad.

"She talked a little with the lead cameraman. I saw them joke around, but he didn't seem tight with her like I was. Her PA kept close by her side. The second female lead talked to her a little, but not too much. She wanted to get over a broken heart. She didn't mingle as much during this shoot as she did on the other films that I've worked with her, but I understood her reserve. Her last leading man burned her good." Brad savored the last words like a decadent dessert he was clearly happy to dish.

Hank looked over at him and shrugged. He shook his head no. Hank finished by giving Brad his telephone number and inviting him to call if he remembered anything important.

"He shed a little light. Very little. Someone in the film industry who's big and famous. That could cover Hollywood. Most guys in Tinseltown think they're big and famous." Hank picked up his notepad and crammed it into his pocket.

"I agree. This case has been nothing but frustration. Let's take a break. Get lunch. Bill could find something while we're gone." He motioned for Hank to lead the way, but he wondered if she made up with her last lover, Tony Strete. That description fit him. He'd been an A-list actor for several years now.

"Best idea I've heard today." Hank turned to leave, and he followed.

## 17

Paige walked into the Best Buy at Seventy-First Street and the Mingo Valley Expressway to check on Betty's computer purchase. The trip quickly turned into a dead end. The receipts confirmed the purchased laptop, but no one remembered her specifically. The whole experience played out as she expected it would.

In large stores, too many faces passed through. Many customers helped themselves and didn't speak to anyone but the checkout cashier. The security camera recording of Betty confirmed the real estate agent proceeded through the front register after she conferred with a clerk about the internet purchase. Paige wasted an hour and a half to prove the receipt led nowhere.

Finally, she took the copy of the hand-written receipt out of her pocket. She glanced at the number from the house rental and dialed it. The phone rang ten times and went to voicemail. She left a message and gave her telephone number for a call-back. Her phone displayed six o'clock. She'd been busy since early this morning, but she still needed to run by and file her reports for Captain Underwood. After that, she planned to grab takeout for herself and make it an early night. She hoped to hear from the rented home number before morning.

When she arrived at the department, she spotted a small sports car parked next to Hank's vehicle. A man sat inside it. The silhouette of his head seemed familiar. It took her a few seconds to place him.

She got out of her car and strode toward the main entrance. She didn't get far before Peter Faulkner got out of his black Miata and walked toward her. She wanted to ignore him but figured he would stop her. She prepared and clicked on the phone recorder she always kept in her pocket.

"Good afternoon, Detective. How does Hank feel since his . . . shall we say, spell the other day? Or shall we call it an incident?" His expression ranged from confident to overbearing, but she remained calm.

The reporter positioned himself in her path. She attempted to step past him, but he countered. She stopped and glared at him. She moved again to get around him, but he continued his maneuvers.

"You're about to push past your luck. Get out of my way."

"I learned your boss chewed your ass the other day, but you were most helpful. I will use you again because I witnessed Hank's secret." He got right up in her face. The stale cigarettes on his breath offended.

"I think you're mistaken, Mr. Faulkner." She didn't budge from her spot, stench or not.

"I don't think so. We both understand why Hank shouldn't be working on the job. He's not healthy enough. If the secret gets out, they will force him to retire or set him behind a desk for sure. You wouldn't like that, would you? Hank is all about being a cop twenty-four seven." As he threatened her, he sneered, making his homely face uglier.

"You need to let me by. I want to go inside." She motioned to the right again to get around him.

"Give me something more on the Heather Balentine case. I don't want to see Hank put out to pasture, but we both know I will if I have to." He grabbed her arm.

"I'm not on the case anymore, but I wouldn't give you anything either way. Let me go." She stared directly where his hand held her.

"No chance. Not until I get new information on her case." He squeezed tighter.

She pulled her phone out and flipped the switch. The sound of their conversation played from the small device for several seconds before she shut it off. "Go ahead, try to black-mail me. I'd love any excuse to arrest you. If you want more information, stalk somebody else. Get out of my way, or you're going inside with me in cuffs. I can always add an assault on a police officer." She stared him down. His grip loosened a little. She shook off his hand and freed herself. Then she walked past him and didn't care what he did with the information he imagined he possessed.

She left paperwork for the captain to explain what she covered during the day. Tomorrow she would face him, but today provided an opportunity for him to cool down. He would see she took him seriously. Hopefully, in the morning, he would listen to her explain her concern for Betty Greenway. She knew the woman was dead. She could find no sign of her anywhere, and women didn't leave their purses behind—not on purpose.

HE'D DISCOVERED where to find Caroline Montgomery on her calendar. She'd booked taping sessions for her TV show tonight. The schedule worked perfectly for his plan.

The Oral Roberts University campus was deserted this late at night. A security car made a loop occasionally. He used his watch to measure them, but he didn't detect a pattern in their appearances.

He found her car by the back entrance to the Mabee Center and parked nearby where six cars sat haphazardly in a group. He wanted to check out the situation.

She'd booked the studio until twelve thirty. He wasn't sure if the time frame would hold. They might finish early or run over. In his work, both happened frequently. He'd planned to park out on the street and wait. Once he arrived at the location, it didn't seem feasible.

So many exits presented too many options for her to take when she left the parking area. If he blended in, he would follow her out, and no one would notice. If someone recognized him, he'd go on his way and take her from another location. Not good, but doable.

This hunt and capture challenged him. He found he enjoyed the excitement that stirred his anticipation to a new level. The apprehension of getting caught amped him up. *Every Breath You Take* played on his iPod. He listened to the beat pulse through his veins. In only a few more minutes, he would claim her. Berlin's *Take My Breath Away* replaced The Police, and the fantasy played on in his head. He lowered his zipper and took his penis in his hand.

He imagined Caroline naked on the gurney with her eyes closed. He would restrain her hands and feet, then he would tape her eyes open. One time he'd lost his favorite moment. Since then, he always taped the eyes open.

Because he didn't get a chance to romance her through the

internet, she wouldn't know her captor. She would wake up, and he would see her eyes fill with surprise and recognition. After all, he was famous. She would understand who enslaved her once she attempted to move. The next stage would take her confusion and turn it to fear. That moment was the most delicious. His skin grew clammy. The beat of his pulse accelerated.

He'd place the scalpel between her breasts. She'd sense the instrument on her chest. It rested there to taunt her. She would see it, and her eyes would fill with terror. Panic and fear would drive her screams to fill his ears and give him such pleasure.

Then he'd position his fingers and thumb around her neck and begin the element that always brought him his greatest orgasm. His hand on her throat tightened, and his cock got harder. In his mind, his hand continued to squeeze her neck tighter. He grew larger and larger until death entered her soft brown irises. When life departed her eyes, he exploded in rapture while sweat formed on his brow. The smell from his release filled the vehicle, and he came back to reality.

His memory relived carving the precious heart from Heather's left eye. He saw his hand force the scalpel into her right eye, and his satisfaction was total and complete. It made her *his* work of art.

He carefully wiped himself with tissues and stared at the back door Caroline would use to exit the building. The clock on the dash showed 12:25. Only a few more minutes until she came out the door and imagination turned into reality.

~

*Eight weeks earlier*

TONY STROLLED into the living room of his aunt's old house. He hadn't sipped a beer in two weeks. The dry spell meant tough going, but he vowed to slow down. He didn't like to think anything could get a hold on him. So far he'd missed it, but the situation wasn't unbearable. He hated to stay away from the guys after the day's shoot, but they usually drank beer when they hung out. He didn't like being the odd guy out. Before, Josh always fill that spot.

He sat on the old maroon sofa, which reminded him of his youth. His Aunt Gina never gave him any slack. She worked him hard the year and a half he'd spent here. Looking back, it didn't seem so bad. The eighteen months with her made him a better person, a turning point in his life. If he'd stayed here, his life would undoubtedly be different—probably married by now with two point three kids and horse poop up to his elbows.

He smiled and remembered Becky Qualls. She'd been cute. He wondered for a moment where her life took her. He might have settled for Becky, but he wouldn't say he experienced an undying affection for her. Mostly a schoolboy crush, and she'd made herself available.

It seemed appropriate to cull drinking from his life during his stay here. He picked up the script and studied it once more. He'd memorized the lines for the shoot the next day. To make the words fresh as you delivered them was the trick. He often used this process. He learned early on it worked for him.

He heard one quick knock at the door before it opened. The leading lady walked in, blonde and beautiful. They'd worked together before. He knew what she wanted but played dumb.

"Hello, Silvie. Why are you prowling around this late at night?" He glanced up.

"I noticed the light and figured you needed company."

"I'm afraid I'm not good company tonight. Today scorched like a sauna, dry and hot. I took a long shower but still feel dust in every pore." He placed the script on the old velvet sofa.

"You might persuade me to wash you all over again. We always did take a good shower together." She stepped closer.

"I remember." He smiled.

"After we scrubbed each other, we had an even better time." Her eyes searched his.

"Is that right?" The idea got more tolerable.

She nodded and opened another button on her top, which barely covered her breasts.

He licked his lips and raised his eyebrows. "I suppose the water has reheated by now."

"I'd race you to the tub, but I don't know where your bathroom is." She popped another button loose.

"Oh, there's no need to rush. We've got the whole night." He took her hand and pulled her into his lap.

"Sounds about right to me." She placed one palm on each side to cup his face and lowered her lips to his.

He figured Ben would kill him, but what the hell. He'd sworn off alcohol, not women.

He followed her car at a safe distance from Oral Roberts University. Since he knew her home address, he passed her on several occasions, then dropped back again. About a mile from her residence, she turned into a convenience store. Her action bought him a chance to go on ahead of her.

He parked in the alley several houses down from her garage apartment. He slipped quietly through the night and made his way up the stairs to unscrew the light bulb above her door. Lack of lighting helped. If someone saw him, they couldn't identify him.

He stood under the stairs and ignored the nocturnal animals that scrounged for food and the tree branches that rubbed on the old building. Darkness had been his friend for several years. Before Donna, he'd never paid attention to what delightful events happened at night.

Car lights announced Caroline's arrival. His tools, prepared for their job, awaited use in his pocket. She turned off the engine. Shadow engulfed her vehicle. She gathered her purchases and got out of the car. Several seconds after she closed the door, the automobile's interior went dark.

"Shoot. The bulb burned out again," she murmured.

Hands full, she approached the stairs slowly. As she stepped on the fourth rung, he silently positioned himself behind her. He placed the damp cloth over her mouth and nose. She dropped everything to fight him off, but by then, she was too late.

He threw her unconscious body over his shoulder like a bag of feed and took her to his SUV. There, he bound both her feet and hands with duct tape. Then he covered her mouth. A syringe lay ready beside her. The drug would keep her out long enough to prepare her for the performance ahead. He covered her body with a dark blanket and returned to pick up her belongings.

He threw the purse and sacks into the back with her and climbed into the front seat. Then he drove his vehicle out of the alley and parked it on a side street where the lights couldn't penetrate the canopy of the enormous trees that grew nearby.

PAIGE STOPPED to pick up takeout Chinese, then remembered she duplicated Betty's actions from several days before. The case bothered her. The woman appeared to have no one. Betty vanished, and not a single soul cared she might no longer rest among the living except one employee. In her heart, she believed Betty Greenway had taken her last breath.

She arrived home and switched on the computer. She left it to boot up while she got a bottle of water from the fridge. She came back into the living room and entered her password. Then she moved back into the kitchen to get a paper towel.

She sat down to eat in front of her computer and pulled up Google search. She entered "real estate lady missing" and hundreds of suggestions popped up on the screen. She worked her way through the list. No names sounded familiar, but several cities did. A couple matched the same places where Heather's killer left victims.

She decided to check further and clicked on one to see what the case entailed. It appeared to contain several similarities to the Betty Greenway case. She clicked on another. She jotted down the names of the ladies and the cities from which they disappeared. Her heart quickened a beat. She dug through the papers lying on her desk and picked up her copy of the victims' ViCAP printout from Heather's case. Then she returned and searched each city from the list. Near the dates they found each victim, at least one real estate agent had a report on file. The authorities didn't locate any of the women or their bodies.

She gazed up at the blank wall above her computer. The old saying Hank always repeated popped into her head. *There's no such thing as a coincidence.*

If she excluded Donna Barnett, who Hank and Trin believed was an accident, that made Mona Lansing the next victim. Mona hosted a radio talk show in New York City. She was often called the female Howard Stern. They found her body in Central Park on Saturday, July 12th. On Friday, July 11th, someone called about Greta Carson, who owned a real estate business. The woman was absent from her work, and no one could locate her. She lived in the New York City area. Greta, the petite redhead, was last seen the previous day. She told her assistants she planned to go home.

Christine Long, a TV news anchor from New Orleans, had been found Saturday, December 13th at the feet of Louis Armstrong's statue near the French Quarter. She'd received offers from the national news networks the week before her death. Her coworkers said what a shame this happened after she'd recently received an invitation to the top.

No one seemed concerned about Elizabeth Monroe, a 55-year-old brunette real estate agent. A co-worker reported her gone on Friday, December 12th, but he last saw her the day before when she departed her New Orleans real estate business.

In Chicago, Bridgette Mallory completed the small part in her tenth feature film. A few weeks passed before she came due on the set of *Delicious*. Police found Bridgette's body Saturday, July 11th at a park. An aunt called the police on Friday, July 10th about Celeta Jones, a black woman in her fifties. The woman said her niece failed to pick her up for a doctor's appointment. An employee told the police the agent left her Chicago real estate office the day before. Nobody had contact with Ms. Jones since.

The killer laid Sheila Gaines' body out beside a fountain in Las Vegas on Saturday, December 12th. The singer recorded a one-hit wonder several years before. "Love Me Tonight" sold another million downloads following her death.

Brown-haired Susan Grace, a 48-year-old real estate agent in Las Vegas, went unnoticed at the time she disappeared. Friends reported her gone on Friday, December 11th, but no one had seen her since her last appointment on Thursday, December 10th.

She got up from the computer and paced. If she mentioned

this to Hank or Captain Underwood, they'd get mad all over again. They'd think she was trying to find a way back on the Heather Balentine case and wouldn't believe her. She prowled for several more minutes back and forth by the computer.

Finally, hunger won out. She grabbed the sesame chicken with rice and warmed it in the microwave, then sat on the sofa and flipped on the TV. She made herself finish every bite since she'd barely eaten today. She couldn't concentrate on the TV program, so she got ready for bed.

The next morning she flipped on the television to catch the news. While she got ready for work, a bulletin flashed on the screen. *Local Televangelist Caroline Montgomery Is Missing*, it read in big block letters.

**18**

───────

When Paige arrived at the department the next morning, she'd made it to the top of Captain Underwood's hit list. She wished she'd found a good reason not to show up. He called her to his office the moment she walked in the front door. His complexion was the darkest red she'd ever seen on a human.

"You had to talk to the press, didn't you? Now, look what's happened. Tulsa's locked in fear. They've never been this afraid before, not like today. If you hadn't told them a psychopath murderer ran loose in our midst, they wouldn't have panicked because Caroline Montgomery disappeared. The headlines crucified us. Did you see the national morning shows? They're all concerned with Tulsa, the most frightening place to live in America. Look at the things they said about our city." He stopped to catch his breath. He took three steps then turned on her again.

She saw the TV news show flash a headline along the screen's bottom. *Tulsa Loses Another Celebrity to Serial Killer.* She bit her lip as she read the caption.

"You better keep yourself away from my sight for the next few days and *find* Betty Greenway. Do you hear me?" He pointed his finger in her face. It shook with his fury.

"Yes, sir." She could not believe it happened again. This time she did nothing wrong, and she still found herself in deep trouble. She couldn't bring herself to mention her theory on the case. Besides, what did Caroline Montgomery have to do with the Heather Balentine case? The perp didn't take more than one victim in a city. At least, he hadn't before if you didn't count the real estate agents, and the captain wouldn't count those women. He wasn't aware of them.

The people in Tulsa didn't know that information, but her captain would. How could he blame her for something she had no control over? She struggled to identify the right path to take.

She believed the correlation between the real estate owners and the celebrity murders meant the cases somehow connected. If she mentioned her suspicions, she felt doomed by her superior who was on a rampage. If she didn't tell him, and further people were harmed or strangled, she would never forgive herself her cowardice.

"And furthermore, when we get through this situation, you will learn to keep your mouth shut. Are you listening to me? If I didn't figure it wouldn't about kill Hank, I'd can your ass. I can't tell you how disappointed I am with you. Get the hell out of here and find the missing real estate lady." He stopped abruptly and motioned three different times for her to leave his presence.

She turned and hurried out the door. Her ears rang. Everything seemed surreal. Still, she didn't understand what had happened. She'd worked hard yesterday on her case, stayed away from everyone, and he railed at her again for something she didn't exactly do in the first place. Tears formed, but she forced them away, determined not to cry. It took every bit of control she could muster not to let one drop slip down her cheek.

She rounded the corner, and there sat Harley Judd on the edge of her desk. He was the last person she wanted to see. Why must she continue to deal with him? His sneer made her want to rip his eyes out and stomp on them. Because he had a handsome face, he assumed all women thought him irresistible. He strutted around the office while his minions followed. She hated his sense of entitlement. He'd asked her out several years ago. Since she turned him down, he made her life impossible. The promotion only made it worse.

"I can't take time for your stupid games. Get the hell away from my desk," she said.

"Oooh, mama bear is mad."

"You are a poor substitute for a human being. I don't know why you're hanging around me. You're not wanted here, but, oooh, I forgot, all the women tell you that."

His expression turned to fury. "You bitch. No wonder no man will have you. And neither will the department before long."

Trembling, she finally whispered, "Asshole," as he stomped down the hall.

She wanted to kick herself for responding to his bullshit. She should've ignored him, but he'd picked the worst time ever to confront her. He did it on purpose and used her trouble against her, the jerk. Oh well. The situation had passed, and she couldn't undo it. She bet he would brag to his buddies about her near demise from the force.

She walked halfway to her car before she remembered she needed to stop by the lab. She still had the blood sample to give them.

She thought for sure the scrapings from the floor were blood, but she needed to see if the sample belonged to Betty or someone else. She hadn't booked the hair she'd taken from Betty's brush for comparison, either.

She went by the lab to leave the samples and then decided to call the number from the rental receipt again. A dozen rings later she hung up. Bill seemed like the most logical next step, and he always gave her moral support. He would get the answer for her in short order, but she needed to stay out of her captain's way. Though she wanted to see Bill at the TU campus, she decided to look it up on her computer. She didn't want to get him in trouble too.

TRIN AND HANK used the back door to sneak out, then found a small restaurant close to work. Trin preferred to talk where no other officers had the chance to listen, and no press would hang out. "Through the glass, it looked like Captain Underwood gave Paige a terrible butt chewing. Is she all right?" he asked as he watched Hank for a tell.

"I didn't make out what he said, but he was the maddest I've ever seen him. I wanted to talk to her to see what happened, but it would only make it worse. Everyone thinks I helped her make detective. What they don't recognize is how good she is. Paige trained longer than most officers. She lived with me for years while I raised her and soaked up everything she could. Her instincts are usually right on." He glanced up from the menu. "I'll call her later to check on her, but she's tough."

He nodded, then pursued another track which needed attention. "I heard about this Tony Strete on several occasions. It's time to see if we can locate the man. People have told us they've been apart for a time, but she might have called him in the last month or so. Besides, he should know her preferences in her sex life. Before the case finishes, we'll find out every personal habit she has. Everyone hides something."

"I got the same nudge several times, but I got sidetracked by this other bullshit. Another female is missing, and it hit the news big time. I'm sure it's the main reason Underwood seemed pissed off this morning. She's not known nationwide, but she's famous around here. With the news full of Heather's death by a psychopath, everyone believes he took the evangelist, too. Of course, you and I realize he only takes one per city, but sometimes situations change on these deals. The public gets swayed a lot more easily than most people understand." Hank finally laid the menu down on the table.

"You mean the woman who disappeared is a celebrity around here?" He felt his expression tighten in concern.

"Yeah. I toyed with the notion, too, but for our guy, the change makes a big one. You think it's possible he has the evangelist?" Hank said.

"I wouldn't rule it out. This whole setup in Tulsa has been a little off. Small differences exist, but they add up. Since we consider his first kill happened accidentally, he might still experiment with what he prefers. Something didn't go as planned. He didn't fulfill his fantasy. A number of issues could account for the change." He held Hank's stare.

"So it's not a fluke. It is a real possibility that he has her?" Hank questioned.

"I wouldn't mention it to anyone. It might come from a separate circumstance altogether, but it is possible."

A waitress walked up and set down two mugs for them. When they nodded, she filled the cups with coffee.

"I hear what you're saying. So how does one find a superstar actor who breaks women's hearts more often than the weather changes in Oklahoma?" Hank blew on his coffee as the steam rose from it.

"You forget I can get us contacts. The FBI has faster ways to find him. Let me check while you make the next phone call on the list by yourself. I doubt the second leading lady, or the cameraman, will add much. We can check back after we finish. What's good to eat here?" He poured a little sugar in his coffee and stirred.

"I don't know. I never eat here. I wanted a spot where we can talk. On this highly publicized case, everyone wants in the loop." Hank picked up his menu again.

"I think we both got the same idea." He laughed.

*Six Weeks Earlier*

THE SILHOUETTE of a mesa in the sunset offered the camera a magical view. Ben finished the last shot for the day. The director called, "Cut." It seemed odd Tony never mentioned how fantastic the evening sun brought the day to a close here.

Grant Windsor walked up to him and preened for attention. "It's been too long since I took a role like this. I've got to say I enjoyed it. It gives me a new perspective on directing."

He smiled and didn't know how to answer him. He didn't want Grant on the project, but Josh couldn't tell the man no. He changed the subject. "What's your opinion of the scenery?

"We got great shots. Caught the evening light to perfection."

"It's fantastic, isn't it? I guess you never can tell what places are like until you stay there awhile." He noticed Windsor worded it like he directed the film.

"So true." Grant stood and seemed posed in the evening sunset. He wanted to walk off and leave the windbag, but he didn't want to be rude.

Grant rambled and commented on various aspects of the film they made, but he tuned him out. He felt tired, sweaty, and wanted a shower. An enormous yawn formed, and he milked it.

"Sorry, I can't stand this sweat any longer. I need to get in the shower before the dust out here turns me into a mud-covered monster. Catch you later." He yawned again for good measure.

"Of course. I understand."

He watched Grant walk away. Then he climbed the small steps of his trailer.

His muscles ached as he sat in his rented RV and stared down at his mother's Bible. He didn't understand why he carried it with him on location shoots. If anyone questioned him about it, he would have denied the truth.

Tonight he remembered the times they were alone together. The house would stay peaceful and calm when it was just the two of them. In those moments, he experienced total peace. That's all that got him through the times his father came home, when chaos ruled.

The flat land out here with the mesas appeared so silent and still. He figured the atmosphere reminded him of her quiet presence.

He moved over to the bed and stretched out on his back. He opened the book to John: 14 and read. In verse two, it mentioned many mansions awaited. He hoped his mother dwelt in a great big one. Nobody deserved one more than she did.

He remembered she read this chapter often to him at a young age. He had visions of stately old homes from *Gone with the Wind*. His tired muscles relaxed, and he drifted off, but the familiar nightmare awaited him.

*Twelve-year-old Ben put his foot to the shovel top and stepped down hard. He threw the soil beside the grave and* repeated the process over and over until he lost count of the times. Black shadows from the tall trees cloaked him while he toiled, but the hole still wasn't large enough. He couldn't believe he helped his old man do such a deed, but if he didn't, his father would kill him too. The only person who repulsed him more than himself was the man who worked beside him, but the job required completion.

Anger fueled each sore muscle as Ben threw the next shovelful of dirt to the side. Sweat beaded on his forehead. He wanted to brush it away, but he dreaded his father's wrath.

His old man murdered her. Ben waited one blow too late in his effort to save his mother. He loathed his cowardice and remembered again how he detested the monster beside him. The torturing fear that held him paralyzed for many years finally broke, but he delayed too long to come to her aid. She wound up dead. Ben's beating forgotten, he forced himself to keep to his task.

The bastard who beat her to death forced Ben to dig her grave. His hate-filled eyes sneaked a peek at his father. He tossed the next scoop to the side. He'd never wanted anything more than to use the garden tool as a weapon on his old man, but Ben knew he still needed his support to survive. He'd manage a few more years, and then he would leave his father behind. At that time, he would reveal to the whole world the murderous asshole, Tom McCall. Not a single neighbor would show surprise.

While the old man lifted the body into the grave, several tears streaked their way down Ben's dirty cheeks. He fought hard to keep from crying, because he figured the old man would only laugh at him for his weakness.

He vowed to bring her Bible tomorrow and read from the scriptures over her. She took solace from the words inside it. He hadn't much understood them, but she'd always received *strength when she read them. The least he could do was comfort her since he'd failed her as a son.*

*Tom McCall stared into the grave for several moments. He didn't appear sorry for his actions. "Hurry your ass up. You got school tomorrow," he said.*

*Ben picked up the shovel and started the long process to fill his mother's grave with dirt. Without a word, Tom followed his son's actions. Shortly, the old man stopped to take a drink from the bottle he kept handy. Then he left Ben to finish the job.*

*Later, he walked from the grave and felt hollow inside. For days after, he sensed the grime on his hands though he washed them repeatedly. The shame he lived with wore on him continually. Ben promised himself he would never forgive his old man. Before forgiveness came, the bastard would be dead a long time, his corpse as rotten as his soul.*

Ben woke up soaked with sweat. His breath labored like he still dug that grave. He remembered the darkness where he'd left his mother, covered in dirt. Regret filled his chest with a heaviness like an anvil dragging him to the bottom of the sea.

**19**

———

Paige ran home to use her computer. After she checked her search engine, she found a reverse directory. She entered the telephone number and waited. Paul Rubrecht came up on the list for the person she'd dialed in vain. She jotted down his address and went back to her car. The address on the east side wasn't far away.

She drove three miles north on Garnett, then turned right for a mile. On 129th East Avenue, she entered a small housing development located in the Union School District. The small ranch-style home looked like a standard three-bedroom with a two-car garage. The dark red brick house looked like someone built it in the seventies. The white trim appeared freshly painted. When she saw the manicured grass, she wondered if the owner reached Betty's status as a perfectionist.

As she put the car into park, an older gentleman strolled into view from the residence's backyard. His clothes stained with sweat, he appeared to be the lawn's caretaker.

She smelled the fresh-cut grass once she got out of her car. He wasn't the reason her boss reamed her out in a rage this morning, so she approached him with a pleasant smile. She slid her jacket's right front to the side to show her badge and offered her hand to shake in greeting. "I'm Detective Paige Stone, Tulsa PD. Are you by any chance, Paul Rubrecht?"

"It's pronounced Rupert. We spell it funny. Everyone makes the same mistake." He shook her hand and grinned.

"Nice to meet you, Mr. Rubrecht. Could I ask you a few questions about Ms. Betty Greenway? She had your number on a receipt for a house she rented. A two-month rental seemed odd to me. Do you know why the short time?" She noticed the older man wore a hearing aid in each ear.

"It sounded peculiar to me too. The cabin sat empty for several years, and I wanted to sell it. No one took an interest in it in all that time. But she came to me the other day and wanted to rent it to someone for only two months. I figured I might as well make some money while it sits there unsold."

"Did she mention who rented the place, or did she plan to use it herself?" She took her notepad from her jacket pocket.

"She said for someone else. She didn't say who. A bigwig wanted privacy. He'd finished a major project and needed a break. Claimed he didn't want anyone to disturb him. There ain't much chance for intruders out there." He pointed to the northeast.

"Did she tell you the man's occupation?" she asked.

"No, I'm not certain. Let me think. Betty said something about publicity. I don't remember for sure. I think she said something about entertainment." He shook his head a little.

"So exactly where do I locate your cabin?"

"I don't understand. Did something illegal happen there? You're such a pretty young woman. I forgot for a moment you're with the police." He smiled harmlessly and squinted.

"Thank you. I'm sorry to say we've been unable to find Ms.

Greenway for several days. Someone reported her missing. I wanted to check out this lead to see if I can find her."

"Well, I'll be. I didn't talk to Betty since she came by and got me to sign the receipt. I signed it less than a week ago." His expression turned thoughtful, and he wiped his brow.

"Now, where can I find the cabin? You won't mind if I checked it out? I want to make sure she didn't get into an accident around there."

"Of course I don't mind. Betty's a great lady. I would hate to think she injured herself out there or something. It's out by Dog Creek near Claremore." He gave specific instructions to get there, and she wrote them down.

"I can't thank you enough for your help. I appreciate it. If you think of anything else, give me a call." She shook his hand once more and slipped him her business card.

"No trouble. Let me know about Betty. I hope nothing happened to her." He shook her hand.

When she got about three feet from her car, her cell phone rang. She glanced at the number. The captain. What did she do wrong this time? She pushed the answer icon.

TRIN WALKED OUT and observed the scene. Captain Bob Underwood tapped on the microphone three times to test if it worked. The captain's voice sounded above the fray from the news personnel that surrounded the podium they'd brought out for the conference. He couldn't believe so much had happened while he and Hank ate one quick lunch.

Caroline Montgomery's parents contacted news sources and wanted to appeal to the kidnapper to let their daughter go. They'd been estranged from their daughter for years and wanted to make amends and to plead her case before the media. Harrison Montgomery IV owned the controlling interest and managed one of the largest banks in Tulsa.

His wife, Barbara Wentworth Montgomery, was the only heir from *the* Wentworth's. The family was well known for its financial endeavors in many industries. Caroline, their only child, disappointed them and joined a charismatic religion. After she turned eighteen and graduated from Holland Hall, they cut her loose to stand on her own. They hoped their daughter might soon tire of her inferior situation. Her parents assumed she'd quickly return to the wealthy support from their home. It'd been over seven years, but Caroline remained independent and lived away from their wealth.

From the information Hank gave him, he figured this performance had more to do with saving face before their friends than a sincere desire to make up with their daughter. They needed to make appearances count before their friends. It wouldn't do to appear callous about their daughter's plight. An unpleasant rumor at the neighborhood country club must be avoided.

He watched the crowd for any individual who didn't belong. He doubted their man had time to appear and questioned the timing between this kidnapping and their case. The last-minute plan for the press conference didn't give the new unsub enough time to find out about it and get here in time. His eyes searched anyway. Hank recognize the local reporters, but most national news agencies also flew in for the Heather Balentine case. So he and Hank and several other police officers searched the crowds for anything that didn't seem to fit.

The captain approached the podium microphones again. "We gathered here today to let her parents speak for Caroline Montgomery. They want to make their voices heard concerning their daughter's disappearance. I want to say Caroline is a great asset to the city of Tulsa, and I'm sure her many followers here and around this nation wait and watch carefully for her return. We want them to understand we will continue to do everything possible to find her. We invite you to join your prayers with ours in this trying time. I want to introduce Barbara Wentworth Montgomery, Caroline's mother."

The petite woman had neatly styled blonde hair. Her flawless face remained unlined. A hint of coldness emanated from the woman, which Trin found off-putting. He figured she never lost one night's beauty sleep to give Caroline her two o'clock feeding. The nanny probably raised her daughter. At least he got that vibe from the woman who stood on the stage.

Mrs. Montgomery hesitated for a moment, then opened her mouth to speak the words that could set her daughter free. Before she spoke, he knew her words were a mistake. Of course, they didn't ask him. This whole event transpired while he and Hank took a lunch break.

"I'm not sure who you are, but it doesn't matter. My daughter is our only child. We cherish her beyond reason. We worry about her as all parents do. Please release our daughter. Let her come home to the ones who love her." Tears formed on the woman's face.

"I cannot imagine anyone would want to take our wonderful daughter. She works hard to help a hurting world. For many years now, she's performed only good deeds. It's unfair you should keep her from her crucial work. Please, please, let her come home. Set her free to help others less fortunate. Don't let her light go out in a world that needs her so desperately. We will wait for her safe return." She bowed her head to appear overcome with care and tears.

If he detected her fake appeal, so would the kidnapper. He only hoped this didn't provoke the unsub to do something worse to Caroline than he already planned. It depended upon the mitigating circumstances, and he hadn't studied this case enough. But if Caroline's disappearance was related to the Heather Balentine case, this could prove disastrous. Then again, if the serial killer took Caroline, the young woman was doomed anyway.

Once Mrs. Montgomery left the stage, the intrusive reporters dispersed. A prominent news anchor spotted him.

"Special Agent Trinity, I assumed you're working the Heather Balentine case. What are you doing here? Do the two cases relate the way people are speculating?" She poked a microphone toward his face.

"Ma'am, we returned to the station and stopped to observe. We didn't want to intrude on Mrs. Montgomery's time. No further comment." He pushed through the crowded reporters and worked his way to the door.

After Hank managed to get in the building, he wandered over to him. "I didn't notice anyone. Did you?"

"No. I didn't notice anybody suspicious."

"Huge time waster," Hank said.

"Yes. It would have gone a little better if we'd helped Mrs. Montgomery with her words, but I doubt even that would help. Sometimes people don't take advantage of the advice that I've spent years in training to acquire. You probably understand what I mean." He stayed quiet for several seconds before asking, "So Caroline's parents are wealthy?"

Hank nodded as they made their way to his desk.

"Then we need to take a serious look and assume money and a ransom make for a great motive. Is there any word or note from the kidnappers?"

"Not to my knowledge, but they only took her late last night. Since everyone assumed it relates to the Balentine case, the kidnappers could hesitate to see how we proceed. Another possibility, our guy took her, but a third party might want to cash in on the money angle."

"I agree. We don't have enough facts yet to know which situation we've got here. I hate the wait and see part. It made me come up short once, and I swore I'd never do it again. Damn it." He got up and moved around, fighting the urge to slam his fist down on the desk.

~

"Paige, stop whatever you're working on. I want you to go over and interview Caroline Montgomery's neighbors. I tell you, the press is on this like piranhas. The detective in charge will assign you where the situation demands." Captain Underwood's voice sounded all business.

"What about the Greenway case, sir? I still have to chase a few leads down." She wanted to say more but didn't dare.

"It'll have to wait. This case has moved up in importance. Way too many Christians interviewed on TV about this catastrophe. The police come off like we don't have a clue. Hays said he needs help desperately. You better assist him in whatever way he wants. Do you understand?" His voice sounded firm, but at least he didn't yell at her like this morning.

"Yes, sir."

"Get your ass moving, Stone." The captain's voice went up several decibels.

"Yes, sir." He disconnected. She feared he'd wear the phrase out on her before the day was over.

She wanted to check the cabin out, but she couldn't bring herself to disobey a direct order. If she did, she would get fired for sure.

At the risk of Hank's disdain, she dialed his number. She'd made it to the car and climbed inside when he answered. "Hank, I want to run something by you. I know you'll think I'm crazy, but I think our cases relate. I didn't figure out how exactly, but I checked on the internet last night—" The call dropped.

She looked down to check her bars, but the battery icon flashed instead. *Shit.* She shook the phone several times and glanced at it again. She pulled out the adapter and plugged it in several times, then wiggled it to fix the connection, but it didn't work. The device turned completely black. Either the battery had died or the adapter did. Great timing. She figured the day could only get worse.

She grabbed the key and turned the ignition. The Cavalier started, and she wound her way through the neighborhood. She left the addition and drove south on Garnett. Hays waited for her to show up, but first she need to get her phone to work. At this point, she remembered she didn't have the address where the detective wanted her.

She drove the few miles to her apartment and hustled inside. She grabbed her charger and plugged in her cell phone. No luck.

She booted up her computer and left an email for the captain to explain the problem. She asked for Detective Hays' location. It took ten minutes to get an answer. Once she knew her destination, she grabbed the cell phone and raced out the door.

She located a phone store about a mile from her apartment and made a quick stop there to purchase a new battery.

After thirty long minutes, the tech smiled and announced the new battery fixed her problem. She drove to south Tulsa. Caroline lived in a large garage apartment behind another famous TV evangelist and his family.

Once she arrived, it took her several more minutes to find Greg Hays, the lead detective. He was interviewing the maid who worked for the Jones family. He briefly excused himself and walked over to her.

"I'm glad to see you. We need interviews completed by the dozens, and my partner stayed home with the flu today." Greg seemed friendly enough, but she didn't like him. He usually flirted with her, and she felt no attraction to him.

"I understood you wanted me to canvas."

"That may be what Underwood said, but I need you to interview. I've got a bunch of people who need a closer look." He tapped his pen on his notepad and gazed up at her with a suggestive smile.

"I'm cold on the case. Give me a quick briefing. Then I'm ready." She smiled and attempted to stay agreeable. Captain Underwood was already mad at her. She couldn't afford another complaint. The last thing she needed was for Hays to report she was "difficult" because she didn't smile enough. She pulled her notepad from her pocket and got ready to take the information down.

"Her crew saw her late last night at the ORU campus. They filmed a few shows for her TV program. Around twelve thirty, they finished. Everyone got into their cars and started home. The last time anyone saw her, she drove away from the Baby Mabee." Greg smoothed his hair and gave her a smoldering gaze.

"What have you found out? Is there anything else I should know?" She avoided eye contact and wrote the information down on her notepad.

"No. I've mostly got her routine. Everyone loved her. Why would anyone take her? Where could she be? Info like that. Here's the list. You start on this side." He pointed to the left half and handed the paper to her, brushing his hand against hers in the exchange.

"Okay. I could use someplace separate where I can work." She gazed around at the state-of-the-art kitchen.

"I'll ask the maid." Greg turned to leave, resting a hand on her shoulder before he walked away.

He came back in less than a minute. "How about the breakfast nook over there?" He pointed to a table and chairs that sat by a bay window.

"It'll work." She left him and moved toward the specified area. The sooner they separated, the better.

TRIN WATCHED Paige pull up and park her car. When she got out with a small sack in her hand, he figured she'd stopped for her dinner. He left his car and walked up to join her.

"You're out awfully late." He fell into step beside her.

"What time is it?" she asked.

He looked at his watch. "A little after nine. How did your missing person case go today?"

"Which one?" Paige shrugged and grinned.

"What do you mean which one?" He put his hand to the small of her back to guide her toward the building. He liked the feel of it resting there.

"I had to help Greg Hays on the Caroline Montgomery case. His partner called in sick. I've been there since before noon. So how come you're slumming in my neighborhood?" By this time, they'd reached her apartment door.

"Your call to Hank got cut off, and you never did call him back. He didn't worry, but I did." He took her key and opened the door for her.

"My phone battery died. I mean completely died, not needed to charge. I was driving my car, so I didn't have a radio or any way to contact anyone. By the time I got a new battery, I forgot about calling back. Sorry. Take a seat." Paige pointed at the sofa. "Did you eat? I only grabbed one hamburger and fries, but I'll share if you'd like."

"I ate an hour ago. I'm not hungry. So how did your cases go today?" He sat down on the sofa where he had the last time.

"I still want to track down several details on the Greenway case. I was about to check on them when Captain Underwood called and told me to drop everything and help Greg. I've interviewed more people today than I can count." Her countenance appeared weary before she walked into the kitchen. He heard the refrigerator door open and close.

"People don't understand how tired it can make you. Did anything important come up in your work today?" He took the water bottle she handed him.

"Not that I could tell. Greg and I will compare notes in the morning if he doesn't call me first. The captain got super ticked Caroline Montgomery disappeared. I got reamed out again this morning. I know you saw it. No one missed it." She sat down on the opposite end of the sofa.

He didn't answer. He smiled and lifted one eyebrow.

"I'm glad you find it funny. I've never been in trouble before, but you show up, and it's an everyday occurrence. Do you jinx everyone or only me?" This time she grinned before she took a bite from her burger.

"Hank and I didn't make too much progress, either. I might go back in later. It seems Anthony Strete came here to the Tulsa area. Tulsa PD went out to round him up. He and his buddies registered at the Hard Rock Hotel. They finished their location shoot out in western Oklahoma and apparently wanted to celebrate for several days." He opened the water bottle and took a drink.

"When did they arrive?" She put the fries on the coffee table between them. "Eat part of these. I won't finish them."

"They arrived before noon Thursday." He picked up a fry and ate it.

"The timing is interesting." Paige took another bite from her hamburger. He could tell her mind worked hard on something. He didn't know what for sure.

"I considered that too, but Strete could have an alibi if his friends were with him the whole time. We wanted to interview him to get more personal information on Heather. Then we found out he was in the area." He shrugged and set his bottle down on the table.

"Wow, coincidences don't happen that neatly and come all wrapped up with a bow."

He heard the wistfulness in her voice and recognized she still wanted back on the case. Since he'd been there a time or two, he empathized. "It would probably make for a long night if they get him to cooperate and come in for questioning." He lifted another fry to his mouth.

"Oh, to be a fly on the wall."

"I certainly don't have a problem with it." He watched her for reaction and discerned none.

"You forget. The captain banished me from his sight. He will kill me if I show my face, not to mention the teasing I would get because Tony Strete is so gorgeous. They'd never quit giving me crap about it," she said.

"I could use my influence." He kept his eyes on hers.

"We've had this discussion."

"I remember. But you could have changed your mind." He took another fry.

"I'd love to be there, but I can't. How's Hank doing? I miss him." She changed the subject.

"He seems fine." He snitched a fourth fry. They both stayed quiet for a short time. He decided not to mention Hank's health scare.

"Are you sure you've eaten?"

"Yep, I like to snack when I work on something." He stopped chewing and smiled at her.

"What are you working on? You mean the case?" Paige picked up her water bottle to drink.

"No. It has nothing to do with the case." His hand reached for another fry but stopped midway.

"So, will you tell me or what? We're getting older just sitting here." Her voice sounded curious, so he knew she didn't have a clue.

"That's true enough." He decided to put all his cards on the table. "The problem is, I find you attractive, but you look pretty young. How old are you, anyway?"

"You're never supposed to ask a lady her age. Where were you raised?"

He thought he caught a gleam in her eye before she looked away. "Indiana."

"So you intend to blame a whole state for your manners." She grinned.

Yep, she was teasing him. "It sounds that way."

"A northerner for sure."

"You didn't answer the question. I'm not sure you're legal."

"Of course, I'm legal. I'm on the force. I turned twenty-four about a month ago."

Before he could reply, his telephone rang. Blast. Bad timing. The defiant look in her eye sent butterflies fluttering through his stomach. Damn, she was cute. He dragged his gaze from hers, took a deep breath, and answered the phone.

## 20

*The previous Wednesday night*

Tony stood before Josh. Condescension emanated from him. He hitched one hip higher than the other and spat on the ground. Then he stared Josh in the eye and turned deadly serious. "Ransom Stoddard, you're gonna die tonight. How will your fancy law books help you now?" He called the line out with confidence and a cruel sneer on his face.

Josh stood his ground and kept his trembling hand at the ready by the holstered gun on his hip. Sweat covered his brow, and determination made him face the evil presence before him.

When his expression turned to one of smiling disdain, his hand went for his gun. The squib exploded in his chest, and the startled look that came to his face created pure perfection. He stumbled down three steps and fell to the ground. His leg failed to find purchase twice before it became motionless in death.

Ben holstered the rifle to his saddle, the horse stomped his hoof in the dry dirt on the side street, and Josh stood with his gun in his hand. The smoke drifted from the pistol that pointed where Liberty Valance once stood. The dust from the street wafted softly across the scene while the other actors spilled out from the hotel and cafe. The director called, "Cut."

Tony knew he'd gotten it perfect. He didn't want to repeat the scene. The next one wouldn't turn out as good. His eyes searched for the director to see if he needed to redress and shoot another take. If Josh and Ben did their parts correctly, they would get away from this damned heat. He noticed the director give a thumbs up.

This was it. They were through until they got back to LA to finish the interior scenes. It always took time to move the equipment. *So, Tulsa, here we come.*

For him, to return home felt odd and uncomfortable. He'd left for Hollywood and hadn't come back. He always flew his parents out to LA. His old buddies from here probably landed in jail or died. He'd never been one to keep in touch, but his mother often updated him about the ones she remembered.

Ben strolled up the street toward him and unbuttoned his shirt along the way. The sun scorched everything in its path. During the shoot, most days the temperature reached over a hundred degrees.

Tony was glad to finish the location filming. Party time had arrived, but his ambiguous attitude lingered about that too. He'd returned to his home state, and he couldn't shake the feeling. Liberty was his first truly evil part, so he questioned if it affected him. In his early career, he'd only taken roles where he was more of a lame bad guy.

Ben stopped in front of him. "Hey, we're through." Ben's smile brought one from him.

"Yeah. I've got to get a few clothes together. Then we can leave. Is the crew ready to take everything back to LA?" Tony snapped out of his mood.

"Since when do you concern yourself with such matters? You want to steal Josh's job?" Ben stared at him weirdly.

"Since I invested so damned much money, and I'm not worrying. I want to enjoy myself in Tulsa and know everything got settled and on its way. I'll relax more." He wouldn't look Ben in the eye.

"What's the deal? You've acted strange since we got here. I figured the reason might have to do with you and Silvie O'Brien. I was certain you hit that, but now, I'm not so sure." Ben pulled his shirt off and shook the dust out.

"You weren't supposed to find out about us, and before you say another word, she seduced me. I didn't start it. So I don't want to hear any more about it."

"Two whole months seems a long seduction. You're awful touchy on the subject." Ben shook his head and laughed.

"I remember when you and Josh gave me hell about it when we discussed leading ladies. You probably blame me because Gwyneth didn't take the Hallie role, but I swear I've never messed with her." This time he stared Ben square in the eye.

"Silvie did great, and she cost a lot less. If we can get the interiors shot and edited without long delays, we may not require much more money to finish it. At this point, we're still on target. Let's keep it that way." Ben tossed the shirt over his shoulder.

"That's music to my ears. I hope we don't need to pour any more money into it." He saw Josh head their way.

"If it isn't Buzzkill," Ben said.

"I think that name belongs to Tony after this stint. He's been quiet the whole time we've been here. Of course, he played house with the fair maiden." Josh handed Ben a cold beer.

Tony rolled his eyes. "Thanks for the news flash. I didn't do anything you wouldn't if she'd come to you like she did me." He noted Josh didn't bring a beer for him but was glad. He'd been dry for two months, and the craving had lost part of its power.

"Minor point in your favor." Ben rubbed his cold bottle around his neck.

"Why are we discussing Tony's love life when we could be heading for the casino?" Josh tipped his bottle up for a long drink.

"Good question, Josh. Let's get out of here." Ben opened his bottle and took a swig.

"Why don't we take our separate vehicles? We can meetup there. I'm not ready to leave yet."

The other guys agreed.

"Stay on US 412 the whole way through Tulsa to the 193rd East Avenue Exit. Turn left, and you're there. I'll meet you sometime Thursday. You'll start without me, anyway."

"You know us too well." Ben slapped him on the back as they split up.

He strolled toward the old house. He had several items to prepare and pack before his special trip to go home. He saw a dark SUV heading out. Surely Ben and Josh wouldn't leave without a shower first. Several crew members owned similar vehicles. The SUV probably belonged to one of them.

He sat down on the bed and thought about what the next few days would bring. A younger crowd would fill the old haunts. His parents would expect him to visit the aunts and uncles during his trip home. They'd probably prepare a huge get-together for everyone.

It had been good to stop by the old place again. Everything was simple and straightforward here. He missed the unpretentious life from his past. The house was old and run down, but he hesitated to leave it behind. Though he owned the place, he didn't know the next time he would visit again.

Maybe that's why he'd suggested they come here. He'd

always stayed grounded here. He'd learned the value of hard work and come to love an aunt he'd barely known. He didn't feel ready to leave yet, but plans awaited him. Plans he wouldn't cancel.

He lifted his carryall bag from beneath the bed and sat it on the floor. Then he filled it with his possessions.

~

PAIGE WALKED Trin to the door and locked it behind him. They'd located Tony Strete. Hank required Trin's presence to begin the interrogation.

After he left, she strolled to her computer, sat down, and shuffled through the papers she'd printed the night before. She must tell someone about the connection she'd discovered between the real estate agents and the celebrity deaths. It would bring disaster if she didn't. She should have trusted Trin with the information, but the agent had completely thrown her with his unexpected comments. Still flustered, his words kept running through her mind.

*I find you attractive.*

She didn't like the way that sent a warm rush through her. Better to focus on work. She got her cell phone and hit the speed dial for Hank. He'd be busy interrogating the actor, but she could leave a message.

Tony Strete. How surreal Hank would interrogate him. She would give anything to observe but didn't dare. The captain would tear into her again if she showed up.

Hank surprised her by actually answering. "What do you want, Paige? I'm busy."

"I need to tell you something. I think I've found a connection between the serial killings and Betty Greenway." She hesitated and listened for anything that would give her an idea about his reception to what she said. "Hank, are you still there?"

"I don't see how that's possible." He sounded preoccupied.

"I found other women who disappeared about the same time as the serial killings. They were all real estate agents."

"Listen, I need to go. We can talk about this later. I'm not sure I follow you, but I need to get to this interrogation. This whole case could break open with these interviews. Gather what you found together, and we can look at it tomorrow. " Hank hung up.

She paced up and down her living room floor. In police work, coincidence didn't turn out to be a fluke the majority of times. If she figured out what happened to Betty Greenway, it could help lead to the serial killer.

The items she found made perfect sense. A burn phone that only traced back to Betty Greenway. A computer with an internet connection that led directly to the agent. A house rented in the boonies traceable only to the same woman. The situation made the perfect setup for someone looking to hide, and offered a way to contact the victims without anything that tied back to the killer.

The woman had vanished. Every piece of evidence led to a dead end. She felt certain their killer had used the cabin and needed to get there quickly if there was any chance one of his victims was still alive. He was probably already gone. But if she could save a life, she had to try. She moved back to her computer and sat down. While she reread her notes that matched the women reported missing with each victim the serial killer took, her phone rang.

"Hello, Paige." Greg sounded exhausted.

"Sorry, Greg. I forgot you said you would call me tonight. My evening got busy since I left the scene." She put down the paper she studied.

"I got sidetracked myself. Did you get your partial list finished?" She heard Greg tap his pen in the background. She'd observed today he did that a lot.

"The ones I could round up. I missed the gardener and one cleaning lady who comes in twice a week to do extra work. Who knew they needed so much help to keep a household together?" She got up and walked to her sofa where her note pad lay.

"I got through most of mine, too. Did anybody witness something that might help?" Greg's pen stopped its tap dance.

"No. Not one person noticed anyone watching the neighborhood. They didn't see her with any guests. It's like the darkness swallowed her up. Did the campus security uncover anything? Were there any vehicles parked around the Mabee Center last night that didn't belong?" She attempted to concentrate on this case, but the cabin nagged at her.

"They weren't sure. A few cars parked nearby, but they never counted how many and never recorded any license numbers," Greg said.

"So we got nada?" She bit her lower lip.

"We got zilch." Greg tapped the pen again.

"I've got to tell you. It's not a good time for me to show up with nothing. The captain is already pissed at me for circumstances beyond my control. We need to catch a break, fast. What leads did you find about this case?" she asked.

"Nothing." His pen tapped again.

"What's her background? Anything there?"

"No. Not for years. Her life turned up clean. I didn't discover anything significant, but it's early. If the serial killer has her, we don't have much time left to do her any good," Greg said.

"You think he has her? I figured the press only attempted to sell papers." She didn't think the killer would change his MO this much in such a short time. Would he?

"We don't know for sure. Do we?"

"I guess not." She sat quietly for a moment. "Greg, do you still need me tomorrow? I need to check out a lead on my other case if you don't, but I think Underwood wants me to help you until you don't need me. So say what you want me to do. I'll do it." She needed to get to the cabin soon, or the reason to go might have left. But the techs still might find trace if he killed Heather there.

"I need the help. I'm still not sure about my partner, whether he will come in or not. I caught parts of your interviews. You did great. So I'd appreciate it if you kept helping me."

"Okay. I'll see you in the morning. You want to meet at the station?" She wanted to sound excited, but the cabin worried her.

"That'll work." Greg hung up.

She checked her cell phone. Ten after eleven. If she didn't find time to make it to the cabin tomorrow, she would go in the evening. No matter what time.

She went into the bathroom to get ready for bed. As she stared in the mirror, her eyes searched for her father's picture. Then she remembered the photo lay face down. For two days, it remained unchanged. The pain faded a little, but still, she left the picture in the same position and walked out the door.

TONY SAT with a ten of clubs in the hole, and a four of diamonds face up. He nodded for the dealer to hit him. A six of diamonds joined the four. He motioned he would hold. The dealer moved on to the next player.

He glanced up and saw a police officer not far away. The officer appeared interested in him, but he drew a lot of people's attention. He continued to hold his cards until the hand finished. His twenty beat out the dealer's nineteen. The chips in front of him increased.

He'd been acting for years, but he was still uncomfortable when people watched him. He gathered his chips, got up to leave, and strolled toward the cashier to exchange them. Gambling wasn't his thing, but he knew Ben enjoyed it. So they'd agreed to celebrate the completion of their location shoot with time spent here. He figured he'd wasted weekends in worse ways.

After he swapped in his chips for cash, an older man approached him. He didn't know the man, but he seemed like a cop, though he wore slacks and a jacket.

"Hello. I'm Detective Hank Gettering, with the Tulsa Police Department." The older man offered his hand.

He shook it. "How can I help you?" He figured they wanted him to do a favor. Often, people asked him to visit sick people or various other kind acts. If he could help, he usually did.

"I suppose you've heard about Heather Balentine." The detective scrutinized him.

"I'm sorry. I haven't been in touch for a while. We just finished a shoot out in western Oklahoma, and I haven't seen the news recently. What's happened?" He kept his expression neutral.

"An officer found Ms. Balentine dead early Saturday morning." The detective continued to examine his expression.

It took him a moment to comprehend. "She's dead?"

"I understand you and Ms. Balentine dated not long ago." The cop looked at him like his face belonged on a fugitive poster.

"Yes. We made a movie together, but I haven't seen her in close to a year." He hadn't felt this nervous since he got in trouble with the law during his teenage years.

"It would help us if you would come down to police headquarters. We need more details about her personal life. We want you to answer a few questions. Your cooperation would help us out a lot."

Tony recognized the innocent and persuasive manner. He figured the situation would be much less complicated if he left with them. "I guess. Will it take long?"

"Probably not."

They walked toward the door, but he wanted to notify Ben before he left with them. "Let me call my friends and tell them where I'm headed. I don't want them to worry."

The detective nodded.

Tony pulled his cell phone from his pocket. It rang five times before Ben answered.

"I'm going downtown with the police. They want to talk to me about Heather. She died over the weekend, and they need personal info about her. They said it wouldn't take long. Don't leave town without me." He couldn't shake the uneasiness, but acting was his strong suit. Outwardly, he remained calm.

"I saw something on TV about her death. Do you think it's wise to talk without a lawyer?" Ben's voice remained light, but Tony detected real concern, too.

"You're hilarious. I'll see you later. Don't take off without me. I'm not sure I want to drive the whole way back alone." He disconnected and followed the cop out of the building.

When they reached the parking lot, a white car with a Tulsa Police logo on the side waited. They helped him inside and drove away.

## 21

Trin arrived at the department and parked while the police unloaded Anthony Strete. He walked close behind them once they entered the building. They had to handle this situation carefully before expensive lawyers got involved. He wanted to do the interview, but he didn't want to embarrass Hank in front of his coworkers. If he could get Gettering alone, he figured they could work it out.

He watched Tony shake hands with everyone. The guy hadn't yet realized they took an interest in him because he was a suspect. The situation looked good. Cooperative suspects often revealed issues they wouldn't want to go public.

After a few minutes, the detective ushered the Hollywood star into a room with a camera. The video feed connected with a monitor in the next space. Since he performed before a lens in his work, Tony might stay comfortable—unlike the average person. He replayed in his mind the various techniques he used for interrogations, contemplating which would bring him the information desired.

When the homicide detective came back out from the

interview room, he got his attention. He motioned for Gettering to move near the desk where he stood.

"What was he told?" He sat down so the older man would do the same. He remembered Hank always rubbed his legs.

"Strete didn't seem to know Heather was dead, but he acts for a living. I said we wanted to get personal information about her from him. I mentioned he'd been close to her about a year ago. He claimed he hasn't seen her since they worked on their last movie together. I think he's going to cooperate." Hank's exhaustion hung on him like a worn coat.

"He acted surprised by her death? You think Strete didn't realize until you told him?" He listened and made a few notes in the file he carried with him.

"Yeah. If the guy wasn't a performer, I would believe him. I figure he might try to outfox us."

"Would you care if I interviewed him? I don't want to steal your thunder, but I would like to take a run at him. If you wouldn't mind." He watched for any contentious sign.

"He's done police movies so he'll recognize a good cop, bad cop," Hank said, and he stood up to stretch his legs.

"Great to know." He remembered the movie, *Catch or Kill*, but sometimes it worked smarter to play dumb. He and the homicide detective maintained a better relationship than he did with most law officials. The cop's ego didn't appear too touchy —probably because he kept his health issues secret and wouldn't want to make any trouble. He'd let Gettering do most of the interviews for this exact reason. This time, he hoped it paid off.

"The captain shouldn't mind. I'm tired enough I might not be at my best. Go ahead. Take the lead," Hank said.

"Thanks. You'd do a great job. I appreciate the trust, though." He took the file, tucked it under his arm, and moved closer to the interrogation room.

"Special Agent Trinity will interview him. He's had more time to study the information on Strete," Gettering announced to the policemen who stood around the department.

He watched the monitor for about ten minutes and attempted to get a read on his suspect. The only tell he spotted was his thumb, which tapped the tabletop. If not for the display, the Hollywood star seemed comfortable in his skin, a trait difficult to pull off in front of a camera over an extended period. They made him wait a half hour.

When Trin entered the room, Strete still drummed his left thumb on the table. The actor gave the impression of outward calm, but Trin planned to change the situation before he finished.

Strete glanced up, his expression curious. "Where's the other cop?"

"Hank ran an errand. I'm Special Agent Jordan Trinity." He offered a cordial handshake.

"How much time will this take? My friends are waiting for me back at the casino. We're supposed to leave for LA early tomorrow." The man flashed his movie star smile and shook his hand.

"Hopefully, not long." He sat down and opened the file.

"How did Heather die?" Tony asked.

"You didn't hear about her? The story flooded the media."

"I've been on a shoot, isolated and away from the news." Strete tapped his thumb a few times, then stopped.

"A serial killer got her. At least, that's what the tabloids said." He observed the actor's eyes for the slightest reaction, but the man didn't show remorse.

"You're kidding. How did the guy get her alone? The press followed her everywhere. Constant battles with reporters and photographers were something I hated while I dated her. They track me too sometimes, but they don't harass me like they do her.

And we've been camped out in western Oklahoma for two months. No one followed me out to the middle of nowhere." Strete's charming grin came back, but his hands remained motionless.

"We need to gather more personal information about Miss Balentine. Did you know she kept a separate computer that only she used?" He turned the page in the folder, so Heather's photograph during autopsy was visible. Tony's eyes didn't peek toward the image. They played to the camera located behind Trin's left shoulder.

"Yeah. Heather owned a laptop at the time I dated her, but I'm not into online junk much. I refuse to use Twitter or Facebook. If she wanted to tell me something, I always told her to call. I don't do text. If I got anything to say, I prefer to talk, not type the damn words. What about you?" Tony stirred to a more comfortable position.

"It's not my favorite way to communicate." He smiled. "So did you have her private number? A few people mentioned she used one." He moved the photo to the bottom of the stack, revealing and a photo of her body at the dumpsite.

"It might still be on my cell. Let me see." Tony took a phone from his pocket and scrolled through the numbers. The actor found what he wanted and handed the device to him.

"That's the same one we have. We learned Ms. Balentine used a newer number than this."

"Could be. I haven't talked to her in many months, possibly a year. After we finished *Far From Alabama*, we split up. She was still mad at me the last time I heard." Tony's expression wasn't repentant as he shoved his phone back in his pocket.

"What caused the problem?"

"She fancied forever. I wanted we're through. Ben says I should have let her down gently, but I'm not sure it would have helped. I was seeing another woman. That ended things."

"So she broke it off?" He rotated the second photo to the pile's bottom and left Tony's information sheet on top.

Tony nodded. "Of course. She caught me with a young actress. Her opinion of me was *not* good."

"Now, a few questions I ask will seem really personal, but I need to ask. We have to learn everything we can to help figure how and why the killer contacted her." He stared down at the paper in the open folder for a few seconds. He brought his eyes back up to Tony's and asked. "What erotic fantasies did she like to play out during your time together?"

Tony hesitated for several moments. "I'm not one to discuss details. We had a sexual relationship. That's everything you need to know."

"I assure you it's not. Our killer prefers a particular deviance. It's essential we find out if Heather shared the same proclivity."

"I'm not comfortable going into details. I don't want to talk about this." The actor put his hand on the table and pushed himself upward.

"Mr. Strete, you won't tell me anything I haven't heard before. I've been with the FBI for a while. We come across circumstances you would not believe. What did Heather like to do that made you uncomfortable?" His stare remained steady on Tony.

"It isn't that she made me uncomfortable. I don't want to discuss it with you."

Trin remained silent.

Tony sighed. "What? You want to hear positions? Things like that? She liked extended foreplay. Occasionally oral but not much else. Nothing kinky." The actor's cheeks fired up.

"She begged you to strangle or choke her, didn't she?" he pushed.

"No. Where did you get that idea?" The actor's brows furrowed.

"I ask the questions, Mr. Strete."

"Well, they aren't polite ones, and if she did that with others, she didn't with me."

"I'm afraid it's my job. You sure Heather never mentioned she liked you to squeeze her neck during sex? It's not uncommon."

"It's *not* common for me."

"So you want me to believe you never choked a woman to increase her pleasure." He gazed up from the file into Tony's eyes.

"No. Never."

"You've been in Tulsa since Thursday afternoon. You sought her out to take part in an illicit affair. You strangled her and left her in Woodward Park." He leaned across the table closer to Strete and crowded his space.

"What the hell are you saying? You think I killed her? I haven't seen her in a year." Tony gripped the table's edge until his knuckles turned white.

"So you say, but she came here to meet someone. Someone she cared enough about not to mention to anyone where she went. You, the love of her life, show up but we're supposed to believe you didn't give her another go?" He leaned in so close, he could smell Tony's breath.

"It wasn't me. I tell you. It wasn't me." The actor's frown deepened.

"You want to stick to this lame excuse that you haven't seen her for a year?"

"I didn't count the months. It's somewhere around that."

"You can bet we'll investigate your story, and after we find out you lied, I will own your ass. When did you arrive in Tulsa?"

"Thursday. I'm not sure what time. I got here in the afternoon. The hotel should have my check-in info." The color in Tony's face returned to a more normal tone, but his thumb tapped.

"It tells us when you checked in, but not when you arrived in the Tulsa area."

"I came here to help you, and you act like I'm the guy who did it. What the hell is your problem?" The actor sat up straighter.

"At what age did you get involved with gangs in Tulsa?" He watched the surprise spread over Tony's face.

"I never ran with any gangs."

"That's not what this file says." He pointed with his index finger to the paperwork in front of him.

"I was fifteen, and I met this kid named Jedediah Smith. I don't remember his street name. Too many years since I hung around him." He paused. "I think they called him Beemer. He loved BMWs. Someone beat him up real bad. I got him help. After that, he wanted to hang out. The whole thing caused way more trouble than it should have. I never joined a gang. He introduced me to his friends. That's it." Tony emphasized his speech with his hands as he talked.

"Is that how it started with Heather? You got carried away? What happened? She liked the tight squeeze, and you craved the look in her eyes when you snuffed her lights out. Does that make your world explode? You can't get it up unless you choke the female's life from her? Is that your thing? You must dream about it every day." He leaned across the table, right in the actor's face.

"I'm out of here." Tony pushed up from his seat.

"Sit your ass down. We're not done." He stood and faced him.

"Do I need a lawyer? Either book me, get me an attorney, or

I will leave." He sat back down and crossed his arms over his chest. Strete stared him square in the eye and shut his mouth.

He understood this round finished without a winner, but he wasn't satisfied they had their man. Street didn't peek at the pictures once. The young actor never showed interest in his handiwork. The whole situation hadn't played out the way it should have, but neither did it prove his innocence.

Trin sat back down and wrote nonsense while he studied the file like he had all the time in the world. He wouldn't ask their guest any more questions since the man had invoked his rights, but head games were another matter. The silence in the room thickened.

PAIGE WALKED into the department at ten to seven. She wondered how the interviews went the previous night. She sat at her desk. A newspaper laid where she could read it.

*Does the Celebrity Strangler Have Caroline Montgomery?* The large letters formed the headline on the Tulsa World's front page. She dropped into her chair. Someone had used a yellow highlighter to emphasize the essential points in the article. She hadn't seen a reporter except for the sleazeball, Faulkner, and she told him nothing. Her colleagues believed she did this. Harley Judd would celebrate her downfall. *Shit. This was so not funny.*

She'd barely read the byline before the captain appeared in the doorway. She got up and moved in his direction, not allowing him an opportunity to yell at her. He waited for her to enter his office, then he slammed the door behind her.

At this point, she doubted she would ever wake from this nightmare. What the hell happened to her life? Someone else in the department leaked material for cash to the media, but who would sabotage a case to get at her? Surely, Harley Judd wouldn't stoop so low, but Hank said they paid big money for information on high-profile stories.

The captain's fist shook with fury after she glanced up at him. He stared at her. She wanted to melt into the floor.

She put her hand up in protest. "I don't know where the leak came from, but it didn't come from me."

"Several patrol officers witnessed you with a reporter in the parking lot." His cheeks flushed red, but his voice remained calm.

"Yes. One waited outside when I returned to leave you a note on my progress, but I refused to talk to him. He got aggressive, and I threatened to arrest him for assault on a police officer. He grabbed my arm to stop me. I never told him anything. The creep hasn't been around since." Her hand searched her pocket until it snagged the recorder in case she needed it.

"It's difficult to believe you because you originally leaked the information. Officers saw you with a reporter, and the press found out someone strangled and mutilated her. What will I wake up to tomorrow?"

"I haven't a clue, but I recorded the conversation between myself and Mr. Faulkner. I don't want to produce it, but I made a copy." She hesitated for several seconds. "Besides, I didn't leak it the first time. The reporter grilled me about something to do with my father's death. Then off the subject, he suggested a serial killer murdered Heather. I never said a word, but my face revealed the answer. He caught me unprepared. By my expression, he figured it out. He got lucky, or he had foreknowledge and searched for confirmation. Either way, he received what he wanted, but I've been careful ever since. He's gotten nothing further from me, sir." She shut up and kept her military stance.

He stood still for a moment. "Why not say something

sooner? Why not tell me the other day when I took you off the case?"

"I felt partially to blame for the bad press. I didn't guard my reaction. We use the same technique here on our perps. I've been trained to do better." She stared down at the floor. Then she brought her eyes back up to his.

"But you said nothing to him about strangulation or mutilation?" Underwood's color slowly returned to normal.

"No, sir. I wouldn't." Her body relaxed a tinge. Did he believe her? She really didn't want him to listen to the recording. It would mean the end for Hank's career. She couldn't carry the weight for that too.

"Let me do a little checking, but don't you repeat a word. If everyone realizes I'm not on your butt about this, the guilty party will figure I suspect someone else. I intend to get the SOB who blabbed our secrets to the world. He'll regret the day. Do you hear me?" He raised his voice at the end of his words, pointed his finger at her, and shook it like anger still controlled him.

"Yes, sir." Relief began a slow journey through her body. He trusted her.

"I want you to walk out from here and pretend I tore you a new one. I won't put you back on the case until I discover who opened their mouth. You understand why?" His expression was the first decent one he'd directed her way in days.

"Yes, sir. I do." She didn't smile, but she wanted to.

"This means you can't tell Hank, either." His countenance remained stern.

"Yes, sir." She swallowed.

"Now get out of here," he yelled, then muttered quietly, "The last I did for show."

She nodded, turned, and left. She wouldn't look anyone in

the eye. She needed to keep the captain's confidence, or he would never trust her again.

She walked down the hall. Harley Judd leaned against a doorway then stepped away from it to block her path. Great. Just what she didn't need. His smug grin irritated her. "Don't you do any work? All I ever see you do is follow me around to harass me. Get a life."

"My life's fine. I can't help it if you fall into the crapper every day. The job should have been mine the first time."

"I know you've convinced yourself and most of the force, but I've seen no evidence to prove it's true. Why don't you bother someone who wants your opinion and do your work? That's why they pay you."

"Hell, your time's about up. I won't need to wait long until I get what's rightfully mine. Hank can't protect you forever."

"You keep him out of this. I carry my own weight." She pushed past him, but in her heart, she understood her mentor's influence played a big part in her promotion. He'd watched his partner implode after Glen's children died, and it took a considerable toll on Hank's health. If only they'd worked together longer. She'd hoped his fitness would improve, but this homicide came their way too soon.

Now he was partnered with a stranger, and the pressure from this high-profile case wouldn't allow him to hide his condition from Trin for long. She felt like someone lit a fuse, and she waited helplessly for the explosion to go off.

Paige sat at her desk for fifteen minutes, then Greg showed up. He'd been out later, so she figured he deserved the extra wait. He appeared worn out. These types of cases often caused weary days and nights.

"Someone said you've got a scheduled appointment with the captain every morning to get your ass reduced. Have you acquired a new diet technique I never heard about?" Greg's smirk bordered on the juvenile.

"You're so not funny. My ass is just fine."

"I noticed."

"Don't go there or hassle me today." She wanted to stay strictly business.

Greg opened his mouth to say something, then closed it without speaking. She figured she didn't want to listen to his opinion, anyway.

She brought the conversation back to the case. "So what have we got? What do you need me to do?"

"I plan to go back out to the house and toss the room myself since the crime techs have finished. I'll see if I can find anything to tell us who she is and what she was into," Greg said.

"I toyed with an idea. If you don't mind, I'll run out to Oral Roberts University and talk to the security guard who worked on the night Caroline was last seen. But if you need me to do something else, say the word." She watched him as she pulled her keys from her pants pocket.

"It wouldn't hurt. I won't get time to question the man today." Greg walked beside her as they left the building.

"I guess I'll head his direction. You want to meet with me later? Or you can call me. Tell me what's up next on my list. I don't think this will take too long." She separated from him to go to her car.

She drove down Riverside Drive most of the trip and enjoyed the Arkansas River with the wildlife statues along the way. The mama bear with three cubs who fished in a waterfall had always been her favorite. They'd searched in the water without a catch since 2002 near the intersection where the thoroughfare she traveled meets Seventy-First Street.

She wanted a chance to savor her redemption with the

captain. She couldn't tell anyone, but at least she knew he believed her. After the last few days she'd endured, it meant a great deal.

She turned off Riverside and headed east on Eighty-First close to the River Spirit Casino. The traffic stayed moderate this morning and made her drive time pleasant while she took the longer route.

After she arrived at the ORU campus, she got a feel for the last known location of her victim. Though she was familiar with the place, she liked to go back and visualize it through the perp's eyes. How would she do it if she planned the crime?

The parking lot was huge and surrounded the Mabee Center and the Baby Mabee, which attached to the backside of the arena. In its day, the great rock bands and legends performed in this arena. These days, with the much larger BOK Center, mostly Christians held events here.

For anyone who followed a target, the number of exits to the main streets from Lewis and Eighty-First Street presented a problem. Then other roads led back into the campus, so Caroline's exit options ran too high. The perp probably waited near her vehicle.

Once Paige gained perspective on the area's layout, she searched through her notes to get the phone number for the security guard. She figured he didn't work the day shift, but she wanted to call first to discover if he was home before she made the trip to his residence. Once the man agreed to speak with her, she drove to his place.

John Sullivan lived in a large apartment complex near the campus. She knocked once, and he answered the door. Tall, slender, and on the geeky side, the young man motioned her inside.

"Hello. I'm Detective Stone. I want to ask you a few more

questions about the night Caroline Montgomery disappeared." She offered her hand to shake. He completed the greeting.

"Yes, ma'am. I apologize, but I didn't notice anything unusual. Nothing." He peered at her through his black-rimmed glasses.

"Why don't we sit down and try to visualize it. Maybe you can help me see what you saw the night you patrolled. You never know what might happen."

"You won't hypnotize me, will you?" He seemed horrified.

"No. I've never done that to anyone." She shook her head and wondered where he got such an idea.

She surveyed the room. His apartment was the complete opposite of Betty's home. Various items laid everywhere and mostly where they shouldn't. She picked up a stack of school papers and moved them to the floor with a bunch of others. Then she sat down on the cleared chair.

"So you're a student at the university?" she said.

"Yeah. I took six hours this summer. I want to get done early."

"What's your major?"

"Science with a math minor. I start my senior year in the fall semester," he offered.

"Sounds like you've got your head in the right place."

"Oh yes, ma'am." His serious reply confirmed her next move.

"I'd like you to close your eyes, and try to remember your rounds the night Caroline went missing. Keep them shut and visualize what you observed on each trip you made. How many cars did you notice parked outside the Baby Mabee?" She kept her tone casual.

After a prolonged pause, he answered. "Somewhere between five and ten."

"In your mind, drive back by the vehicles and count them."

"Six, I think. Six people worked there the night she vanished," he said.

"No, don't use reason. I need you to search in your memory and visualize what you witnessed that evening. Can you do that? It doesn't matter what the number is. I only want to know what you saw while you moved along your route." She kept her tone soothing.

"Let me envision it. The first few times I drove by, I saw six. I'm sure I counted that number." He sounded confident about the quantity.

"What about later? Did you still count the same total? Only picture them in your mind." She kept her voice uniform and controlled.

"Wait. Now that I think back, I believe I noticed a dark SUV parked near Ms. Caroline's car. Yeah. That's right. I noticed it because I was thinking I couldn't possibly afford something like that right now. The color was black. I don't know why I didn't remember that before." He sounded amazed.

"Did you recognize what make and model?" She barely dared to hope.

"Oh, yeah. A Cadillac Escalade. I wondered who worked there who could afford such an expensive car. I figured I might have the wrong job at ORU." He shrugged in embarrassment at his tangled words. "I guess my little joke helped me remember better."

"Yes. I've done something similar before. I'm glad it stuck out to you. Did you get the tag number? Again, try to visualize the numbers. Don't push it. Drive by the vehicle another time like you did on the night in question and tell me what you spotted. Let it come to you."

John sat for a time. "I can't read you the lettering, but it didn't have a regular license. At least not the main Oklahoma one. We sell so many tags for the Native American Tribes here.

I'm not sure, but the plate was not a match for mine. I have the one with a sculpture of an Indian shooting the arrow skyward on it. You know what I mean. It might have been from another state." He shook his head.

"I recognize the one you described. Did you get a good look at the person driving the Cadillac?" Her recorder stayed on, but she took out her notepad to jot down the pertinent details.

"It had dark tinted windows. Impossible to glimpse inside." His lids remained closed.

"Were you close when the group came out from the building?"

"No. My next round, the cars were gone." John opened his eyes and stared at her.

"You've been most helpful, and you gave more information than you believed you could. Thank you for your time. I'll get this reported to the other detectives. It may prove valuable." She handed him her card, shook his hand again, and left his apartment.

Now she knew where the perp waited. Maybe Caroline's workers would remember something else after they received this new information. She hoped at least one could give more details about the Cadillac.

Betty Greenway's neighbor mentioned a dark SUV in her alley. Could that have been an Escalade too? Was it the same vehicle?

Today was turning out better than expected. She still wanted to go to the cabin tonight, but for now, she needed to help Greg.

Paige's cell rang before she drove away from the apartments. She glanced to see who called. Greg. He probably wanted her to chase down a new witness and question them. Since she'd finished with the security guard, he caught her at a great time.

"Hey, what's up?" she asked.

"A patrol officer found Caroline's car." The excitement in his voice felt contagious.

"Wait, don't tell me. Woodward Park. Right?"

"How the hell did you know that?" He sounded surprised.

"Actually, I was half teasing, but everything points back to that place. With your discovery, I might be convinced the serial killer has Caroline. I didn't believe it before, but with her vehicle found there, it's too much coincidence. You need to phone Gettering and let him in on your report. He'll want that info ASAP. I'm on my way. It may take me a few. I have to drive from ORU." She took her foot off the gas and slowed for a corner.

"Hank's your partner. You call him. I'll meet you there."

She figured Greg understood homicide's best detective didn't like him much.

"Okay." She accelerated again once the road straightened.

They both hung up, and she hit the speed dial for Hank. It rang ten times before he answered.

"Hello, Paige. What gives? I'm in the middle of something." Her mentor sounded annoyed.

"They found Caroline Montgomery's car at Woodward Park. I think your perp could have our girl." She got the words out before he disconnected. If the detective was busy, he often hung up on you.

Hank paused for several seconds. "You're sure it's her vehicle?"

"Greg called me. I'm on my way, but not there yet."

"Call me after you arrive. If it's true, our whole perspective is likely to change. Verify and get back to me. We're in the middle of something, but I want to know as soon as you find out."

"Okay. Will do. It's good to hear your voice. I miss working with you." She waited for his response. She hoped he wasn't pissed at her. The Peter Faulkner incident hurt her future more than his.

"I've missed you, too. Once this case wraps up, you come over for supper. You might as well put it on your calendar, 'cause I won't take no for an answer." She smiled broadly, huge relief coursing through her. The invitation to Hank's told her everything was fine.

"I don't intend to tell you no. I can hardly wait. Your cooking is great."

"It's good you do. I raised you on it." Hank went back to his no-nonsense self.

"In case I didn't say it in a long while, thanks. I love you. I'll call you later." She disconnected, and tears formed in her eyes. He could always tell when she cried. She both loved and hated it about him, but she missed her time with him every day.

Several police units already congregated in the Woodward Park parking lot. Five uniformed officers surrounded the parked hatchback. Greg stood in their midst.

After she walked up, Hays lifted his head and motioned for her to join him. "We've verified the vehicle identification number. It's her Ford."

She inspected the older model blue Escort. It didn't seem flashy enough for a TV evangelist. If Caroline Montgomery preached on television, why drive such an old car?

She stopped beside Greg. "Are forensics on their way? Did you find anything helpful yet? You need to keep everyone away until the techs go over the vehicle."

"They haven't gone near it." Greg assured her.

"You're absolutely certain on this? I'm supposed to call Hank back, but he will kick my butt if we waste his time with misinformation."

"I matched it myself." Greg nodded and pointed to the windshield on the driver's side.

"The gates close at eleven. How did he get the car in here? Caroline didn't leave the Baby Mabee until twelve thirty-five. Any sign of tracks around the entrance gates?" She stepped closer to the blue Escort and tugged latex gloves from her pocket.

"We hadn't got that far in our assessment. You think the guy pulled it in once the access opened again?" Greg said.

"It's possible, but he would probably use the darkness for cover. Do the people who lock the entryways check to see if the place is empty first? We need to pinpoint how long this car has been here. Did he park it today, or has it been here since he took her?" She glanced back at Greg, who'd stopped in his tracks.

"I can't answer your question, but we *will* find out." He gazed up at her and nodded. She thought she saw something close to respect in his eyes. A nice change.

She slowly circled the car. The vehicle was spotless. She figured forensics wouldn't discover much, but the killer had to mess up sometime. At least, she hoped he would.

She noticed Greg still watching her. "I need to call Hank back, but the sooner we confirm how long the Ford has been here, the better. The minute you hear something, phone me." She walked away toward the Cavalier but turned around.

"I re-interviewed the night guard at ORU. He remembered he saw a dark, possibly black, Cadillac Escalade, late model. He didn't get the plates, but possibly out-of-state." She strolled to her car for privacy to confirm the information with Hank. He needed to know ASAP. It could determine how he proceeded with his interview.

## 22

Trin continued to stare at the file in his hands. Occasionally, he pretended to write something to look legitimate. Anything to keep Tony in his chair a little longer.

"How the hell long do you plan to hold me here?" The actor glared across the table and spoke to after ten excruciating minute's of silence.

He'd hoped Strete would break the silence first. It sometimes got them talking again without a lawyer. He kept writing in the file and ignored the suspect. He figured being ignored rarely happened to the pampered star.

After another five tedious minutes, Tony got up and moved toward the door.

"I wouldn't if I were you." He sounded confident as he wrote on a form that meant nothing.

Strete stopped and stared back at him.

He looked up from the file. "A whole department of cops awaits you out there."

"I know my rights. You need to book me or let me go. I'm not an idiot from Podunkville."

"Suit yourself, but I wouldn't leave." He kept his expression calm, his voice neutral.

"I have places to go. This hold up will cost me money. We've got to leave for California today." Tony remained standing.

"Who's we?" he asked while he still pretended to write.

"I'm sure you're already aware, but Josh Stuart and Ben McCall. We made a movie together."

"What's it called, *A Reunion of Heather's Past Lovers?*" He quit writing and glanced up. The performer's reaction revealed uncertainty.

"Why do you say that?"

"I told you. I'm the one who asks questions."

"And I'm the one who left out the door." Tony reached for the handle.

"Go ahead. If you want." His smile insinuated he understood something the man didn't.

"I wanted to help you, but you can't blame me for this one." Strete came back around and sat down again. "What information do you want from me? Make it fast or I'm gone."

"Surely, California won't disappear if you don't get there tomorrow." He finally stopped writing and stared across the table.

"More than likely it won't, but every day we waste the soundstage we've rented, it costs us money. I must get back. Ben and Josh won't like the cash we blow if we don't." This time, the movie star didn't play it cool when he glared at Trin.

"Is that so? You a mama's boy who has to do what he's told?"

"Oh, good grief. It's not your money." Tony slammed his hand down on the table.

"So what about Ben and Josh? Did they kill Heather?" He made his expression more serious.

"Now you sound crazy. Those two are my friends. They would never hurt anyone let alone kill them."

"Your buddies arrived Thursday afternoon too?"

"I'm not sure. They both left the set before I did, but they came to Tulsa sometime Thursday."

"Why didn't you three ride together?" He made another note in the file.

"I told them they would need wheels in case they got lucky. We don't like to step on each other's toes. Besides, I needed to take time to spend with my parents and family."

"You were all okay with being Heather's past lovers?" He looked up from his notes.

"I had no problem with it. They didn't seem to either." Strete moved his hands to the chair he sat on. Then he tucked one under each thigh, palm down.

"But you don't know for sure."

"We've been friends for years. We've never fought about women. They joked with me about it once, when we discussed who to cast as the female lead in our movie. I'm sure they didn't give a damn either way."

"We'll see."

"What's that supposed to mean?" Tony moved his hands to the table once more.

"It means we'll see." He gazed up at the actor and lifted one eyebrow.

The Hollywood star stared back but remained quiet.

"How long did you live in the LA area?"

"Twelve years." Strete didn't move, but he could tell the man had difficulty controlling the urge.

"Did you only work as an actor since you've been out

there?" He appeared uninterested and wrote a few words down.

"Mostly. A few odd jobs to get by until I made enough money to survive on my acting roles." Tony relaxed a little.

"What type of jobs?"

"A convenience store clerk. I waited tables for six months. I worked at construction on sets. The construction job gave me an in with the studios. I can't think of anything else. Oh yeah, I parked cars close to a year." The performer shrugged. "A few jobs overlapped each other."

"Did you ever mule dope?"

"Hell, no. I hate drugs."

"You like the booze." He made it an accusation.

"I've downed a few." Tony shrugged again.

"From what I hear it's a lot more than a few."

"My drinking is in the past." Strete sounded defensive.

"How far past?" He kept the pace fast between them.

"Not far, but I haven't taken a drink since I started the new film. It's been two months."

"Were you ever acquainted with a girl named Donna Barnett?" He watched the man's reaction.

"I don't think so, but I've met a lot of women. I'm not sure." Tony ran a hand through his hair.

"She hung out at The Reel Shack."

The actor shook his head no. "Still not familiar. I don't remember her. What did she look like?"

"Strawberry blonde, green eyes, five foot four, built. She represented the Sizzle Shampoo Company several years ago. Now, do you remember her?" He detested a man who couldn't remember his last conquest, let alone a woman he killed.

"I don't recall her, but I've nailed lots of girls from The Reel Shack. I don't remember each one's name."

"This one you would remember. She wound up dead." He didn't detect a response from his target.

"I already told you. I never killed anyone." Tony glared at him.

"So you say." He smirked like he didn't believe the other man.

"Do I need to go back to the lawyer bullshit? We've wasted enough time on this. I'm ready to go." The movie star got up again and opened the door.

"I think I'll go get your buddies and get this straightened out, because I'm sure one of you three killed Heather."

The actor turned back around and stared at him but never said another word.

"I THINK it's time to pull his friends in and see what shakes out. They've each had sex with her, and there's something strange about them owning identical SUVs." Trin sat in the room where Hank watched the interview.

"Sounds good. Let's do it," Gettering said.

"The three are registered at the Hard Rock. We should find the other two easy enough."

"I'll make a call to get them picked up. Catoosa Police will help us again. No problem. Besides, the sheriff in Rogers County owes me a favor." Hank grinned.

"You know, he didn't seem interested in her photos. Most serial killers would examine the pictures of their handiwork," he said.

"I noticed he didn't." The detective left the room.

Trin couldn't shake the feeling that something didn't seem quite right.

~

TRIN WATCHED Ben McCall swagger into the department's main hall. He wore his confidence like an entitlement. His background portion of the file read sketchy, but at present, he appeared to live the good life in Malibu. He sipped his coffee and hoped it would give him the energy he needed. He'd already had a long night with Tony Strete, and he still wanted to interview Ben McCall and Josh Stuart.

Hank appeared troubled when he walked toward the back. "We didn't locate Josh Stuart. His gear is still sitting in his room, but he isn't. We didn't locate his vehicle, either. Tony talked to one guy by phone at the time we picked Strete up. I think Stuart's in the wind."

"Josh might have taken up with a woman. Let's not jump to conclusions." He didn't like the situation, but he didn't want to make assumptions, either. "McCall should know where Josh went."

"He could. Many young women these days are impressed with the celebrity crap."

"Yeah, the information highway and reality TV influence many people, but I suppose a certain number of women will always run wild." He watched Hank and thought his new partner appeared worse than he did earlier.

He nodded. "You want me to take the first run at McCall? You look tired. I bet I'm not in much better shape."

"You've looked better, but go ahead. I enjoyed the observation. This makes a nice change. I always run the action." Gettering nodded then rubbed his leg longer than usual.

"Are you sure you're okay? We can take a short break if you need to rest." He sensed Hank felt too tired to go on. Otherwise, he wouldn't let go of such an important interview.

"Nah, I'm fine. Let me fill my coffee cup, and then I'm ready to go."

By the time Hank got his hot drink, Trin had finished his and picked up the folder on Ben McCall. He grabbed Heather's photos from Tony's file and started for the room with the monitor. The detective followed right behind.

He watched their subject for twenty minutes through the computer screen while he waited for the freshness to wear off and the worry to begin.

PAIGE DROVE TO THE DEPARTMENT. She wanted to talk to Hank about Caroline's car and to explain about the connection she'd found between the real estate women and the other victims. If she could get him to listen, she hoped he would want to go check out the cabin with her.

She knew they needed to get there soon. She might have waited too long for Caroline. If she'd realized sooner that their killer had taken Caroline, she would've already stormed the place. Hank needed to listen.

She pulled her car into the lot, and hurried inside. She didn't want to attract attention, but she had to find Hank. Their desks sat empty. She assumed her mentor and Trin interviewed Anthony Strete, but a lot of time had passed. Surely, they'd completed the questioning by this time.

She scanned the room for someone who could give her information about the interviews. She spotted a group of uniforms down the hallway. They should tell her if Trin and Hank still worked on Anthony Strete, but she hated to ask. They would think she wanted in on the grilling.

Her mentor would get mad if she interrupted them during

an interrogation. They'd just made up. She didn't want to alienate him again so soon. *Shit. What to do?*

She moved toward the bathroom to call Hank on her phone when Bob Underwood spied her. He walked toward her. She wanted to hide but where could she go? So she waited for him.

"What the hell are you doing back here?" His eyes stayed friendly, but his voice sounded loud.

He did it for show, but it embarrassed her anyway. "I got something I needed to discuss with Hank. Where is he hiding out?" She whispered so no one else would overhear.

"He's in the observation side for Interview One. He and Trin have been at it since late last night. I watched for a while, but I had to go home and rest. The special agent's good, but we got nothing helpful so far. You can't talk to them. You can catch them later." His voice got much louder. "You get back out there and help Greg. I don't want to see your face until you bring Caroline back." For effect, he stormed off.

She walked out to her car and hit the speed dial for Hank. The phone rang and rang and eventually went to voicemail. "Hank, the car they found belonged to Caroline. I have something important about the case I need to tell you. Call me back as soon as you can. I need your advice. It's important. It can't wait. Please. Oh, and the security guard at ORU remembered he saw a dark, possibly black, Cadillac Escalade, late model. Please call me back." She hung up.

What next? The captain told her to help Greg. She didn't want to share her information with him. Her trust for him and his ideas ran toward nil.

Hank would know what to do with it. He would figure out how to handle the situation and send reinforcements out to the cabin. The jurisdiction placed the property in Rogers County, which caused complications. She drummed her thumbs on the steering wheel. Someone had to go out there.

Her tires screamed when she left the parking lot. She called Greg after she got on the street.

"What's up, beautiful?" Greg's answer made her skin crawl. She hoped to never work with him again.

"That's what I'd like to know. I couldn't get in touch with Hank, but I left a message for him on his cell." She waited for a response and continued to drive toward Woodward Park. She figured Greg waited there.

"We're sharing our statements. Then I'll plot our next move." His voice trailed off.

"Do you still need my help? I've got a lead I want to follow up on my last case." She turned on to Twenty-First Street with its towering trees and stately old homes and drove closer to the park.

"I still need you. You're the only help the captain gave me who has a clue what's going on. We're at the Olive Garden at Utica Square to get out of the heat for a bit. Then we will regroup."

"Okay, but I have to leave early today. I have something important to do, and yes, it's about work." She wanted to stop his suggestion before he mentioned a hot date. His type always wanted to go that direction.

She took a right turn and entered the Utica Square Shopping Center. Food sounded good anyway. She glanced at the clock on her dash. It read twelve thirty. She hadn't eaten yet today.

**23**

———

Paige's cell phone rang as she parked her car on the Olive Garden's east side at Utica Square. She couldn't find a spot any closer to the restaurant.

"Hi, good looking. I'm afraid I got bad news."

"That's not what I wanted to hear." She'd hoped the phone call came from Hank, so she'd answered without a glance at the caller ID. It took her a few seconds to realize the caller was Bill Graywolf.

"The cell phone number I traced back led nowhere. Heather probably bought a new one on purpose, so she could talk to her secret lover with a device nobody had access to. Everyone I contacted from this number you gave me did not know her new one. I called every single number myself. " He sounded frazzled.

"I can't say I'm surprised. Nothing has been easy on this case. Thank you seems so inadequate. Even though I'm not on the case anymore, I'm glad you called me to report back." Sweat formed on her forehead. She'd already shut off the car, so the AC went with it. The heat this summer scorched unbearably.

"I didn't have any better luck with the traffic cams. I've searched every one that works properly in the area. I couldn't find Heather on any recording. He took her out another way or used side streets. It's not impossible to do either one." Bill cleared his throat.

"I was hoping the perp wouldn't think to do that, but obviously, he did. Thanks for giving it your best shot. I'm banished from the department right now, so you'll need to tell Hank yourself. He was still working in the interview rooms when I went by the department not long ago. You might catch him there."

"I'll try, but it's a pain to drive over there, especially in this heat. I'll probably phone him." Bill ignored her suggestion.

"I already did, but I got voicemail. If you talk to Hank in person, tell him to call me. It's important. Okay?" She used her special voice. The one Bill couldn't resist.

"All right, I'll make the pilgrimage downtown in a few. I'll give him your message, but you know how Hank is. If he's on a case and doesn't want to stop for anything, he doesn't call back until he's ready."

"I know. Got to run. I'm late for a meeting with Greg Hays, but I do appreciate the hard work. Catch you later." She figured Bill's effort might waste his time, but Hank often didn't listen to his messages for hours.

"Paige." Bill hesitated. "I wanted to say I'm sorry I pressed you about Bobby and Crissy. Everyone deals with issues in their own way. I wanted you to know I care, and I miss them too. The whole department," he took a deep breath, "had difficulty with the loss. I know you were closer to both of them than most on the force were. I guess I wanted to push you through your sadness. I didn't let you go at your own pace. I'm sorry."

"I will get through this, eventually. I'm not there yet, but I know I will make it through. At least I've gotten that far.

Thanks for the support. Say, I just thought about the other number. Can you run it quickly to see if they ever turned on the device?"

"Let me check. It won't take a minute." She heard his key strokes. "I don't show any activity yet. Sorry."

"I'm not surprised. Nothing else on that case panned out either. Thanks again. I owe you a big one." She disconnected.

She sat in the car, and for an instant, she could still see Bobby's flashing eyes.

She remembered they'd ducked into the storage closet in the department's back hallway early Christmas Eve. For the first time in the thirteen and a half years she'd known him, he finally saw her as a woman.

"You know we can't stay in here long. The captain will expect me to get back out on patrol. I wish I could leave with you both, but Hendricks called in sick at the last minute. I didn't get a choice when the captain phoned me, but I'll go out to your parents after I get cleared from duty."

"I know, but in the meantime, I need something to sustain me." He grinned, and his eyes shone until their lips met. Her heart shifted and settled like she'd found a permanent home, warm, fuzzy, and content. She'd never wanted to leave the tiny room and her first romantic kiss.

Two hours later she heard radio static for a second. Then the dispatcher's voice announced, "Someone reported an accident near the intersection of US 169 and Forty-First Street. A tractor-trailer is involved. Any patrols in the area, please proceed to the scene."

Snow had drifted down for hours and measured a good eight inches deep. In this weather, patrol ran Operation Slick Streets. The division couldn't begin to handle every fender bender so only the ones with injuries received call-outs. She lifted the radio transmitter and announced she'd proceed on her way. She flipped on her light rack and progressed toward the accident.

White powder still drifted down at a decent rate, and the streets weren't treated or plowed in this area. Though Forty-First was a main thoroughfare, the snowfall kept the plows and sand trucks busy with the interstate and the inner-dispersal loop. The untreated road left Forty-First to turn into an icy, snow-packed sheet after the late shoppers finished for the day.

She'd already worked three injury accidents in as many hours. She fishtailed her way to the new location. If the tractor-trailer needed a tow, she'd stay stuck here for hours in this cold, wet place. Bobby and Crissy would have wait. If she made it to their father's farm before midnight, it would turn into her Christmas miracle.

Once she arrived, she saw a semi had jackknifed off the Mingo Valley Expressway, the wreckage a snarled mess. A black pickup lay mangled beneath the big rig's trailer. The dark truck looked similar to Bobby's. Before she could get her cruiser in park and open the door, the wreckage blew. Her breath caught in her throat. Flames leaped twenty feet in the air. Smoke billowed through the snow that fell steadily to the ground.

She hurried toward the conflagration. Then a license plate landed near her feet. BTT BONE. Bad to the bone. Oh my God. The tag belonged to Bobby. Her voice keened a wail she'd never heard before. She staggered a step then ran toward the inferno.

By that time, the second patrol car had arrived on the scene. Officer Berelli grabbed and held her before she could hurt herself. They called for the fire department and HAZMAT. Ambulances drove up, and the procedure to dismantle the wreckage began.

She'd waited an eternity for the love of her life to notice

her, but he was gone. Her best friend who might understand her loss died too. She felt like she couldn't go on, but each morning she got up, showered, brushed her teeth, and pasted on her life, then buried herself in work.

Hank didn't take it lightly, either. Glen Youngblood, his partner, lost himself in a bottle of bourbon. When both his children died in the fiery crash, depression overtook him. Glen finally retired a month ago. Hank refused to pair with anyone until Paige. Though they never talked about it, she knew Hank needed a partner who wouldn't say anything about his health condition. In exchange, he would groom her to become the best homicide detective in Tulsa. She watched helplessly while their plan collapsed around them.

PAIGE SWELTERED in the heat that poured over her after she got out of her car and walked to the restaurant. Once she went inside, it didn't take long to find the guys. They sat around a table in a semi-private nook in the back. She joined them and ate from the soup and salad menu to save time.

"Glad you could make it. We were discussing the method the perp used to take Caroline. What's your theory?" Greg gazed at her as if he already anticipated what she would say.

"I know he watched her leave the Baby Mabee. He blended in with the other vehicles parked there. When they left, he followed. Somewhere, he either waited until she stopped, or he forced her off the road. My best guess, he followed her home. She doesn't live far from Woodward Park. It was late, dark, no one would notice. He probably gave her something to drug her and tied her up. Then moved her car." She drummed her fingers for a few seconds until the waitress arrived with her soup and more breadsticks.

"It sounds plausible. I like it better than what we discussed. We couldn't decide how the perp got the car to Woodward Park unless someone helped him." Greg seemed thoughtful for several moments. Then he nodded in agreement.

"It's a theory. We won't know for sure until we find Caroline or catch the perp." She bit her lip. The killer had held Caroline a long time. He'd killed Heather in only a few hours. So far, no one had discovered another body.

Greg nodded. "Maybe we'll catch a break today."

"So what do you have planned for this afternoon? I need to get away early," she reminded him.

"I want you to question more family members and the people she worked with." Greg pulled a sheet of paper from his shirt pocket and unfolded it. "Other than this list, we've got nada." He gave a copy to her.

"I've never talked to so many unhelpful people in my life. No one knows anything. I swear Caroline Montgomery lives a near-perfect life, to hear them tell it." She stared at the list in her hand and sighed. The names ran long. She looked back up.

"Get through the ones you can. So far, we've got nothing helpful except a black Cadillac Escalade, and that's thanks to you." Greg's smile seemed sincere, but she didn't want to encourage him.

"I'll do what I can. Did you find out if anyone at Woodward Park checks for parked cars when they close the gate at night?" She glanced up at Greg.

"They don't. So we aren't sure when someone parked the car there." Greg shrugged, dismissing the lost information's importance.

She finished eating and left to get started. The afternoon promised to run long, again.

～

TRIN SHOOK Ben McCall's hand. He'd been a fan for years, but this concerned murder. The time had come to sort the situation out with these three men. With Josh Stuart missing at the most convenient time, the whole mess still nagged at him. The unsub might not have anything to do with these guys, but he had to make sure.

"Take a seat, Mr. McCall. I'm Special Agent Trinity. I've got a few questions for you about your friends and Heather Balentine. We heard you had a relationship with her."

"Yes. I worked with her. We made a film together. *Deserted Dreams.* You may know of it." Ben's charming manner felt a little too smooth. He could tell the actor used it to disarm people and get out of unpleasant situations like this one.

"I understand your friends also shared a relationship with Ms. Balentine. Were you aware of that?"

"Yes. I was aware they both saw Heather after she and I parted company. The job often leads to the leading man and his female partner getting caught up in too many steamy scenes together. Sooner or later you want to find out how much is acting and how much is real. In our case, it turns out we mostly acted." The performer smiled and extended his hand palm up.

"I see. You never saw any hostility between the three of you over Heather?" He opened the file and shuffled the pages inside. Heather's crime scene view landed on top. He left it there to get his pen out from his jacket pocket. Ben didn't appear interested as he wrote on the paper's margin.

"We didn't discuss it, but I couldn't tell that it bother anyone." The man hesitated. "Well, we did mention it when we talked about casting our Hallie."

"Who's Hallie?" He knew, but he didn't want McCall to know how much he understood about the three.

"She's the female lead in our latest movie. We financed it ourselves, so we discussed who we wanted to play the part."

He let the picture stay visible, but the star didn't glance at the photograph. He watched Ben's eyes. The actor didn't try to sneak a peek. "How long have you known Anthony Strete?"

"I'm not certain. Ten or twelve years. We made an early film together. We weren't the leads in the movie, but we got along great. The friendship lasted." McCall's smile got old. He wanted to wipe it from the man's face.

"Do you know where Josh Stuart went? We've been unable to locate him."

"He may have gotten lost in his shower. Since we came to Oklahoma, we've been covered in dust most of the time." McCall grinned at him. He didn't smile back. "No. I think the last time I saw him was yesterday. It's difficult to remember what time or day when you're in a casino."

"So how did you hear about Heather Balentine's death?"

"A while ago Tony called to tell me you took him in," Ben answered. "Then I called Josh and relayed the message."

"It's been on the news for several days." He made the statement sound like a question.

"I've been in the casino and asleep. Oh yes, and the shower." McCall's smile turned to pure innocence. It made him trust the man less.

"So how did you boys come to Tulsa?"

"In three black Escalades. Tony insisted we buy them before we left LA. I'm afraid we got drunk to celebrate our new movie. He chewed us out the next morning since we listened to him." Ben's laugh seemed sincere, but they paid him mega money to act.

"What I meant to say is, what brought you three to Tulsa? Why did you come here?"

"Again, we celebrated the completion of the location shoot. We only need to do the interior shots back in LA to finish up. We decided to take a short break before we start that phase."

"So you decided to drive across the state to gamble. Why not stop in Vegas on your way back to LA?"

"Tony's from Tulsa. He wanted to see his family." McCall shrugged.

"Why did you three buy the Escalades?"

"I told you, we got drunk. Tony insisted we could drive them at the Little Sahara Park. It's close to where we shot the movie, but it turns out we didn't get to use them for that purpose. No big deal."

"Why not?"

"We sobered up the next morning, and Tony said we could only drive real four wheelers there, not Cadillacs. But we used them to get around, and the local people liked to drive them when we paid people to run errands. So it worked out."

"I'm certainly glad. We wouldn't want you to waste your money so foolishly. At the time you dated Ms. Balentine, you were lovers, weren't you?" He changed the subject and hoped to catch Ben off guard.

"For a short time." Ben nodded and moved his hand to a more neutral position.

"What was your sex life like?"

"I wouldn't want to appear indiscreet." Ben's gallant smile flashed and lingered.

"I'm sorry, but I need to know what she preferred sexually. It's important to find out how the killer lured her to Tulsa."

"I never participated in anything kinky with her. I liked the passion, but nothing other than the ordinary, as I recall. It's been a long time. Several years, I think." Ben shifted in his seat.

"So she wasn't into erotic asphyxiation when she had sex with you?" He stayed on point.

"No." Ben shook his head and wrinkled his nose. His left hand found his pinky ring and rubbed at it.

"But you've heard about it." He kept the pace brisk, so it allowed McCall little time to prevaricate.

"Yes, I've heard the term." Ben seemed hesitant.

"Did you ever try it?"

"That's awfully personal." This time the movie star did manage to evade for a second.

"I often need to get personal." He stared at McCall like the man should expect difficult inquiries.

"I'd prefer not to say."

"And Heather would prefer not to be dead. Answer the question."

"Once with a starlet. I don't remember her name. She later did the commercials for a shampoo brand. She enjoyed it big time. I only dated her once. She liked it the way you described." The actor's face turned red. His hands moved to his lap, and he twisted the gold ring on his right pinkie.

"Why did you only date her once?"

"I felt uncomfortable. She liked to take it too far. She called me several times after, but I always made excuses. I never went out with her again." Ben put his hands up as if he remained innocent.

"You didn't like it?" His voice sounded like he didn't believe McCall.

"I said she wanted to take it to extremes. I was afraid she would wind up dead, and I didn't want to wind up the schmuck who did it. The sex didn't thrill me the way it did her, anyway. Th whole thing made me feel gross." Ben shrugged like he didn't understand other people's tastes.

"So if it felt good for you, you wouldn't mind if you killed her?" He pushed more.

"That's not what I said." The actor twisted the ring again.

"It's what you implied."

"I didn't mean to imply what you think I did." Ben acted

insulted, but he still rotated the ring, and the large diamond flashed several times in the light's reflection.

"We've got a dead body, killed by strangulation, probably during sex. You admit you've done it before. You had an affair with the victim. You can see, it lines up well for us." His confidence returned.

"It can't line up. I didn't have anything to do with anyone's death. You've got it wrong." McCall sat up straight and stopped every movement with his body.

"I don't see how I've got it wrong." Trin continued to smile but something shook Ben. The color drained completely from the man's face and the perma-smile plastered on his face melted. Something had changed. Trin felt certain that in his last statement, Ben had lied.

"I tell you. I didn't do anything but gamble and sleep since I got here. The casino's probably got me on film. You can check at the Hard Rock." McCall hunted for a way out. You could see it in his eyes. He twisted his jewelry harder than ever.

"Why would I do that?" He kept at it as if he found his man.

"Because I'm innocent. I didn't kill anybody. I tell you, I didn't kill anybody." Ben's demeanor changed, and his voice pleaded.

"Admit it. You did it. She liked the squeeze, and you obliged her." He rose from his chair and shoved the table a little. It stopped against Ben's chest.

"Heather? No, never. I never did. Not with her." The fear seemed tangible on Ben's face. His forehead appeared damp with sweat.

"You took a scalpel and carved her up like she didn't count for anything." He picked the photograph up and held it in front of McCall's face.

"I tell you, I never touched her. Never. Never that way."

Ben's statement trailed off at the end, and he sat down. He buried his face in his hands. The performer sat in the same position quietly for a long time.

He didn't know if the actor cried or what, but the man refused to lift his head again. McCall wouldn't look at him and kept his face buried until he finally asked for a lawyer.

He grabbed the scalpel from the floor and marched toward the gurney. With both hands raised high above the table, he used the instrument like a dagger and smashed it down.

He stared at the scalpel, which rested only two inches from her abdomen. *That* song. He continued to hear the words to *that* song from his youth. Jesus didn't love him. He couldn't possibly. He'd dropped the religious crap from his life eons ago.

The first round from the Eagles' "Somebody" trailed to its completion. The second round would follow immediately. He programmed the CD to play the song six repetitions in a row. With her eyes taped open, he knew she could see the scalpel that hovered over her stomach, but she remained calm. Her hands stayed relaxed beside her nude body.

Though he'd turned the volume up, the words to the childhood song echoed through him. He couldn't figure out why he heard it in his mother's voice as it repeated in his brain. He gripped the surgical instrument tightly in his hand and plunged it again and again, but always he stopped short above her body. What the hell went on here? Why did he lack the balls to go through with it?

Her eyes observed him and didn't seem confused. He saw her lips form "Thank you, Jesus." Then she smiled and relaxed. He could see the muscles in her body loosen up and go limp.

She might not be confused, but he was.

Her vision focused on him, and she smiled. "You don't understand, do you? Jesus loves me. He won't let you hurt me." She turned her head away from him.

He attempted one more time to stab her, but he didn't succeed. The scalpel fell from his hand. He walked in a daze and sat down in a chair across the room. He watched her breath turn shallow again.

He could still hear his mother's clear musical voice sing. "*Jesus loves me. This I know, for the Bible tells me so.*"

My God. How did one deal with this? It messed with his fantasy, the ritual he craved now flawed. She'd ruined everything. Never did the words to "Somebody" seem more appropriate. He sat there and studied her. The lyrics to the song tormented his mind with tombstone images and a crow who called him home. The darkness and the music blared on and isolated him in a world where he felt doomed.

**24**

———

Paige glanced at the address on her list again. The numbers matched what she'd written. Though she'd expected a showplace, the palatial house surprised her. She parked her modest Cavalier in front. When she walked up the steps to the massive Greek revival, sweat from the hottest summer in a decade popped up on her temples and forehead. She blotted it away before she knocked on the door.

She speculated about the life Caroline lived while she grew up in this storybook mansion. Was she happy here? Did the young Caroline get dirty and play like she did with Crissy? Probably not allowed. Had she grown tired of her lavish surroundings? This place comprised a whole different world than the small track structure where she grew up. The one fact she knew, from her work on the force and her life with Hank, behind closed doors, no family was ever as perfect as they seemed to others.

She reached to knock again, and the door opened to reveal a petite woman with platinum blonde hair. Her impeccable presence brought the word 'elegant' to mind. The classically beautiful face, ravaged little by time, belonged to Caroline's mother.

"Mrs. Montgomery, I'm Detective Paige Stone with the Tulsa Police Department. I'd like to talk to you about your daughter." She offered her hand to shake and displayed a pleasant expression. She hoped to put the woman more at ease.

"You may come in." The woman opened the door wider. Caroline's mother led her to a parlor in the home's front. Never did she see so much wealth displayed in one room before. The woman motioned for her to sit down on a white brocade settee. Mrs. Montgomery then seated herself opposite in a matching one.

"I'm sorry to ask questions at this time, but we need more information about your daughter to help get her safely home to you." Again, she attempted to appear charming, but the woman's face didn't hide her distaste.

"So I understand. Ask your questions." Mrs. Montgomery made the words seem more like a command or permission granted from the queen.

She let it slide. She might elicit more information if she acted like the woman expected.

"Did Caroline make many friends during her school years? Did she have a friend who seemed closer to her than others?" She played into her youthful looks and attempted to stay impressed with the woman's demeanor like she thought the woman expected. Her examination of the room with its treasures made her deliberate again about Caroline, who played here in her childhood. What did the young girl experience with the coldness the room exuded from walls covered in powder blue damask? She kept her expression awestruck.

"Caroline has always been a pretty child. She remained popular until she wandered afield into this religion we do not —" The woman's voice stopped mid-sentence.

"I see. Do you remember her best friend? The one she hung around with at the time she lived here? Someone with whom she remained close from her youth into adulthood?" She continued to pretend to stay impressed with her surroundings as she examined Caroline's mother.

The victim was in her mid-twenties. Why would her mother call her a pretty child?

"I couldn't say. I haven't contacted my daughter in the last eight years." Her voice held no emotion.

"In what extra-curricular activities did Caroline take part while in school?"

"She made cheerleader, though we didn't approve. She later acted wild to get attention, but we did *not* think it proper to reward her offensive behavior. It seemed the wrong way to handle her actions. Then the next we found out, she got into this whole religious cult." By this point, Mrs. Montgomery's eyes filled with fury. Her voice turned cold. Contempt roiled beneath her scarlet cheeks.

"Can you identify any current friends? Did you ever hire a private investigator to check on her since she has been on her own? I don't mean to sound disrespectful, but a few parents do in your situation." She watched the woman work to control the hatred her daughter's choices brought.

"No. We left her to her own devices. She appeared to manage until this happened." Again, the woman offered little insight into any bond that might exist between Caroline and herself. Only the hatred for this religion her daughter preferred.

"Does Caroline possess any money of her own, like a trust fund or something she will inherit after she reaches a certain age?"

"A small one. About twenty-five million or so. I'm sure it's increased over the years. My husband manages it, but she won't inherit until he's assured us she can handle the money properly. We wouldn't consider it now since she's attached to the religious affiliations we discussed earlier. My grandmother set it up for her. You know, Harrison's parents set one up too for a similar amount. It's been so long since they started the account. I forgot about it." She nodded her head and confirmed her words.

*Forgetting about twenty-five million must be nice.* "But your husband could make the funds available if a ransom call came in?" She closely watched the woman's reaction.

"Someone told me the serial killer has our daughter." The woman appeared uncertain for the first time.

"We aren't positive yet. Not for sure. Several possibilities exist."

"I thought they found her car in Woodward Park." The woman appeared to want the serial killer to hold her daughter captive instead of kidnappers. Was she that upset about paying a ransom? How did she already know about the car?

"Yes, ma'am, but it might turn out to be a coincidence. I'll admit the two cases might share a connection, but we have no proof. We need to cover every contingency." The woman's complacent disregard for the welfare of her daughter's life was beyond anything she'd dealt with before.

"You think Caroline remains alive?" Curiously, the expression on Barbara Montgomery's face didn't register relief. She questioned what mother would not show joy at the idea her child did not die at the monster's hand.

"I couldn't make any claims at this time. We don't possess enough facts to support any theories. We need to get the facts we can to better assess what happened to Caroline. Do you remember her best friend's name from her younger years?" She wanted to get away from here. The coldness from the woman gave her creepy vibes.

"Valerie Carter. She lived several homes over from ours. I understand she married and has several children. I'm uncertain of her husband's last name. We traveled out of the country at the time she held the wedding. Her mother and I were never close, so I lost track after Caroline moved out."

"Did your daughter ever get engaged or show serious interest in someone? Anyone she remained close to that she might run to in an emergency?" She added Valerie's name to her notepad.

"No. I don't have their names. The ones I remember are married and have families of their own. I guess a few remain single, but most live busy lives and work at important jobs. I don't know if she still keeps in touch with anyone. Since she left here, her life got swallowed up with *those* people. I can't understand why she would choose to make such a decision." The woman made no attempt to disguise her bitterness. *They* committed the unpardonable sin. She figured the woman before her was at least one reason Caroline chose her new path.

"Did she take her possessions with her when she left or did she leave a few belongings behind?" She glanced up from her notes.

"She took most everything. The rest I threw out years ago." Again, Caroline's mother answered only with the facts. She wondered, who would throw out every trace that her child had lived with her?

"If you remember anything that might help us find your daughter, please call me." She handed her a personal business card and offered to shake hands. "Thank you for your time, Mrs. Montgomery."

Caroline's mother told her goodbye and escorted her to the front door as if she might steal something valuable. She wanted to believe somewhere inside the woman cared about her daughter who vanished. But the woman made that difficult.

~

TRIN LEFT the interview room and joined Hank next door. Hank held his cell phone to his ear. He was eager for Hank's take on it but waited for Hank to finish his conversation before he asked his opinion.

In the meantime, he wanted to review the portion of the interview where he was convinced Ben had lied to him. He rewound the footage and replayed it three times.

Several minutes later Hank shut the cell phone off. "I'm sorry. I had messages out the wazoo. Several with interesting information. They found Caroline's car at Woodward Park. The best detail for us, a dark, probably black, Cadillac Escalade the guard spotted at ORU the night Caroline went missing."

"This information could bring a break if our man has Caroline Montgomery."

"I saw you mess with the video. What did you find so interesting?" Hank tucked his phone into his pocket.

"Ben lied in one answer, but then later after he reworded it, I'd swear he told the truth. I wanted to reexamine the difference between the two. Here, take a look. See if you can tell what I picked up." He backed it up a little and reran the small portion from the interview.

"I caught it, too. Ben lied at the time he worded it *have to do with anyone's death*. Then later, when the actor claims his innocence, he appears not to lie. Something happened McCall feels responsible about in the past, but he didn't kill Heather. Or Ben might know who killed her, but he didn't do it. McCall's a damned good actor. Hell, he won an Oscar. He can screw with us any time he wants."

"The situation puzzles. You said officers found the car at Woodward Park," he said.

"Yeah, Caroline's car. Then we've got a dark, let's say black,

Escalade that the guard saw right before she disappeared. What little evidence we've got adds up against our guys. Then we can't locate the third party. Josh Stuart is still missing. We need to find him." Hank rubbed his leg.

"Yes. We do. Let's find out if we got enough for probable cause to get search warrants for their vehicles and their rooms. It's time to apply pressure."

"I need to call Paige back sometime. She says she has something important, but it will need to wait until after the searches. These guys will get hotshot lawyers before we can turn around twice," Hank said.

He stopped pacing for a moment after Hank's departure, but he often worked issues through better if he stood and moved. He figured he'd wear a hole in the tile by the time Hank returned.

"I got the captain to work on the warrants. It depends on which judge and how long it takes to find one. So what opinion did you get from our superstars?" Hank sat down in the chair he'd used while he watched the interviews.

"Neither one seemed interested in our photos. Many serial killers like to see their work. More than one has gone back to visit the body dump itself to relive the experience." He stopped and faced Hank.

"Yeah, I've heard about cases where the perp did so, and you're right, neither showed the least interest in the pictures. They're the only leads we've got, and they own the right vehicle. We could get lucky and find something in the searches." Hank absently rubbed his left leg.

"Tony seems the best choice. He instigated the Escalade purchases and talked them each into driving their vehicles here. Strete was the last one from the three to carry on an affair with Heather, but if he's guilty, he's the best actor I've seen." He leaned his hip on the back of the other desk in the room.

"I got the same ideas, too. Strete appeared helpful, and after he invoked, too. I got to say, Josh Stuart still missing bothers me. Did the FBI keep a file on him? What did it reveal?" Hank got up, stretched his leg, and sat back down.

"I received a file, but it didn't contain much in it. Sometimes information gets lost. More than likely, a paper pusher threw these together since I asked about one. At any rate, Mr. Stuart's file reads thin and sketchy. They redacted much of it." He frowned, picked up a file folder, and read through it.

"I guess I'd better see if I can get through to Paige." Hank moved to pull out his cell phone but hesitated. "You know these three guys got women who trail after them most of the time. Normal sex probably got boring for one of them. When Donna Barnett came along, he found something he liked and couldn't turn it off."

He continued to peruse the folder's content. "It sounds plausible."

They both sat for a time. Hank rubbed his leg again.

He figured every muscle in Hank's body screamed tired. They'd been at this for a while. "I think I'll wait to pass judgment until after we get a few hours of sleep. What about you? We've been at it with no sleep for too damned long. Do you have a place we can nap for two or three hours? My thoughts will run much clearer after I rest." He watched the older man for any sign Hank figured out what he attempted.

"We keep a room in the back with a few cots. They aren't much, but if you're tired enough, they'll get the job done." Hank led him out the door and down the hall past several interview rooms.

After they arrived, he wished he hadn't suggested it. They were cots with one pillow and a spare blanket. Like Hank said, they would work if you felt tired enough. He figured he was.

$\sim$

THE TV REPORTED ninety-three degrees at ten in the morning as he walked down the stairs and woke Caroline up. He'd removed the tape from her eyes hours ago. She dozed off. How did she sleep like she had no cares? If he hadn't seen it with his eyes, he wouldn't believe it possible.

Her eyes looked sleepy once she gazed up at him. "You got breakfast? I'm hungry."

"You've got a lot of nerve."

"Actually, it's you who has the nerve. You brought me here against my will." He found her confidence amazing since she remained tied to the gurney.

They didn't speak for a time. Finally, Caroline asked, "When will you let me go?"

"I don't plan to let you go." He shook his head and pointed his finger at her like a gun.

"You might want to change your plans since your original one didn't work, and you can't keep me forever. So it only leaves one option."

"I suppose I could keep you forever if I wanted to." He figured his comeback didn't convince, but he must keep a little control. His mind boggled at what happened last night and attempted to write it off since exhaustion made him too excited about the beautiful Caroline. But inside him, uncertainty ruled.

"I have business to do. Crusades to plan, people to save, children to feed, and lots of work ahead." She stared at him for a time. "Why do you waste your life with this?" She moved her head and indicated the whole basement and his sick plans.

"I found I liked it." He shrugged.

"It's not a worthwhile hobby. You should give it up."

"Still, it brought us together." His smile leaned toward suggestive.

"Your comment will impress me how?"

"I've turned heads."

"Then why do you need this? If you've got no problem with the women, why do you need the butchery?"

"I said I found an appetite for it."

"Bully for you. I bet the women didn't much like it. For instance, I'd much prefer my clothes back. Now is a good time," she commanded.

"You've got a mouth on you, don't you?"

"I suppose, but I'm not comfortable with my nakedness, and I don't like yours either. Why don't you, at least, cover yourself?"

"You're not the least bit afraid, are you?"

"No. Why would I be? My choices remain good ones."

"You have no choices. *I'm* the one in charge." He moved closer to her, and his voice got louder.

"You only think you are." She smiled.

"What's that supposed to mean?"

"What I said. You want to believe you're in charge, but inside you know you're not. Last night changed you."

Her words marked his soul, but he would not give in to them.

"How can you say that? You're naked and tied to a gurney."

"In your heart, you're convinced I'm right." This time her smile held conviction.

"I don't like the subject of our conversation."

"I'm sure you don't. It makes you uncomfortable, but it's the truth."

"Shut the hell up. I'm going to dig your grave." He stormed from the room and up the stairs.

～

AT TEN MINUTES PAST SIX, Paige ended her last interview. After a promising start this morning, the day resulted in nothing but frustration. Everyone on the list turned into a complete time waster. She drove around much of Tulsa and interviewed the cook, her PR advisor, and several others, but no one offered anything helpful.

Caroline lived like a saint. She rarely dated, or she didn't date period. She didn't have a single bad habit. Her life neared perfection, to hear everyone tell it.

Only Paige knew differently. No one came close to perfect. She'd worked for the police long enough to understand the truth. Everyone had a weakness, a secret they hid. But Caroline hid hers better than most.

The evangelist's secret rested with her family. Her mother was the perfect icy bitch. Undoubtedly, the evangelist had issues with the situation. She hoped to interview the father tomorrow. She wondered what man could live with Barbara Wentworth Montgomery year after year.

The heat made her uncomfortable and sticky. Once she showered, she wanted food. Hot food. After she arrived at her apartment, she walked straight to the bathroom and stripped. The steaming water pelted down on her and refreshed her. She felt much better afterward, but she longed to skip the food and crawl straight into bed. The trip to the cabin still waited for her. She'd put the journey off longer than she should.

While she dried with her favorite fluffy towel, she spotted her father's picture. It laid face down in the same place where it had for several days. When she'd moved into this apartment a year and a half ago, she'd put the shelf up and placed the framed photo there. She picked up the image to examine the face and uniform for the first time in ages. She looked like her father. He'd given her his blue eyes. She fought with the same determination, but she wondered if she'd inherited his reck-lessness.

Would she wind up the same way her father did? The cabin was out of city limits. She didn't dare wait any longer, but he'd been so wrong in his decision. Could her choice to visit the cabin be as flawed as his turned out to be?

No one would listen to her. Hank wouldn't take time to answer her. But she sensed it in her gut. She believed the killer held Caroline captive there, figured Heather died there, and poor Betty Greenway might remain buried there. Someone must check it out. By events beyond her control, she'd got the job.

If she were wrong, she'd only waste her time. The property sat a fair distance from the city, but the killer had time enough to make the trip and kill Heather in the slot allowed. No one saw Heather after six thirty in the evening. Danny found her after one in the morning. Six and a half hours. Time and plenty to get there and return, plus several hours to torture and kill Heather Balentine.

She placed the photo back on the shelf. It didn't lay face down anymore. He hadn't been perfect. Few people were. But he remained her father. The truth would never change that. Her resolve hardened. No matter how tired, she would check out the cabin this evening.

She walked back into her bedroom and yanked a black T-shirt off the hanger in her closet. She pulled it over her head and snatched navy blue jeans.

Darkness would come soon after she arrived. If the killer remained on the property, this might make her less visible. She shoved her badge in the front pocket of her jeans and pulled her service weapon out from its holster. After she tucked the Glock 27 at the back in her waistband, she strapped her throwaway, a .22 Beretta, to her right ankle and covered it with her pants leg.

By the time she left her apartment, hunger gnawed at her stomach. She stopped for a burger and a soda. Then she drove up Garnett and got on I-44.

She took her phone out of her pocket and speed-dialed Hank one more time. It went to voicemail. His phone habits frustrated her. When he didn't want to answer his phone, he didn't. *Dammit.*

"Hank, I'm on my way to a cabin near Claremore. Since I can't get anyone to return my calls, I'm going alone. I could sure use backup. I believe your killer has Caroline Montgomery there. Would you call me, *please?*" She disconnected, put the phone on silent, and set it to vibrate. While she stuffed the cell phone back in her T-shirt pocket, she kept her course steady toward Claremore.

She punched the button that turned the radio on. Bruno Mars sang "Talking to the Moon." She'd heard it for the first time right after Bobby's death. It made her long for a connection to him—like he might remain out there somewhere trying to talk to her too. Several tears rolled down her cheek as she took the left curve near the Hard Rock Casino. She kept an even pressure on the gas and drove northeast on old Route 66.

**25**

Trin awoke from his rest with an ache in his left knee. He automatically glanced at his watch. They'd slept two hours. His muscles felt a little better, but his head remained groggy. That combination only happened when he entered a deep sleep.

He put his legs over the military cot's side and peeked over at Hank's sleeping form. He attempted to push up, but the cot wobbled under the additional pressure. He wanted to laugh at the ridiculous bed, but he really needed to urinate. He put his hands on each side of the support bar and used his calf muscles to push to his feet.

Out in the hall, officers milled around. He searched for the captain, but he didn't see Underwood anywhere. His eyes spotted a bathroom down past the interview rooms on the left. Relief was in sight.

After he used the john, he splashed water onto his face to clear the cobwebs. By the time Hank walked in, his body felt closer to normal.

"Better?" Hank passed him on the way to the urinal.

"I'm beginning to feel human again." He glanced in the mirror, to his regret. Haggard didn't come close to describing his current state.

"I dozed a little. My cot wasn't much better than the floor." The older man finished, washed his hands, and splashed his face.

"I guess we should go find out if Underwood got the warrants served. It would turn out great if they found something. I don't want to spend another night like this last one." He threw the paper towels he'd used in the trash as they walked out the door.

"Me either. Home in my bed sounds a lot more comfortable," Hank said, and the egress closed behind them.

They went to the captain's office, but he still wasn't there. The detective reached into his pocket for his phone. He held the device out to arm's length, then hit a button. He moved the cell to his ear and waited.

After he spoke into the mouthpiece for several minutes, Hank gazed back over at him. "We'll be right there." Hank's voice rose a decibel.

"What did you find out?" he asked.

"They found a red hair in Tony's Escalade. Forensics is examining the strand for a match ASAP. So far, it's the only item they've discovered." Hank led him around the corridor toward the parking area.

"The color's right. Where are we headed?" He rearranged his jacket and brushed it off a little while they walked.

"Down to the action. They're taking the vehicles apart. The lab techs started on them during our nap. The guys found a single red strand on the passenger seat headrest in Tony's Caddy, but they've got Ben's vehicle to search, too," Hank said.

"This might give us the break we've waited for. Last night I was exhausted, but I would have sworn there was no way Strete murdered anyone. Today with that hair for leverage, who knows what he'll admit." He felt his heart rate increase. The new find acted like a tonic. He felt energized and ready to give Tony another go.

"My thoughts exactly. You never can tell what the next day has to offer. I hope ours gets better."

He saw two black vehicles in various degrees of dismantlement. "Did we document these with care? We don't want them to use mishandling evidence as a technicality. Please label every nut, bolt, and whatever." He raised his voice to the detective over the noise caused by the many electric drills and machines used in the search.

Hank approached the captain and relayed the message. Bob nodded his head during their discussion. He observed the two with uncertainty. Neither suspect fit the profile he'd worked up for the killer of these women. Something seemed off here, but the best lead they possessed pointed to Anthony Strete. He had no choice but to go with it and push it to the limit if he could. It appeared Tony would return to number one on the list.

He and Hank watched them work on the Escalades for thirty minutes without another significant discovery. The detective got a call on his cell. The forensic techs found nothing in the rooms to help—a few fibers, no fluids, and no prints from either victim. The guys seemed to live like hermits since they arrived at the casino.

He doubted they lived in such a manner. The three were handsome, loaded, and famous. Women would climb over each other to get a chance to date them. No way someone didn't take advantage of the new wealthy men in town.

"I think it's time to give Tony another go. The actor didn't seem right, but you never can tell. Strete resembles our man more every minute." He glanced at his watch—a little after six.

They'd eat something quick and then get started. More trace or prints might turn up while they ate.

"I got the same idea. My gut doesn't like him for it, but the evidence supports his suspect status. It's difficult to argue with facts." The older man stretched his leg out and rubbed it.

"Let's find a good place for breakfast. That sounds good since we missed it earlier. We can see what turns up during the time we get food. Then we'll go at him again." He figured Hank had been on his feet long enough.

The detective nodded, and they both left the building. After they walked to the car, he heard Hank's cell beep. "You should check your phone. I think you've got messages."

"It's Paige. She has an absurd idea her missing real estate agent relates somehow to our killer. I'll call her back later when I can carve out more time to listen to her. I know it's her first case by herself since she received her promotion. We'll more than likely talk about it for hours. She likes to jaw at me about my health, too, and I don't want to discuss the issue while I'm on this job. After last night, my age is screaming enough." Hank grinned, but he didn't believe the excuse the detective gave equaled the main reason the older man avoided his protégé.

He remembered his first solo and his eagerness in those days. An exhausted appearance wouldn't mark him then as it did now from missing sleep. "If you want her to speak to you again, you'd better not wait too long. She seems intense."

"Intense doesn't begin to describe it, but she *is* special. Next time she calls, I'll pick up," Hank promised.

He still struggled with the idea she believed her case related to theirs. That puzzled him a great deal. Why didn't the detective mention it earlier?

~

He opened the cabinet door and saw the heart-shaped piece of iris from Heather Balentine's eye float in contact lens solution. The clear vial sat next to various cans. He would serve her his chicken noodle. The soup's flavor was his least favorite.

The piece of eye occasionally reflected the overhead light and caught his attention. He toyed with the idea he could put it in her broth with noodles. Wouldn't it get her engine revved up if he told her she ate Heather's eye? Initially, he had plans for the tissue, but tomorrow if nothing changed, she might receive it for lunch. A smirk crossed his lips while he stirred the liquid in the pan he heated.

He carried the bowl of canned soup and a few crackers downstairs to his captive. She would soon die anyway, but this should stop her complaints. The events that happened last night still unsettled him. He told himself he dreamed it, but the children's jingle continued to run through his head. Why did she pick *that* song? His mother used to sing it to him each evening at bedtime. He often fell asleep to the melody.

When he opened the door, she smiled. It aggravated him.

"There you are. I wondered if you would feed me. I've always had a healthy appetite." Caroline acted as if he should serve her a banquet.

"I know you want to appear brave, but let's not overdo it. I'm still in charge here."

"You sure?" Her voice sounded innocent of guile, but it grated just the same.

He remained silent and set the soup bowl on the cloth-covered table.

"I see you wore clothes. You look much better." Her cheerful manner pierced him.

"Don't push it. They may come off again."

"Why not wear them? You've got nice apparel. I deal with many people who own almost none."

"Oh, boohoo. Like I'm supposed to care."

"It wouldn't hurt you to think about someone else. Your selfishness got you into this mess. It always leads to no good."

"So when did you achieve sainthood?" He'd listened enough. He wanted to change the subject.

"My parents raised me in a mansion and spoiled me as your mother did you. Then the Lord saved me. He gave me a chance to repent." She opened her mouth for a spoonful of soup.

"You never killed anybody." He gazed at her with a hint of regret in his eyes.

"No. But I grew bored and stole an expensive necklace, which might have landed me in jail. I wanted to embarrass my parents who didn't give a flip about me. An opportunity came to return it, and I repented. It changed me forever. If you let Him, He can change you." Her voice softened and pleaded with him.

"You can peddle your words somewhere else. I'm not interested."

"This won't end well for you. Eventually, the law will catch you. At least you could get saved before you go to meet your maker. It's not too late to fix this."

"The morning I woke up with a dead woman in my bed, the time for salvation had passed. By then, I'd already gone too far." He scoffed at her idea and swung his arm dramatically.

"I suppose that situation would present a problem," she admitted.

"The actions I've taken are way beyond anyone's help. Eat the food and shut up." He fed her another taste of broth, but his eyes avoided hers.

∼

TRIN'S FOCUS returned to the case after they finished bacon, eggs, hash browns, and toast. He drank a second cup of coffee, which changed everything as far as his sleep-deprived world was concerned. He walked into the interview room with confidence and laid the file down with force.

"You've survived, for now, pretty boy. You should do great in the slammer. They will name you queen bee in no time." He hit Tony front and center. It rattled the actor. He recognized it in the man's eyes.

"I assumed we'd gotten past this. I didn't kill anyone. So why do we still go in circles?" Strete said.

"I told you several times already. I'm the one who asks the questions. You're the one who answers them."

"Look, I don't know what you want from me. I haven't seen Heather Balentine in a year, give or take a few. We never had sex the way you described. I didn't kill her."

"Why did you three buy matching black Escalades?" He continued to stare without a blink.

"Right before we left LA, we got drunk. I can't remember too much. Josh said, and Ben agreed with him, that I insisted we purchase them to use at the Little Sahara State Park. My memory from the night we bought the Cadillacs is gone." Strete shrugged like the lost recollection counted for nothing.

"Do you black out often when you drink?" His mind raced with possibilities.

"I have a few times, but I haven't consumed any alcohol in over two months. So I wouldn't get my hopes up." Tony seemed to possess more control over himself than he did in the other session.

"If you can't remember, how are you certain?"

"Because it takes several drinks to take me there. I never took the first one."

"Are you acquainted with Caroline Montgomery?" He changed the subject.

"I don't think so." Tony's expression filled with hesitation.

"A guard saw your SUV at ORU the night she disappeared from there." He observed Strete for a tell. The actor never showed one.

"You can't arrest me in Heather's case, so you try to get me for someone I've never met?"

"How are you sure you didn't meet the televangelist? You said yourself you black out."

"I told you. I quit drinking. If I did something so stupid, I would be certain."

"Would you? We found a red hair in your vehicle. The techs are testing for a match with the two victim's strands right now. I'd say it's convincing." His tone made it sound like he had closed the deal.

"It won't match either of them. I want a lawyer." Tony's voice was tempered with steel. They would play no more head games.

Eventually, he figured Tony would ask for an attorney, but to get what information he could without his representation present remained his job. The actor appeared a lot more confident this time around. He wondered where they put him during their two-hour nap. For whatever reason, Tony's act stayed together.

He did not bother to go the distance. He understood it wouldn't do any good. They'd back off and let the lawyers handle it. He got up and left the room and Tony alone with his thoughts.

Time to get serious and find Josh Stuart.

## 26

Paige followed the instructions in her notes. After she turned off Route 66, the drive got more grueling. The blacktopped surface continued with patches on top of patches. Her Cavalier shimmied and shook as it continued down the rough road. After about five miles, it changed to gravel. Oaks and pecan trees lined the way and made a canopy overhead as she proceeded on for another half a mile.

When she found what she believed was the correct driveway on the narrow lane, she stopped to reread her instructions. Off to the left, through the dusk, she could make out a cabin. The home covered in mock logs looked large enough to contain three bedrooms, with a double car garage.

Twilight still lingered while she turned her Cavalier around. With barely enough light to see now, she figured it would only be more difficult in complete darkness. The moon's sliver rose without providing much light. After four forward and reverse movements and a stiff wrestling match with the steering wheel, she finally got the Chevy parked where it faced the way she'd come.

Flashlight in hand, she left her automobile on the road and walked toward the house. She didn't press the ON button for her Maglite and relied on the evening glow to guide her way. She moved her cell phone to a more secure pocket in her jeans. Her nerves tingled. This location topped the most remote she'd ever visited for work.

The private entrance extended about a quarter mile, topped with the same gravel that covered the road. She heard various movements in the knee-high grasses that bordered the drive to the right and left. She ignored the sounds and walked briskly. Her eyes adjusted to the darkness. A small rodent scurried across her path ten feet in front of her. Her pulse quickened. An owl screeched in the distance, but she only picked up the pace. She would rather search anywhere else than here.

No vehicle sat in the drive, and the garage door remained down. She examined it once she walked closer. No windows. She couldn't see if a black SUV lurked in the interior.

She traveled to the closest dark window of the house and switched on the flashlight. She aimed the lens through the glass. The area appeared vacant. The knot in her stomach eased a little.

She moved to the next one. She used her Maglite to sweep through the room. Her gut churned when she noticed a sleeping bag in the northeast corner. Near the bedroll's end sat a small stuffed duffel. She continued to check each casement until she worked her way around to the kitchen.

She moved the arc of light across the barren room until she spotted a pan on the cook stove. A cracker box on the counter sat beside a pot. Everything looked unremarkable until she noticed a pink backpack. It lay on an old, scarred table. The corner of a laptop stuck out from the opening. Her heart seemed to beat double time as she staggered away from the window. It belonged to Heather. The pack matched what she'd seen Heather carrying in the airport security footage. *Oh my God. It's him. I've found him.*

She silently retraced her steps and stopped outside the room that had appeared empty before. Her hand shook as she took her cell phone from her pants pocket and speed-dialed Hank. He'd better pick up, or she would kill him herself if she got out of this alive.

It rang five times before Hank finally answered. "Hank, I found him. He's at the cabin. I saw Heather's pink backpack. I need backup, now." Her voice barely rose above a whisper as she tried to impress the severity of the situation on Hank.

"Hold on. You don't make any sense. What cabin?" Hank asked.

"The one Betty Gre—" The light departed from her world.

Trin sat across from Hank when he answered the ringing cell. "Hold on. You don't make any sense. What cabin?" A slight pause followed. Hank lowered the device from his ear and stared at the screen. "Shit." His pallor turned gray.

"What's going on?" He got up from his seat in the observation room.

"I think he has Paige." Hank stood too.

"What are you talking about?" His stomach sank.

"The damn killer. She said she saw the pink backpack. First, she claimed she found him at a cabin. I asked her what cabin, and she said 'Betty Gre.' She didn't get the rest out. It might have been Green or Green-something. I don't know since her line went dead." Hank opened the door and started down the hall.

He knew Hank would go to Bill for help, but would he find a way to save her? The question stopped him, and he realized the two suspects they'd grilled were still in lockup. Who the hell had her if they didn't? They'd never found Josh Stuart.

Tense with nerves, they drove in silence to the University of Tulsa campus. He parked the car, and they raced into the building.

Bill glared at them like they'd gone crazy when they burst into his office. "What gives?" The IT tech turned his whole body around to give them his full attention.

"He's got my Paige. You have to find her. She called me a moment ago. Bill, locate her. Hurry." Hank thrust the phone into his hands.

Trin stood there horrified. He could maintain distance from the other victims, but with Paige, he'd shared her dinner. He was attracted to her. She was beautiful, vibrant, and alive. The son of a bitch got her. The serial killer grabbed Paige. He attempted to stay objective, but it felt so damned personal. Pain raced through his chest. When Bill called his name, it took three times before it registered.

"Trin, damn it. What resources does the FBI have that we can use to track her phone?" Bill's fingers banged hard against the keyboard.

"Is her cell equipped with GPS?" His brain searched for anything he figured would help.

"Yes, but someone has turned it off. I can't get a signal for Paige's number. The creep must have taken the battery out or broken it somehow. I've got nothing to work with." The tech stayed busy. His fingers moved quickly over the keyboard. "I don't find it." Bill stared up at them, his face bleak.

"I'll call them, but they'll only tell us the last tower her phone used. If they can track it in time to do us any good . . ." He worked his speed dial and started the process. "Is her car equipped with LoJack?"

"No, the Cavalier isn't new enough," the IT tech answered. His fingers still worked the keys.

"Bill, can you produce a listing for the numbers she's called in the last week? One might lead to the cabin. It's the only other idea I can think to try." They couldn't sit here and do nothing. Paige would die.

Bill's fingers moved again. "I need to hack into the phone company. It will take too long to get a dump on her number."

He gazed at Hank, who sat quietly. The older man slumped in his seat, and his complexion looked pasty, his expression dazed. He was in the middle of an episode. *Shit. They didn't have time for this.*

"Hank? Hank, are you all right?" He moved toward him. Hank fumbled with his pocket as if struggling to remove something. Trin walked over to him and helped. He pulled out a bottle with medication and read it was for the heart.

"Here." He shook a pill from inside and gave it to his partner.

Gettering relaxed slightly but didn't speak yet. He continued to monitor the old detective.

After a few more minutes, Hank finally spoke. "Put out an APB on Josh Stuart. He's the only one left. The asshole took Paige." His face took on a more sickly pallor.

"You have to quiet down. She will need you once this is over, and we bring her back. Calm yourself and stay alive for her. I got the same idea a few minutes ago. Something should break soon. It has to." The last he spoke only to himself.

"I've printed a list. It's lengthy. Why don't we divide it between us?" Bill broke into his thoughts.

Finally, he could contribute and help. He picked up the printout and divided it into three equal parts with pencil lines. He asked Bill to copy it twice. That left thirteen phone listings apiece to work through. They got to it.

After forty-five minutes of dead ends, they had nothing. The only good to come from their effort was the list got shorter, and Hank's color returned to normal. Trin paced, continued to dial numbers from his paper, and asked questions of the people who answered. He felt certain their time had ran out, and his insides turned frantic with fear.

"I'm afraid I have to move you." He prodded Caroline awake. "I need your space for another guest. She came to me unexpectedly, but she'll make a tasty morsel. Come on. Wake up." He shoved her again, and she mumbled.

The evangelist dragged her feet. He hadn't given her anything to induce sleep since he first took her. The whole slumber farce seemed a ruse, but if she plotted a getaway, it wouldn't do her any good. If help had arrived, he'd just captured it.

He removed the battery from the officer's cell phone so the authorities couldn't find them—at least, not for a long while. He'd still make time for his fantasy. Caroline didn't work out, but the new detective would present a significant challenge.

Tall and slim, her breasts were full, not like the skinny actresses from California. He envisioned a feast on her nipples until they stood at attention. Her long neck would handle a good squeeze until they both came together. Her blonde hair would contrast with the blood-soaked tendrils, but he'd wash it clean and arrange it to perfection. Yes, the police officer would do great. He nodded, licked his lips, and smiled to himself.

He pulled Caroline's body up from the gurney once he released her wrists and loosened her ankles. He took the Glock from his back waistband and pointed it at her. "Stand up."

Her legs folded under her weight when she attempted to

obey him. He grabbed to catch her. She leaned on him for a moment.

"My calf muscles are asleep. You've kept me tied up too long." Caroline lifted each leg and moved it around. She clenched and unclenched her hands three times to make the circulation begin again.

"I'll give you thirty seconds to get them awake because you *will* walk up those stairs." He motioned toward the doorway with the hand that held the Glock.

After several more attempts to shake out her limbs, her movements grew stronger. He forced her up the steps and into a dark bedroom. The previously vacant room contained a lone chair.

"Take a seat," he commanded and pointed to the piece of furniture, nudging her with the gun.

Caroline stretched first and then moved near the ladder-back with arms.

"Quit stalling and put your ass down here. I don't have time to waste anymore. Sit." He poked her side with the pistol and motioned again toward the wooden piece.

"Why not? What's changed?" The evangelist shuffled closer to the armchair but dawdled before she sat in it.

"Your rescuer used her phone before I could knock her out, but she didn't tell them exactly where she was. I'll have to shut you up permanently when I'm through with her."

He took the duct tape that laid nearby on the floor, ripped off a piece, and covered her mouth. He bound her feet to the legs and hands to the arms with the adhesive and left her there alone in the room. The time had come for his last hurrah. His new play toy waited for him to release her into eternity.

## 27

Trin glanced at his watch. Two hours since the phone call, and they still had no indication where the unsub held Paige captive. The FBI had located the tower from her call in Rogers County on the east side of Claremore. They'd called all the numbers from Paige's phone but a few had gone unanswered. Not one contributed any information about a cabin. He figured the solution remained in the unanswered calls.

He stared at the paper again. Three non-responses. He walked back over to Bill and placed the list down before him.

"Is there any way to find which person from these three numbers owns a cabin in Rogers County? Only these didn't answer. One number should belong to our guy. It's the only idea I've got. Hank, have you got a better plan?" He looked over at the detective.

Hank stopped mid-stride and gazed up at him. He shook his head. Hank paced a six-foot area beside the nearby bench again. After three trips back and forth, the older man staggered and half-fell, half-sat on the seat.

Trin grabbed his cell phone and dialed 911, then peeked over his shoulder at Bill. "Get started on that search! I'll handle this."

He helped Hank stretch out on the floor and loosened the man's tie. The dispatcher answered the phone. "I've got a middle-aged man in his fifties, I'd guess. He displays symptoms of distress. He's currently being treated for heart problems. I need a bus or anyone in the building to bring him help immediately. We are at the University of Tulsa, Cyber Crime Unit. In the tech department near Bill Graywolf's desk. Please hurry. His coloring isn't good." He laid the phone down to help Hank get comfortable. He unknotted Hank's tie, unbuttoned his collar, and rolled his own jacket to use for a pillow.

"You can't worry right now, Hank. I need you to pull yourself together. Relax. Take a deep breath. Can you breathe normally?" He hovered over Hank and racked his brain for how to find Paige.

Hank nodded. He observed the detective for a minute. The older man's breathing seemed better. In another few minutes, two officers came into the room.

"Is this where the emergency call originated?" the officer on the left asked as he moved closer.

"Yes. Hank Gettering is here on the floor. He seems more responsive, but I want him checked out no matter what he says. Make damn sure a doctor examines him." He figured Hank would give them a hard time, so he'd repeated the specific instructions.

The men left the room then came back with a stretcher. It took the officers no time to get Hank loaded and ready to go. He picked up his jacket from the floor, shook it out, and put it back on.

He leaned over Hank. "I will find her. I promise. Go get well for when she comes home."

Hank looked back up at him, his eyes filled with uncertainty. "I taught her everything I know. She handles herself like a pro. Don't let Josh Stuart get away with this. You and I both know he's got her."

"I will find her. You go get help. Paige will need you after this is over." He stood up and went back to where Bill continued to break the law in his searches.

Paige opened her eyes. The room was poorly lit. Once she grew more aware, she made out wavering shadows dancing along the wall, cast by lit candles. Their cloying smell filled the room. She moved her tethered arm and tried to rub her sleepy eyes, but a restraint held her captive.

At first, she didn't remember where she was. Then she remembered the cabin and the pink backpack. She vaguely remembered she'd called Hank. *Oh my God.* He would worry until he knew she got away from this place safe, but she might as well hide in outer Mongolia. No one would find her here.

More than likely, the psychopath had already destroyed her cell phone. He'd have taken her guns, too. She was on her own. She pulled against each restraint and checked to see the extent of her movement. With her restricted range of motion, she couldn't do much.

She tried to focus her thoughts. She had to think of something, anything to get out of this. Otherwise, she would wind up like Heather and the other victims. Fear clawed at her insides as she remembered Heather's corpse. Hank must never see her that way.

She had to plot more lethally than her captor. She must not show fear. It usually fed into the serial killer's fantasies. If she failed to get free, she didn't want to give him that satisfaction. She intended to die without begging or screaming.

She saw movement in her peripheral vision. She wasn't alone. He must have stayed down here with her. Terror flooded through her and brought darkness too deep to fathom, but she had to conquer her fear as much as she needed to conquer him. She had to stay strong and not give in to him or the paralyzing horror. She'd seen his results on Heather. "What did you do with Betty Greenway?" she demanded.

"Ah, so that's how you found me. You are a clever one, aren't you?" He stepped closer to her. She recognized him immediately but refused to acknowledge it.

"You didn't answer my question." Her voice cut through the eerie atmosphere he'd created.

"I didn't think I had to. I'm the one in control here, in case you haven't figure that out."

"Is it so important to you? Control? You like to dominate other people? Is that what gets you off?"

"I developed a taste for it. Playing God can feel luscious."

A hint of insanity appeared in his eyes while he savored his own words.

"I wouldn't call it anything close to that. I'd call it sick. You still didn't answer my question. Where did you put Betty Greenway?" She kept the command in her voice robust and examined his every move. Tall and massive, he must stand six foot six. His biceps bulged. They probably measured close to twenty inches in diameter. His broad shoulders and chest rippled as he walked closer to her. Thank God, he still wore his jeans.

"She's around, the poor darling. She got too greedy. It didn't do her any good. Most people take the materialistic route." This time he answered her with laughter and ran his finger down her thigh until her leg twitched in reaction.

"It's hardly an offense worthy of death. Did you already kill her?"

His hand caressed her foot, making her skin crawl. The size of his formidable body intimidated her, but she worked to keep her voice steady.

"You know I did. I trapped you here, didn't I?" With only a look, his eyes promised her she'd die next.

"Where did you put her?" She continued to question and hoped for more time to think.

"I said she's around. What difference does it make? You won't tell anyone, anyway." He delicately ran a finger over the arch of her foot and reveled in the information only he believed humorous.

"You never can tell. Nothing is ever a done deal until it is." She sounded more confident than she felt, but it was the only weapon she possessed. The longer she got him to talk, the greater the chance Hank would come through with a miracle.

"Did you enjoy your encounters with Peter?" He searched her eyes and continued to stroke her foot.

"Peter?" It took her a second to place the name.

"You might remember him better as the annoying news hound." He lifted her foot slightly and ran his finger over her toes.

"You fed him the information." She refused to acknowledge his suggestive behavior, though goosebumps slithered up her spine from his creepy touch.

"We've known each other for years. He covers the Hollywood crowd. I'm afraid it's more lucrative than the police beat here in Tulsa. I enjoyed tossing him a bone. The reporter couldn't latch onto it fast enough." His face turned toward her. He finally got tired of her foot and put it down.

"You mean you chose Tulsa since the reporter came from

here?" She wanted him to talk longer before he touched her in worse places.

He nodded. "I figured it might arouse more interest. I certainly got more press here than anywhere else. I wanted to try something smaller. Besides, I read somewhere Tulsa has over an eighty percent closure rate on homicides. I wanted to test that, see if they really are that good."

She grew quiet for a moment and remembered the trouble the reporter caused. It seemed trivial compared to her present situation.

"You didn't comment on my identity. My girls usually do." He examined her face.

"Others might be impressed. I'm not. Especially when you intend to kill me. And I'm *not* one of your girls."

He turned away and walked to a CD player across the room. He glanced back at her. "So you do acknowledge who I am."

"Of course I recognized you, but you can't stand for too much if you need to get off by strangling famous women. I'm *not* famous. It's a shame you're stuck with me, but there you are." She kept all emotion out of her voice, but her pulse raced. She felt she might drown in her fears.

"Oh, you're utterly delectable. You'll do fine. In fact, you're a nice surprise. I've never had one search me out like you did. I've always pursued my women. Except for the first one. But she was an accident anyway, so she doesn't count."

"I doubt she would agree with you. Of course, she's dead, so we'll never find out, but still, it's a fair assumption."

"Besides, she wasn't famous really. She got more attention in death than she ever did in auditions. I'll make you famous, too. I'll make you my newest creation." He waved his hand as if *no problem.*

"Please, don't do me any favors. I don't like to join clubs.

And I doubt she wanted that kind of fame." She moved her hands enough to keep the feeling in them.

"You're probably right, but she came up with the idea the first time, and she did turn me on to this whole new game for pleasure." He shrugged and pushed several buttons on the CD player.

"That's such a pleasant way to put it. You kill people for fun and games. That's hardly your average game for pleasure."

"It's brought such interesting responses. Take yourself, for example. You know no help will come, but you cling to the idea someone will rescue you before I complete my quest. We both understand that won't happen. I will leave long before anyone comes to claim your remains. Long gone, Paige." He licked his lips, using her name for the first time.

Of course he'd found her name. He had her possessions. "I'm glad to see you don't have sex with strangers."

He laughed, and she glimpsed a hint of his madness.

"How did you manage to lure Heather Balentine here? When did you first meet her?" She needed to distract him somehow. His behavior suggested the ritualistic patterns she'd read were common in serial killers. He'd set the stage for his next victim. Her mind wanted to panic, but she forced herself to turn away from those horrid visions. She only had her brain to save herself.

"Why so many questions? But you are a detective. I forgot for a moment. I first met her at a party. She still believed herself in love with Anthony Strete. I consoled her. We became best friends on her private Twitter account. She loved to tweet about everything. Sometimes we talked on her private cell phone, but mostly we tweeted. Next I suggested a clandestine weekend where no one could find us. Who would think about Tulsa? No one. Perfect. Right?"

"I doubt it felt perfect for her." She wondered how she'd ever considered him handsome in his movies.

"At first, she thought so. Sad to say, her attitude did change." He licked his lips .

"How can you expect anything else?"

"Oh, but I didn't expect anything else. Miss Balentine did exactly what I needed her to do. Her screams were incredible. They still echo in my ears." His eyes glazed over as he relived the experience. The smile on his face twisted with gratification.

"Surely Caroline Montgomery didn't tweet with you. She didn't agree to meet you. How did you get to her?" She changed the subject. She didn't want to watch his sickness another second. If she could keep him talking, maybe she could buy some time. She didn't want to die here in this God-forsaken basement, alone with this psychopath. She also knew Hank wouldn't survive if she became the next victim.

His face changed instantly, the dreamy smile replaced with a scowl. "I don't want to talk about Caroline. Do you hear me? I won't talk about her."

Something went wrong with Caroline. But what? Maybe this could be the key to her survival.

"Why? What happened with Caroline? Is she still alive?" She needed to get free. Caroline could be here somewhere, bleeding out. She needed to help the evangelist.

"So many questions. I will not talk about her." He came around the top end of the gurney and messed with something out of her line of vision. Then he jabbed a syringe filled with God knew what into her thigh. She was helpless to prevent the oblivion that overcame her again.

～

"Did you find anything helpful? We've got deputies on standby in Claremore. I should head her way. Give me your number so I can stay in touch with you." Trin stared at Bill and waited to input the new contact.

"I'm working on it. Try to call those three numbers one more time," Bill suggested, fingers flying over his keyboard.

"Good idea." He stepped away from Bill to use his phone. After he redialed the numbers, he grew more frustrated. He worried about Hank's mental health in addition to his physical ailments. This nightmare with a madman holding his surrogate child captive would only exacerbate his issues. Hank knew only torture and death awaited Paige. Trin couldn't imagine what played through the man's mind right now.

"Did you get around the firewalls? Anything new? Did they locate Josh Stuart?" He couldn't stop himself from asking the questions again.

"Same answer I gave a minute ago. I'm working on it, and no one has seen Stuart." Bill looked aggravated with his repeated questions.

He paced for several more minutes and ran his fingers through his hair. The waiting made him crazy. He turned back around and walked over to Bill, focusing on the screen for a few moments.

"I've got to do something. I can't stand here another minute. I'll drive to Claremore so I can be nearby when you find her location. I've got GPS capabilities. If you can get me the address, I'll find her."

"I'm on it. The minute I know, you will," Bill assured him. His fingers hardly ever ceased their movements.

"Okay then, I'm off."

He went straight to his rented car. He climbed inside and programmed the GPS for the sheriff's department in Claremore, Oklahoma. The gas tank was low, so he filled it. He wanted no problems once Bill contacted him with the information.

With his nerves shot, he forced himself on. He cared about Paige, he admitted to himself. She wasn't just another victim. He believed she could be the one he'd waited for these many years. And he wanted the chance to find out. She was a bright, intelligent woman who made one great detective. The world needed more people like her. He pushed the pedal to the floor.

PAIGE TRIED to rub her dry, itchy eyes but couldn't reach far enough. Something stopped her hand. Where was she? The blurriness lifted, and the dimly lit room came into focus. She also became aware of her nakedness.

She felt exposed in a way she had never experienced before. The sensation terrified her. She tried to close her eyes but couldn't.

She remembered Heather's eyes. The bastard had taped them open. She struggled to close her own but they remained forced open, drying in the air.

Fear like she'd never known before grabbed her. Panic set in as she glanced at the table and the objects on it. She knew exactly how he'd used each item on Heather. She'd examined the results from his carnage. Her teeth chattered and blood raced through her veins as her heart raced. She didn't want to die like this.

He'd used something to knock her out, then removed her clothes, had seen her naked. Anger fired within her, burning away the fear.

"There she is." His voice sent shivers across her bare skin.

She knew what happened next depended on her ability to outsmart him. Mentally, she needed to remain calm, no matter what. She held perfectly still while he fondled her toes, fighting the urge to scream. Or puke. He would assume terror gripped her.

His fingers slid smoothly up her ankle.

Her first time wouldn't happen this way. She'd prefer to die than allow him to degrade her in such a manner. She fought the demons in her head until they cleared.

"Is this the best you can offer?" She didn't know if goading him would work, but she had to try something.

He moved directly into her line of vision. "It's always so much more interesting when my girls wake up. Are you going to try to fight? I'd prefer screams."

He was naked, a giant mass of solid muscle. He was moving faster than she'd anticipated. Savoring the ritual should take more time.

"Is that what happened with Caroline? Did she wake up, and you didn't impress her with your advances? She wouldn't scream for you?" She kept her voice calm despite his nearness.

"We will *not* talk about Caroline. Do you hear me? I will *not* talk about her." His body shook as he yelled the words.

"Why? Did she laugh at you and your pathetic attempts at seduction? I'm not impressed with your equipment either." She dropped her gaze from his eyes, deliberately staring below his waist.

He slammed a fist on the gurney and turned his back to her. Then he walked over to the CD player and pushed the PLAY button. She recognized the song the Eagles sang about "somebody following me." She didn't get it at first, but then the lyrics made sense.

After he returned, he laid a scalpel on her chest between her breasts and sneered down at her. This time it took every ounce of fight in her to hold the horror at bay. In her mind, she pictured him carving her body with the instrument. Would he kill her first or keep her alive through the agony?

"Is that tiny thing supposed to scare me?" She chuckled, sure the double entendre wouldn't be lost on him. "Didn't scare Caroline, did it?"

He slapped her hard enough to make her see stars. She shook it off.

She knew Caroline was the key to breaking his concentration."What happened with Caroline? Tell me what happened. What did she do to you?"

He moved his arm up to slap her again, but then dropped his hand to his side instead. He turned and sat in a chair several feet away from her. His head hung as if in despair.

She allowed herself a breath of relief. She'd struck a nerve. Something went wrong in his scenario with Caroline. If he hadn't killed the evangelist, where did he put her? Was she still here in this house?

Quietly she tested the tethers that held her, but they didn't budge. She tried to get her mouth close enough to undo her hands, but couldn't reach. She pulled as hard as she could to extract her hand from the restraint, but it was too tight.

He seemed completely distracted. She forced herself to look again at the instruments beside her on the gurney. Though intended for her torture, could she manage to use one to release herself? No matter how she twisted and stretched, the tips of her fingers barely brushed the cold metal.

But the scalpel still lay on her sternum.

## 28

While her captor sat with his head down, Paige continued to maneuver her body. If she got the scalpel to slide a bit closer toward her head, the tool would lay where she needed it to rest. She pulled in her upper torso, thrust her hips higher, and jiggled her bottom enough to slip the blade nearer her lower jaw. Thank God, it positioned itself in the correct place.

She pushed the back end of the surgical instrument down as tightly as she could with the tip of her mandible, raising the sharp end into the air. The restraint was long enough that she could just reach the blade with her wrist. She dragged it across the edge. The procedure was awkward, and she cut herself several times, but slowly the layers came loose.

Blood dripped to her shoulder before her wrist finally found freedom. Carefully and silently, she grasped the scalpel with her right hand and worked to free her left. The Eagles' music throbbed through the basement, and the candlelight swayed to the gruesome beat. By the third time through the melody, she understood the lyrics. The lead singer sang about how evil he had been, and how he would pay the devil for what he'd put his victims through. Her second arm gained independence.

Could she cut her ankles loose without rousing the killer? The music replayed for the fourth time. The song's vocalist felt bad, but not enough. He had it coming because he played too rough. She pulled her mind away from the lyrics and gradually inched her head up from the table. Bit by bit, she bent her frame in half to maneuver her hand down to saw at her fetters. After she got her left leg free, she noticed him move in her peripheral vision. He looked up at her. She sawed faster to hack the other binding in two, but he covered the distance between them too quickly.

He yanked her body down to the gurney's end. Her slight frame was helpless compared to his strength. His fingers and thumb surrounded her neck, and he stared into her eyes. The squeeze tightened. Her instinct screamed at her to grab his hand around her throat, but she knew his grasp was too powerful. With his other arm, he held her in place. His hold gripped like a manacle made of iron. Her lungs ached with the need for air. She would give anything for her next breath.

She longed to close her eyes, but the tape forced her lids open. She pounded on his back with her right hand. The scalpel she held came up bloody each time she stabbed the short blade into him. Still, he didn't allow her to breathe. Her chest burned in pain.

He continued to gaze into her open eyes. She recognized his desire only strengthened. She turned her head away. He wouldn't get his thrill when she died. In this, she refused to let him win, but with her lids forced apart she couldn't shut out the sight of the items on the table. She stared at every article on it and remembered again what he did with each one. The tree loppers he would use to cut out her ribs as he did with Heather's. She prayed the condoms remained unused.

"Look at me. You'd better look at me," he yelled and lifted his other arm to pull her head around.

The next stab went into his armpit. He finally flinched, but unconsciousness surged toward her, threatening blackness. With everything she possessed, she stabbed him once more and buried the blade so deep her hand returned without it.

She felt death close in on her. When oxygen rushed into her chest, hope came alive.

He shot up from the gurney at the same time his fist reached to pull the scalpel from his body. His face contorted with fury as the sharp instrument flashed in his hand. Blood trickled from his wound.

She sucked air deep into her lungs. She kicked him hard in the groin with her left foot, then struggled in vain to get her right one free.

He moaned and writhed in pain and covered his genitals. The color in his face turned somewhere between red and purple.

Her ankle remained attached to the gurney, but the force from the action caused the whole contraption to collapse on its side and brought her back into direct contact with her captor.

His hands still protected his private parts, and he rolled in agony. The scalpel lay there on the floor. She snatched it up and cut her right ankle free. She rolled over, nothing but escape on her mind.

His hand snagged her left foot and took her down hard on the concrete.

The music wailed. She saw stars from the force of her fall, which knocked the air out from her. Stunned, she couldn't focus enough to regain an upright position. He pounced on her again. Somehow, despite his injuries, he was only more powerful. His hands gripped her neck. She lost the ability to breathe. In her dazed state, confusion reigned. She had to stop him. And the only way to stop him was to kill him. *If I can only get one breath . . .*

She stared at the ceiling as her hands flailed.

"You stupid bitch, I want to watch your eyes. Look at me." His hands tightened more.

Her flailing hands found his face. She dug her thumbs into his eye sockets and pushed with everything left in her. The force was enough. He let her go.

She only took small amounts of air into her lungs. She remained weak, but he groaned and held his face. She stood, wobbled a bit, and kicked, landing her foot in his groin again.

She ran for the stairs. Her gun. She needed her gun and her handcuffs. Anything to stop him permanently.

Her wobbly legs gave out, so she crawled up the steps. Blackness threatened, limiting her vision. She shook her head, hoping to clear it. With each step, she worried those huge hands would clamp down on her again.

By the time she reached the top of the stairs, she'd regained a little strength. Her vision returned to normal. She pulled herself upright, and leaned against the wall for balance. She found a light switch by the back door and flipped it on. Brightness flooded her eyes. She ripped the tape away, taking few lashes with it, and finally could close her lids.

She blinked many times until her focus returned, her sight adjusted—and she discovered her phone laid out on the counter with the battery beside it. Hands quivering, she snapped the battery back into place it and turned the cell on. The second she saw it connect, she dialed 9 1 1. She needed to find Caroline Montgomery. She knew the woman must still be alive. Only a coward would leave her here with a madman. She pulled air into her burning lungs while waiting for an operator.

The music blaring in the basement stopped mid-beat.

Trin's cell rang. He answered.

Bill's excited voice greeted him. "Paige's phone just came back on. Someone dialed 911, but no one will talk to the operator. I'm zeroing in on an address as we speak."

"Give me the address! Hurry! If she's not speaking, she must be in trouble." His voice cracked. He wouldn't let himself believe he was too late. Not again.

"Here! I've got it!"

"I'm ready." He keyed it into his GPS and waited for the satellites to make a connection. It seemed like forever before he received instructions. "Will you patch me through to the cell so I can talk directly to the phone if I need to?"

"Give me a few." Bill stayed quiet for several moments.

"Thanks. Tell me the second I have access to the device."

"Sure. It's open . . . now." The tech clicked off the line, and he heard nothing.

He picked up distant music in the background. He followed the directions given on the GPS unit and drove from Claremore. He'd just turned onto a rough blacktop road when he heard the sound of many shots fired.

Paige moved through the house, flipping every light on as she went. In a bedroom, she found her clothes and pulled on her T-shirt and jeans. Her weapons weren't with them. She hesitated, the need to locate Caroline weighing on her. He'd come for her, though. She needed to find her throwaway. Without her Beretta, she wouldn't stand a chance to save Caroline or herself. Once armed, she could resume her search of the house.

Back in the kitchen, she opened the doors of each cabinet. She turned the stove's burner to HIGH beneath a dirty pan before opening door after door. She had to find something to use as a weapon. In her search, she discovered a vial with a heart-shaped iris floating inside. She flinched. Several soup cans sat beside it.

Slow, heavy footsteps thumped up the stairs. She yanked open drawers, forcing herself to focus.

She heard his heavy breathing. Her pulse skyrocketed as she turned to face him.

He leaned against the door frame. Blood trickled from the wounds she'd inflicted and had been smeared across his bare chest. His right eye had swollen shut. He struggled to stay upright and moaned with every step he took, but he lunged forward and managed to advance toward her.

She stood her ground.

"You realize you have to die now. I *will* prevail." He pulled her Glock up from his side and pointed it in her direction.

"You may, but I won't make it easy for you." He preferred strangulation. If he came near enough to grab her neck, she might have another chance to get loose. Since he had her cornered, the only way out was through him. "What have you done with Caroline? Is she here somewhere?"

"Forget her! You're the one who will die. Right now. Here, in this kitchen."

She pulled open another drawer and hoped to discover anything useful. Her throwaway was stashed inside, but the holster mocked her. Her finger wouldn't be able to find the trigger fast enough.

"I know what you're thinking, but the gun is inside the

holster. I'll kill you long before you can use it." He moved up next to her and rammed her police issue in her side.

With his left hand, he encircled her neck for the third time. Pain radiated like wildfire into her every nerve cell. Her lungs burned. Darkness threatened to envelope her.

She reached for the stove, hand flailing. Finally, her fingers found the handle of the empty pot. She smashed it into his face and pressed the blistering metal hard against him. He stumbled back, screaming. The stench of burning flesh filled the kitchen.

She gulped huge gasps of oxygen and went for the Beretta in the drawer. She ripped the holster from the firearm and seemed to step into slow motion. When she slipped the safety off, her bloody fingers found it difficult to grip the handle. She glanced at him while he moved her service weapon up to fire at her.

She took aim and unloaded the clip into Grant Windsor.

His eyes looked startled the instant the first shot entered his upper side. The power from the bullet thrust him back slightly. The next one pierced him above and to the outside of his stomach. The third hit his shoulder and spun him around. After that, she lost count, but she couldn't get her finger to release its pressure on the trigger. Eventually, the bullets ended after the pistol ran out of rounds.

She inhaled again, but her raw throat constricted with pain. Needles. She breathed needles made from air.

She stepped over him and kicked the handgun away from his body. Sam wouldn't want her to mess with the corpse, but she put her fingers to his neck and felt for a pulse. She didn't find a heartbeat and walked back through the house. Surely, Caroline Montgomery was here somewhere.

She opened one door after another. Inside the fourth, she found the televangelist taped securely to a chair. The victim's eyes filled with relief.

She hurried in and snatched the tape from Caroline's lips and started untying her.

"Thank you. I didn't have a clue who had come to help me, but I worried about you." The beautiful redhead moved her mouth around after she removed her gag.

"I had difficulty, but I put him down. He came close to winning several times." She trembled with emotion. Her voice sounded raspy and gruff.

"I prayed for you." Caroline gazed up at her and winced at what she saw.

"Come on. Let's find your clothes. I think they're in the next bedroom where I found mine. I'm Paige Stone by the way, and I already know your name." She finally got the evangelist completely free. "Let's get you out of here."

## 29

_____

"That bitch. If I have to fill her with lead until she sinks to the bottom of the ocean, she will die," Grant said to himself and attempted to pull his body up from the floor. He used the cabinets for support and managed to climb into a hunched position. While he breathed heavily, he stood there and rested against the cabinets.

Then he reached for the gun on the floor. With his left foot, he scooted the pistol closer and used his big toe to hook it. As he dragged the gun to him, he managed to snag the weapon with his wounded arm since the other still helped support him against the cabinets. The ache from the injuries sent pain throbbing through his arm and shoulder. Blood dripped freely from the bullet holes, but he stayed determined. Paige _would_ die.

The exertion cost him valuable strength. He rested another minute. His upper torso still throbbed.

"The whore ruined my looks, for God's sake. I use my face to earn my living. She will pay for it," he mumbled. Fueled with fury and adrenaline, he took his first steps toward the bedrooms down the hallway. Enraged, he gained strength and momentum as he traveled closer to the women.

They were unaware he stood nearby and watched through the doorway. They talked and worked to get Caroline dressed. Thoughts of him would be their last and would follow them into eternity. Gun in hand, he entered the bedroom.

~

THEY WERE FULLY CLOTHED when Paige noticed Caroline look up.

"Where is he?" Caroline's concerned eyes stared past her.

"You mean Grant Windsor?" she asked.

Caroline nodded.

"He's in the kitchen with several bullet holes in him. He's dead. I checked his pulse." She turned to see what Caroline studied over her shoulder.

Grant stood in silhouette and filled the doorway. The Glock in his hand pointed in her direction. Rage filled his eyes as he moved the gun toward Caroline. "You want to save her so bad. There she is. Save her." He walked several steps closer toward her but kept the pistol trained on Caroline.

Her brain refused to acknowledge what was happening. Windsor wasn't alive. He couldn't be. She'd checked him. Mentally and physically exhausted, she longed to give up. Her body wanted to rest. But she knew she couldn't. Adrenaline seeped back into her system, and a tiny spark filled with hope. If Caroline ran to her car, at least she'd report who killed Heather to the authorities. The evangelist might get away. She would live.

To serve and protect. No decision remained. She had come to save Caroline. She'd get the job done.

The idea of his hand on her throat again filled her with

such dread, she didn't move. She opened her mouth but couldn't form words. With every last bit of resolve she possessed, she forced herself to work past the dark void that nearly swallowed her whole, to work through the fear. It was the only way, she reminded herself—the only way.

"You know it's me you want. I'm the one who gave you so much trouble. Why waste time on Caroline? She's not the challenge, I am. If you go for her, I'll kill you. If I never draw another breath, I *will* kill you. You will never harm another woman."

He seemed to struggle with the correct course of action. His head swiveled back and forth, weighing his options.

She stared him down, breathing heavily. When he made up his mind and stepped toward her, she issued clear directions to the other woman. "Caroline, run. My car is at the end of the drive. Go, get help. Find someone on the force. You have to tell them who he is."

She saw his hand coming for her. He grasped her, picked her up by the neck, and shook her until she went limp. Her throat exploded in sharp, searing pain. Her air supply evaporated into nothing so quickly. With her last strength, she grabbed for the pistol. She wanted to keep him occupied until Caroline escaped the house. She'd never experienced such intense agony in her life. The last of her air extinguished. She fell into the peaceful black abyss and left her body behind.

TRIN FLOORED THE GAS PEDAL. The car swerved to the edge of control when he rounded the next curve. He'd heard so many shots fired in such quick repetition, his pulse rate soared. Whatever had happened, he was certain Paige needed help. He couldn't get to that house fast enough.

The bumpy asphalt gave way to gravel for a short distance. He spotted Paige's vehicle parked at the end of the road. He didn't slow down until he'd turned into the driveway. He slammed the brakes right before it reached the house and shoved the transmission into park. He jumped from the car, raced the few steps to the cabin's front entry, and grabbed his service weapon from his holster, releasing the safety.

He checked the locked handle and kicked the door open. A female nearly stumbled into his arms. He recognized her from the photos he'd seen. Caroline Montgomery. Paige had found her. She pointed at the hallway behind her.

He rushed into the house with his weapon drawn. The evangelist followed hesitantly behind him. He shouted, "Paige!" Caroline pointed to a room farther down the hall.

He entered, gun before him. A naked hulk of a man held Paige by the throat. Her body appeared lifeless. Without thought, he fired.

Paige hovered near the ceiling, not sure what was happening. She looked down and watched Grant Windsor hold her by the neck while he shook her. *Why would he do that?* Everything moved as if in slow motion, but distant and hazy. She could see Caroline run away, though a wall separated them. *How odd.*

She looked again at her body in Grant Windsor's clutches. She stared into her own eyes below, vacant and unseeing.

She was dead.

A light flashed through the bedroom window. Hank had come to save her, she thought, but he'd come too late. Why did she linger here? She knew she couldn't stand the sight of Hank scooping her lifeless body into his arms.

But it wasn't Hank. Agent Trinity burst into the room. He fired a pistol. Grant's brains splattered over the bedroom wall. She saw her body fall to the carpet. Grant dropped on top of her. He landed hard, but she didn't feel it. She wouldn't feel anything ever again.

Trin lifted the lifeless remains from her and threw Grant to the side. She didn't sense any release from Grant's weight.

As she watched, Trin put his mouth to hers. How sad. She wanted to taste his lips on hers, but couldn't. And now she never would. She'd missed her chance.

A light appeared, not far from where she hovered, watching the final events unfold. She'd saved Caroline. Grant could never hurt another woman. Her work here was done. She turned to the light.

A voice stopped her. "Paige. You come back, right now. You can't leave, yet. Paige, you will live and not die."

She turned to see who called her. Caroline had come back into the room, tears streaming. She knelt beside Paige's body, hands clasped, eyes closed.

She watched Trin perform compressions on her chest, then lean over and administer breaths. She watched her chest rise, but still, she sensed nothing.

Fascinated, she drifted closer. He pushed on her chest again as Caroline prayed beside him. He murmured, "Come on. Come on," before leaning over her again for more breaths.

He glanced at his watch before returning to chest compressions. His voice caught as he spoke. "Come on, Paige. Don't do this to us. Come back to Hank. Come back to me." He leaned over her, covering her mouth with his and forcing air into her battered lungs.

And something pulled her toward her body. As Trin breathed life into her and Caroline prayed, the light above her disappeared.

Another set of compressions. This time when he put his mouth to hers and blew air into her lungs, she slammed back into her body. She sensed his lips on hers, the same moment excruciating pain knocked the breath back out of her. She coughed and tried to sit up.

Trin held her down. "No. Don't get up." She heard immense relief in his voice.

"Caroline's okay?" she murmured.

"Paige is okay." Trin sighed and nodded that Caroline was too.

"Check him. Make sure he's dead this time," she insisted.

Trin shook his head. "He will never harm anyone again."

"Thank God." Her voice was nothing but a raspy whisper. She wanted to cheer, but she hurt everywhere.

"Are you okay? You look terrible." Trin took her face between his hands and examined every feature.

"I'll live."

Trin got up and moved to the other woman. "Caroline Montgomery. We've been searching for you." He offered his hand for her to shake.

"Thank you for finding me." Caroline took his hand in hers, smiling warmly as she shook.

"Where's Hank? Why isn't he with you?" she interrupted. Finally, she came around for real.

Trin glanced back over at her, but he hesitated.

When he didn't answer, she struggled to sit up. "You didn't answer my question. Where's Hank?"

"Hey, don't do that." Trin returned to her side, easing her back to the floor. "He's in the hospital. Before you say another word, that's where you'll go, too."

She couldn't argue, even if she wanted to. It hurt too much to speak.

When the ambulance arrived, she was breathing a bit

easier, and she walked without help. She decided her own care could wait while she wrapped up the case.

"I have to give my statement," she said for the fifth or sixth time. "We've crossed county lines. It means tons of paperwork. I fired my weapon. I can't leave the scene until the officials are satisfied. I don't want to lose my job over this."

"Paige, I think you're in shock. You need treatment for it. Your eyes show signs of petechial hemorrhaging. You have terrible bruises on your neck. You're bleeding from the wrist. You need to go with them to the hospital. The officials can find you there." Trin hesitated. "Come on. I'll go with you. So will Caroline. She probably needs attention, too."

"Only if I can stay with Hank. He'll worry about me." She looked up into his eyes. "Thank you. You saved me. I thought I was gone forever." One tear slipped down her cheek.

"Anytime," he whispered.

## 30

Morning sunlight streamed into Paige's hospital room, like the sun breaking through after a violent storm. She felt rested, and if she didn't think too deeply, normal. The sight of her empty zombie eyes flashed through her mind. She trembled and pushed the thought away.

Trin slept in the chair beside her bed. When she moved to get up, he stirred a little. Then he came instantly awake. For a split second, his eyes gazed into hers, and she saw desire before he guarded them.

"Why are you still here?" she asked to break the intimate moment between them. Her expression changed to dismay. She knew she spoke, but the sound she heard didn't sound like her voice. "Will my voice recover?"

"You sound different, I'll admit, but I find it sexy. It should be temporary. You need time to heal."

"Great. I've always wanted to sound like a phone sex operator. It's not like the whole department doesn't already hate me. Now, I'll be a laughingstock."

"I can't imagine you as a fool. No matter what's happened, you're a good detective. With time, you'll be the best. Anyway, I like it." He arched his right brow upward and grinned.

She felt awkward and didn't know how to act since their conversation moved to a more personal area. They needed to finish the paperwork and formalities but mostly the case was over. What did that mean for him? For them?

A nurse entered and broke the silence. "How are you this morning? I understand you want to visit another patient?"

PAIGE COULDN'T WAIT to talk to Hank. She hovered outside his door until the homicide detective sat up in his bed. The night before, she'd arrived in the early hours before daylight. She'd barely spoken to him before they made her leave.

The nurse helped her out of the wheelchair and held up a second hospital gown for her to put on backwards to cover her backside. Then she pushed the door open and walked into Hank's room. She discovered him frowning at the breakfast tray.

"See this crap. No one would eat it without a whip over their head." The second he saw her come through the door, Hank shut up. The nurse silently escaped the room while she could.

"A little cranky this morning, are we?" She moved to the bed and sat on the side.

"Hell, yes. I wanted to wake you hours ago to make sure you weren't in a coma or something, but the Wicked Witch from the West who just flew out the door wouldn't let me. She said you needed your rest." Hank tilted her chin up and examined her face. "You sure you're okay? You sound different."

"I'll live. Do I look that bad?" She gave him a lopsided grin.

"Here's a tip. Don't go near a mirror anytime soon. You might scare yourself." Hank sounded more like his usual grumpy self.

"Now you've got me curious." She hobbled across the room to see her reflection. "Oh my God." Her swollen neck was covered with dark bruises. She saw the hemorrhages in the whites of her eyes and remembered the minutes she'd spent hovering above her body, the emptiness she'd seen in them, and the darkness from the chasm that had waited to engulf her. She didn't care what she looked like. She didn't regret her decision to return. She had more to do and needed more time to spend with Hank.

"I told you not to do that. But you're the same old Paige. You've got to satisfy your curiosity." Hank stared lovingly at her. "It's one trait you acquired since you lived with me. I'm sorry it nearly got you killed, but I love the fact we both need to solve crimes."

"Me, too. I'm glad we share so much in common." She remained quiet for a moment. "So, we still partners?"

"I don't know. The doctors want to do by-pass surgery. I don't think I can go back. If I do go back, I'll probably have to work a desk job. I don't know if I could handle riding the pine day after day." Hank frowned and gazed down at his hands.

"Hank, you can't quit. I'm not through with my training. I still need you." She searched his eyes until his lifted and met hers.

"I think we both know that's not true. You earned solo status with this case. You found the bad guy, and he was a nasty one. I talked with the captain this morning. He wants to get you paired up and back on the streets right away. They need a lot more like you." Hank patted her back. Then he did something he rarely did. He tenderly kissed her cheek.

~

Tony walked out from the detention area where he'd spent more hours than he ever dreamed possible in an eight-by-ten room. He saw Ben leave a similar door down the hall from the one he'd vacated. Ben walked toward him.

"That's one party I don't want to repeat."

He gave a tired smile and stretched. "I don't know how long we stayed here, but too damned long. No retake on this one for me either."

"So what the hell happened? Did they find the real killer?" Ben lifted his arm and smelled. Then he made a disgusted face. "I'm ripe. I need a shower."

"We both do." He rubbed the stubble on his chin. "That's one horrid homecoming. If my parents didn't live here, I'd never come back."

He turned then as Ben said, "Where the hell have you been?"

Josh walked up behind him. "I found a gorgeous girl who liked me fine until the TV and internet broadcast my face over the entire world. I guess the police believed I was this serial killer guy. She did *not* take the news well. Ruined a great romance."

"We've got bigger problems. We needed to start back to LA yesterday. The interiors will cost a fortune if we go over our budgeted time. Is your Escalade still in one piece?" He turned toward Josh.

"Yeah. What happened to yours?"

"The police happened to ours. I don't know how long before the techs put them back together. Let's get on our way. We can pay crew members to fly out and pick them up later," Ben interrupted.

"Where did you park? I don't know if I can stand the smell, but let's get the hell out of here." He walked toward the exit.

~

PAIGE CARRIED the sheets with information about the missing real estate women when she entered Captain Underwood's office. She laid the papers on his desk. "I understand they found Betty Greenway's body on the property at the rental cabin. I figured they would. I brought you a list I found that concerns the other women. If they investigate a little, they'll probably find them, too."

"Thanks. I'm sure they will." He looked over the papers for several seconds. Then he nodded. "You did a fine job on your cases, but don't ever go off without backup again. You know that's how your father died. You're too good a detective to lose over foolishness."

"Yes, sir." She nodded.

"Since the perp is dead, and they won't need to hold a trial, Rogers County officials didn't sound too upset that you went into their territory. I'm sure they would appreciate an apology since you didn't give them a heads up."

"Yes, sir." She stared down at her shoes.

"I will find the right partner for you. Hank will be on my case if I screw up the choice. You know there will be time off involved. Internal Affairs has to clear your firearm use. The shrink will require your presence on her couch for a certain number of visits. After that, you will get back in the thick of it." He turned away to gaze out into the streets beside his office.

"What about Hank? Can't I get him back?"

"You don't want to go there. If anything could blow your career, Hank's heart issue could. It's for everyone's safety we require a police detective to be in good health. We need to trust our partner will back us up at the time we most need it. I hate it even more than you do, but Hank has retired for good." He turned back from the window. The sternness in his expression convinced her when nothing else would.

She figured her distress over Hank's removal showed plainly on her face, but at this point, she didn't care. "Yes, sir."

"And Paige, Hank said he forgot to tell you, this time you've turned the last page. He said you would know what it means."

"Yes, sir." Once she left the captain's office, she smiled and her step quickened. She'd lost her mentor's guidance, but Hank's remark indicated she didn't need it anymore. She'd finished the book. The grin lingered while she walked outside and watched the three biggest male stars of the decade get into a black Escalade and drive west as the sun set.

# ACKNOWLEDGMENTS

Special thanks to William Bernhardt for everything he does for aspiring writers. His teaching and guidance helped me achieve my dream of writing a book.

# ABOUT THE AUTHOR

Maribeth Garrett is an avid reader and has always wanted to create stories like those she loves to read. *The Novice*, a page-turning thriller, is her debut novel in the exciting Paige Stone detective series. A native Oklahoman who grew up around wheat fields, Garrett now resides on acreage in the northeast part of the state, where her children and grandchildren keep her young and active.

# MORE BY ADMISSION PRESS

Looking for your next great read?
Visit www.admissionpress.com

ISBN 978-1-955836-01-2